naughty little secrets

naughty little secrets

mary wilbon

KENSINGTON BOOKS
www.kensingtonbooks.com

KENSINGTON BOOKS are published by

Kensington Publishing Corp.
850 Third Avenue
New York, NY 10022

ISBN 0-7582-0608-9

First printing: August 2004
10 9 8 7 6 5 4 3 2 1

Printed in the United States of America

For Doug, my angel on the second floor

acknowledgments

Thanks to my editor at Kensington Books, John Scognamiglio, for taking a chance on a first-time writer. Without his guidance, you would not be reading this.

Thanks to Doug Mendini for believing in me, even when I doubted myself.

Many thanks to all my theater and nontheater friends and family for their time, kindness, and encouragement, Lynea Adams, Samuel Billings, Willa Coleman (Mom2), Clinton Scott, Cathy Green, Lorraine Hernandez, Sophie Majchrzak, Raymond Martoccia, Kathy Mattingly, Gil Moreno, Rob Pape, Robert Marcela, Joseph Petrecca, and Catherine F. Sutherland.

My most profound thanks to Rich Aront, Rick Brown, Cathy Grega, Patricia Lea Remlinger, Paula Ruffin, Elka Bendit Butterley, Roberta Steve, and Cynthia S. Ross.

To know you all is my light and my joy.

The story you are about to read is a work of fiction. The incidents are not real. The characters are not real.

Names have been made up and real names are used fictitiously.

However, there really is a company named Garwood Paper Board, and an amusement park named Bowcraft.

There really was a cat named Staccato, and she is missed.

There really is a Yorkshire terrier named Garbo, but I'm the only one who thinks she's a Wonder Dog.

naughty little secrets

The Broad Street Players

present

"sorry i missed your birthday!"

An Original Musical

Starring

Rock Scherer as	Michael Ashton
Beautee Holsom as	Elizabeth Ashton
Randall Garret as	Phillip Sinclair
Rachel Brougham as	Darcey Montgomery
Alicia Beavers as	The Maid

Book by	Karson Parker Taylor
Score & Musical Direction by	Sindee Van Sant
Choreography by	Dale Mabrey
Costumes by	Cheri Boone-Blume
Production Stage Manager	Blair Borden
Assistant Stage Manager	David Castrato

Production Directed by Addison Taylor

prologue

Too much Ecstasy and Viagra, too many drinks, not enough men. It was almost the perfect ending to a less than perfect day.

Eugene looked at his watch. The numbers were scrambled at first, making no sense at all. Eugene continued to stare at them until they gradually aligned themselves correctly.

Three in the morning.

He had called for a ride over twenty minutes ago. He was too inebriated to try to drive himself home. Eugene was still glowing and tingling from the effects of the drugs and alcohol and sex. He was pleasantly stoned and exhausted.

He looked around the parking area. Except for his, all the other cars were gone.

Eugene was very often the last to leave. This place was great for men who wanted anonymous sex. With his good looks, Eugene always got every man he wanted. But he always left wanting more. He frequented this rest stop off the Garden State Parkway at least three times a week. He couldn't get his fill.

Normally he would have stayed even longer, but the winter weather and the holidays had kept a lot of men away.

Eugene knew he spent too much time here. He had made a New Year's resolution to cut back. But it was already days into January and he still hadn't altered his behavior in the least.

Oh, well. So much for resolve.

Maybe next year.

He pulled his coat collar up and over the scarf underneath. He had to protect his throat from the cold night air. No matter how cavalier Eugene may have been with his sex life, he was always very protective of his singing voice. He was in a show now, and he had to be at rehearsal later. Even though it was only community theater, Eugene took his responsibility very seriously.

He figured he could kill some time waiting for his ride by going over his script. It would probably help him sober up, too.

Eugene closed his eyes and forced himself to concentrate. Then he started saying his lines and singing softly.

Sotto voce.

He had a wonderful voice. He had some formal training, but that had been done merely to enhance his resume and impress everyone who read it. Singing beautifully just came effortlessly to Eugene.

He walked around the dark, quiet, empty lot, acting and singing to himself, getting into his character as if he were on the stage. The only other sound breaking the late night stillness was the sound of the thin layer of snow crisply crunching beneath his footsteps. He strode up and down, reciting his lines theatrically, even measuring out his blocking and attempting a few of the dance numbers.

A car approached the parking lot very quietly, the driver looking around, careful not to be observed. The driver parked in a remote spot then turned off the engine. Then watched Eugene. Watched and waited. Biding time. Calculating.

Eugene tripped once or twice during the dance routine due to intoxication, but damn, he was good. Why couldn't he be this good in front of an audience? Eugene knew he wasn't a great actor, but he was adequate. And like most actors, he told himself that at times he was wonderful, and at this specific point in time, all alone with no one around to appreciate his gift, he was truly inspired. He was under the influence of drugs and alcohol, of course, so maybe his judgement was somewhat impaired, but he felt this was unquestionably the best he had ever been.

After several repetitions, Eugene was confident that he had mastered all his songs, and that he knew most of his dialogue, but he was not so comfortable with the dance routines. The ability to move fluidly on the stage was not one of his natural talents, but he would not be satisfied until he was sure that he had given it his best try. He was determined to get through a dance number here and now without falling or stumbling.

Focus, Eugene, focus.
And . . . 5, 6, 7, 8
Kick, step, kick, step
Turn in, turn out
Back step, pivot step
Arabesque, arabesque
Double pirouette

On one of his turns, Eugene noticed the car sitting there directly in front of him with its lights off. He had been so deeply into his performance that he hadn't heard it drive up. He felt a little embarrassed. He must have looked very foolish from the car, all alone out here in the darkness, playing out his little pantomime.

But his friend would understand. They were both in the same show.

The car's engine came to life, then its lights came on, centering on Eugene, pinpointing him with two steady radiating beams.

Eugene smiled and waved and started walking toward the car.

He blinked and squinted as he approached, trying to adjust his eyes to the sudden brightness surrounding him.

As he walked closer, Eugene looked into the car and his smile quickly withered. He saw the look of raw unbridled hatred on the face of the driver. The burning rage staring back at him was paralyzing.

At first the driver was nervous about being recognized. There was a feeling of sick excitement. That quickly passed. The driver began to enjoy the eye contact, enjoyed being recognized by Eugene. Now they had another secret connection. It would be Eugene's last little secret.

The driver smiled, and shifted position in the seat, getting comfortable.

Fear came fast to Eugene and it showed on his face. The driver liked that.

Eugene stopped abruptly in his tracks. A sudden chill pierced him to his soul.

He was alone, wasted and vulnerable, with nowhere to hide.

In an instant of crystal clarity, Eugene understood exactly what was about to happen to him.

That was the funny thing. The idea of killing Eugene took shape like a slow moving dream, but Eugene knew he was going to be murdered even before the driver had positively decided to murder him.

Oh, my God, Eugene thought. It was true what everyone had always said.

When you're about to die, your life really does flash before your eyes.

Eugene's life in musical theater was flashing before him!

West Side Story, Man of La Mancha, A Chorus Line, South Pacific, The Fantasticks, Evita, Pippin, Dream Girls, The Sound of Music, Guys and Dolls, The Wiz, Follies, Victor/Victoria, The Music Man, Godspell, Sorry I Missed Your Birthday.

Eugene needed a moment to prepare.

He raised his hand, seeking a temporary delay to the inevitable.

The driver understood and gave Eugene his moment. The car's engine revved once, then twice, then settled down to a regulated continuous purr, contented, it seemed to Eugene, like a cat patiently contemplating its trapped defenseless prey.

Eugene had never spent much time pondering the existence of God, but perhaps, he thought, this would be a good time to pray.

His knees hit the snow.

Eugene didn't pray for God to spare him. He knew there was no chance of that. He didn't ask for forgiveness of his sins, and he didn't dare ask that his soul be welcomed into the gates of Heaven for all eternity.

He didn't pray that peace and comfort be given to the ones who loved him, those whose hearts would mourn his death.

Instead, Eugene prayed that his favorite head shot would be used in his obituary.

Amen.

Then Eugene stood tall and signaled the driver to bring the lights up.

The high beams came on.

With consummate poise and elegance, Eugene took his final bow and made his final exit.

He looked so graceful from the car. It was obvious he was afraid. His body swayed with fear but he never faltered, not for an instant. It was an image that would last forever.

There was the sense that the earth was about to shift. This was the turning point, the threshold.

The driver looked away momentarily, unsure.

For a heartbeat, Eugene felt a twinge of hope.

The moon was so bright, like a great blind eye. It was hypnotic. Focus back on Eugene, there came a detached peaceful trance. Independent hands, possessed of their own will, gripped the steering wheel like they had their own purpose. Somehow the gas pedal was pressed to the floor, and the car leaped forward.

The car came hurtling at Eugene, pitched him into the air, and sped away into the night.

Without hesitating for a second, without remorse, the driver drove off and never looked back.

Problem solved.

Eugene's flawless body shattered internally against the ground in a crumpled heap about twenty feet from impact with the car, and then he felt nothing. He was broken and bleeding. In the remaining shallow breaths left to him, he could smell the acrid stench of stale beer and urine from the pavement rising up through the snow. He almost laughed at himself, knowing that these would be the only earthly scents he would take with him into the afterlife. If there was one.

He couldn't move, he couldn't feel, he couldn't even cry out in his anguish, but he could see the widening pool of his hemorrhaging blood as it flowed and discolored the snow around him.

In this cold and lonely place, armed with nothing more than his frail resignation, Eugene waited to die.

God was merciful.

He didn't judge Eugene for his weaknesses. He rewarded

him for his strengths. He granted Eugene the place in Heaven he had felt unworthy to ask for.

In his dwindling seconds of consciousness, as Eugene slipped into oblivion, all of his departed idols of the theater embraced him with a standing ovation. Judy Garland, Rosalind Russell, Katharine Hepburn, Ethel Merman, Mary Martin, Gene Kelly, Sammy Davis, Jr., Pearl Bailey, Gregory Hines, Bob Fosse. They all cheered, threw bouquets and long stemmed roses, applauded and shouted "Bravo! Bravo! Bravissimo!"

Eugene smiled weakly.

Sotto voce.

Eugene was dimly aware that a gentle winter wind was approaching. It stirred through the trees, tenderly blowing off leaves that had died, but still held on tenuously. He knew this wind was coming for him, too.

Eugene closed his eyes for the very last time.

Slow fade.

Curtain.

1

Laura closed her eyes and let her body relax. She took a long deep breath, and slowly exhaled. She did it again.

In, and out. In, and out.

She began to feel the rhythm inside her.

In, and out. In, and out.

She rubbed her hands together, blew into her palms, then flexed her fingers. Laura was intensely determined to finish what she had started. Even if it took all night, she was going to get it up. She wanted it that badly. The clock was ticking and her desire, her need, was becoming urgent.

She reached over to the nightstand by the bed, and grabbed a bottle of lotion. She squirted some on a few strategic places on her body, then slowly and deliberately rubbed it on her skin. It felt so good against her hot flesh. It was velvety, cooling and soothing.

Laura licked her lips and braced herself for insertion.

Now she was ready.

She lay on her back, squarely in the middle of the bed. Her long blonde hair was in disarray around and beneath her. She found her courage, took another deep breath, and then moved her trembling hands down slowly over her hips. There, on top of her, her hands found their objective. She laughed involuntarily when she felt its sponginess. Still flexible, still doable. It was damp from all the previous attempts, but Laura was confident that she could make it fit.

Beads of sweat formed on her brow and at the nape of her lovely neck. She grabbed hold and started to pull up.

Nothing.

She strained and tugged even harder. She arched her back and moaned.

Still nothing.

Then slowly . . . very slowly . . . it moved.

"Oh, yes . . . yes . . . yes . . . God . . . Oh God," she screamed in abandon.

She started to pump her hips in a bucking motion. She was just inches, mere seconds from the payoff.

"Yes! That's it! Right there! Oh . . ."

"Will you please get a grip on that," said Slick, leaning casually against a post of the canopied bed and smiling down at her. "I wish you could see yourself from here, making a spectacle of yourself like this. All the panting and undulating. Your cheeks flushed. Your breasts heaving in a frenzy. It's shocking and disturbing.

"Have you no shame, no modesty? I'm embarrassed for you. I only hope that in time I'll be able to purge this sordid image of you from my memory."

Without moving a muscle, Laura lay there and asked, "Are you done? Or are you just going to stand there mocking me and making snide remarks at my expense?"

Slick thought this over for several seconds.

"It's very tempting, but no, I'm done. No . . . wait . . . wait . . . I think I've got one more joke left . . . Nah, I've got nothing. I'm done."

Laura, knowing that she had been busted, pulled herself up on her elbows and asked, "How long have you been watching me?"

"Long enough to capture you writhing around like a fish out of water on videotape. It's sure to be a hit at the party."

"Well, you try getting into this stupid thing," said Laura in disgust, collapsing back onto the bed. The tail at the end of her formfitting rubber fish suit crashed to the floor. "It's becoming an aerobic workout. Whose bright idea was it to have a costumed Christmas party, anyway?"

"Someone said 'don we now our gay apparel.' You know our peeps wouldn't let that go by without turning it into a party. But no one told you to go as a mermaid," teased Slick. She walked to the closet and stepped inside.

"It seemed like such a great idea at the time. You know, me being the head of a clam company. I wanted to do something aquatic," Laura explained, reaching down to retrieve her fin.

"Very subtle. And you got me this Sherlock Holmes getup because I used to be a detective, right?" asked Slick, emerging from the closet holding her costume.

"Yes, I was working with themes."

"I see. You will never know how relieved I am at this moment that neither one of us is a proctologist." Slick pretended to shudder at the thought of it.

Slick removed her costume from its wrapping and smiled to herself. She had to admit it was a clever idea. She put on the Holmes trademark deerstalker cap, then put the big-bowled pipe with the bent briar in her mouth. She got into the shirt, and placed the cufflinks into the sleeves. She draped the herringbone cape around her shoulders.

Slick walked to the mirror and struck what she thought was an appropriate Sherlock Holmesian pose. She raised one eyebrow and pretended to smoke the pipe.

"The game is afoot," she said to her reflection.

She did a few turns in the mirror, checking herself out. Not too bad. This could work after all, she thought. She was going to enjoy being Holmes.

She turned back to Laura.

"Would you like me to help you get into your fish tail?"

"Oh, no you don't," laughed Laura. "The last two times you 'helped' me, the damned thing ended up on the floor, around my ankles."

"I can't believe you're still holding that against me." Slick winked and rubbed her chin. "My recuperative abilities are amazing. You'll be happy to know that the feeling is finally starting to return to my face."

"You were the one who wanted to play 'Jaws Meets the Little Mermaid,' " said Laura.

"Yes, but I distinctly remember that you were the one who wanted to play 'The Pussy Hiding Adventure,' " said Slick. "This time I promise I'll be good."

Slick offered her hand to Laura. Laura took hold and Slick lifted her gently from the bed. She grabbed the top of the fish suit and pulled Laura to her. Laura slid effortlessly into the costume. They laughed, and as Slick held Laura close, she looked around the room.

They had shared this room, this bed, this home for ten years. Time had flown. It didn't seem possible, but Slick loved Laura now more than ever.

And now they were about to celebrate their tenth Christmas together. Slick said a silent prayer of thanks, kissed Laura softly, and watched her as she wriggled her way into the final fit of the fish tail. She put her feet through the slots at the bottom and walked unsteadily to the bed.

"I don't get it," said Laura as she adjusted herself. "Bette does a mermaid thing in her show and she never seems to have any problem."

"She's in a wheelchair for most of it, baby," said Slick. "And she's got the Harlettes helping her. Speaking of Bette, do you think she'll be at the party tonight?"

"No," sighed Laura. "I don't think so. She's still a little cranky about her TV series being cancelled."

"She's still upset about that! That was years ago."

"I know. But you know Bette. It's hard for her to get over things. She still hasn't forgiven Barry Manilow for wanting his own career. She swears he'll come crawling back to her any day now."

"What about Puffy?" Slick asked. "Will he be at the party?"

"I'm not sure," said Laura. "But if he does show up, call him 'P Diddy.' Don't call him 'Puffy.' He doesn't use that any-more."

"Why not?"

" 'Puffy' made him sound like he was retaining water," ex-plained Laura.

"Oh, okay."

Slick suddenly became very serious and very still. She stood in the center of the room and slowly looked around. Her eyes searched everywhere, taking in every detail. She absentmindedly gripped her Sherlock Holmes pipe and frowned.

Laura watched her in her transfixed state and knew she was concentrating deeply on something. She wanted to ask what it was, but decided to wait for it.

Ten seconds passed.

Twenty seconds passed.

"I can't find my underpants," Slick finally said in exaspera-tion. "I've been looking all over and I can't find them any-where."

"I was wondering why you were still walking bare-assed around the room. Why don't you just put on another pair," asked Laura.

"Because now it's personal," answered Slick. "I used to be the best looking, best detective in the country and now I can't find my own underpants. It's humiliating."

Laura smiled as she sat on the bed, putting on the top of her costume. "I'll agree that you were the best detective on the east coast, but the 'best looking'?"

Slick sat down on the opposite side of the bed and said, "People used to say to me every day, 'Hey, you look just like Halle Berry'."

"The people you're referring to were criminals, Sweet Cheeks, and you were pointing a loaded gun at them at the time."

"That was the only way I could get them to say it."

Laura turned to face Slick, but all she saw was Slick's naked ass as she bent over, looking under the bed for the missing underpants.

"Gee, what a vision. Where's that video camera? I'd like to get a shot of this made into a tee shirt."

But Slick hadn't heard her.

Laura resisted the urge to reach over and give her a pinch. Instead she watched as Slick's butt bobbed up and down in the air. She had seen that butt almost every day for the last ten years. She hoped she would see it for the next ten years and the ten years after that.

Suddenly Slick stood straight up and said "Aha! Where's Garbo?"

"She went sulking off after you forced her to wear those little reindeer antlers. She wanted to be alone. I think she was embarrassed," answered Laura.

"Well, if we've got to wear ridiculous costumes, so does she. The three of us are in this thing together," Slick said with authority, as she went to search for the culprit dog.

"And you look more like Chuck Berry than Halle Berry," Laura said softly, stifling a laugh.

"I *heard* that."

Laura knew that Slick missed being a detective, and it was no exaggeration that she had been one of the best. She had given it up for Laura because Laura could not cope with wondering every night if Slick would make it home to her. Laura felt that the longer Slick stayed on the streets, the odds were, eventually, there would be a fatal bullet with Slick's name on it.

The world Slick had lived in and worked in before she met Laura was light years away from the lush opulent life Laura was used to. Slick's world was dangerous and violent. Laura knew that Slick had the cunning and intelligence to survive in it, but Laura also knew that sometimes even the best got unlucky.

Slick never said it out loud, but Laura sensed she was bored with her current job. They would have to discuss it soon. Laura knew that whatever happened, they would still be together. There was no problem so terrible that it would pull them apart, but Laura was not ready to see Slick go back to carrying a gun, and risking her life every day.

Slick returned to the room shortly, wearing the stolen underpants and carrying a bottle of champagne. She was preceded by an antlered Yorkshire terrier that jingled with every step it took.

The dog stopped in the middle of the room, shook her head, and flapped her ears in an attempt to remove the antlers. It didn't work. The antlers didn't budge. She stared helplessly at Laura with beseeching, brown glass button eyes, looking for some assistance in her plight.

Laura smothered a laugh, then looked away, not wanting to snicker insensitively.

Resigned to her fate, Garbo gave a short sigh, jumped up on the bed, turned around twice then lay still, resting her head on her front paws.

"Even though it's been years since my last case, I haven't lost my touch," Slick said. "Behold my success and alert the media! Another mystery has been solved. I can still match wits with a crafty canine intellect," Slick said, laughing at herself. "I think we should celebrate."

Her mind went blank when she saw Laura standing there in her complete costume.

After all these years, Laura was still the most beautiful woman Slick had ever seen. The absurdity of the mermaid costume didn't diminish that at all. Her seemingly bottomless blue eyes still left Slick speechless at times.

This was one of those times.

Suddenly it seemed to Slick that all the air had been sucked out of the room. Then Slick felt the familiar swarm of butterflies overtake her stomach, then felt her knees get weak. She was positive that her heart would start to beat again and that she would remember how to breathe any minute now . . . any minute now . . . any minute . . .

She was falling in love with Laura all over again. And falling hard, as if a trapdoor had opened up beneath her feet. It happened regularly. No one but Laura had ever made her feel this way. It had started as long as ten years ago, and Slick had felt the same rush of love for her as recently as yesterday. The original thrill came over Slick with all its desire. All the beauty of that first passion came back to her.

Slick put down the Cristal and started walking toward Laura. Laura started walking to meet her. Laura walked a little lopsided because of her costume and unintentionally started veering off away from Slick, but Slick thought she was the sweetest thing she had ever seen. She reached out to get Laura back and held her tightly. They stood holding on to one another, enjoying the embrace, each replaying scenes of the past ten years in their head.

"Okay," Slick whispered in Laura's ear, "how about a quick game of The Sailor and the Other Sailor," her hands moving up toward Laura's breasts. "Nips ahoy."

Laura kissed her cheek and said, "Silly, as much as I would love to, we're already late for the Christmas party. It started over an hour ago at least."

"Being late is fashionable," Slick urged.

"Not when you're the hosts," Laura laughed. "We've got a house full of people downstairs who are probably eating and drinking us into poverty."

"I'm sure the staff is tending to them. I can hear the music and laughter from here. They don't even know we're not there yet."

"I'll make a deal with you," whispered Laura, putting her arms around Slick's neck. "Let's have a private toast now, and I promise you, those sailors will be standing here to salute you after the party."

"That's a deal, and I'll hold you to it," said Slick, giving Laura one final squeeze.

She hurriedly finished putting on the rest of her costume and opened the champagne.

"Are you sure you're going to be able to walk around in that thing all night? How will you get down the stairs?" asked Slick, bringing her a glass.

"I'm going to ride the motorized seat down the stairs and really make an entrance. After that, if I need to, I can always lean on you."

"Always. Forever."

"Merry Christmas."

"Merry Christmas."

They clinked their glasses, sipped and kissed, then left the room arm in arm to greet their guests.

2

Sindee walked around the set, uncharacteristically humming a Christmas carol in her head, and making sure everything was in its proper place. She was very careful to move silently and unobtrusively. She didn't want to disrupt the dance rehearsal that was taking place on the opposite side of the stage.

She ceased to hum when she found a cocktail napkin out of position. She moved it two centimeters to the left until it was exactly right. She made a mental note to tell Blair, one more time, how sloppy she was in her placement of the props.

Sindee also noticed that the set floor was littered with candy wrappers and soda cans. The idiot hadn't even bothered to sweep the stage. Sindee made another note never to agree to have Blair as her stage manager ever again. Blair was a genius at botching every assignment. Sindee had known at the second rehearsal that Blair was going to be trouble.

An efficient stage manager was a fundamental and essential part of every good theatrical production, and Blair couldn't cut it. She was practically useless.

Blair may have been a decent actress, but a stage manager had to be able to think quickly on her feet, and make critical decisions in emergencies, when things went wrong onstage.

Blair broke out in a sweat from straining to think slowly.

Sindee would be damned before she let Blair oversee another one of her projects.

And Sindee had plans to do a lot of projects here.

Sindee didn't much care for Blair's assistant, David Castrato, either. He was always buzzing around like an annoying little gnat. He was forever singing show tunes as if to let everyone know that he had a good voice and that he wanted to do more than be assistant stage manager.

Sindee didn't think he was as brain dead as Blair, but she didn't like David because he was perpetually and relentlessly chipper. He was always smiling. It wasn't normal. No one was as happy all the time as David seemed to be.

But there was nothing Sindee could do. These were the people she had to work with.

Next, Sindee checked the cables for all the mechanicals that were a part of the show.

Above her, the ceiling was a riot of ropes, pulleys, and other rigging.

Right now Sindee was concerned with the large mechanical champagne bottle that was used in the finale. The cables were crossed inappropriately. This could cause the bottle to malfunction and ruin the whole effect.

Damn it, Blair! she thought. *Like I really need this right now!*

This officially marked the end of Sindee's fleeting moment of Christmas spirit. If poor little Tiny Tim had been in the room with her right now, she would have snapped his good leg like a twig.

God bless us, every one, Godammit! *Crack!*

Sindee had always been the type to obsess over minutia. She understood that it was the attention to every little detail that gave a show its unique look and feel. Blair didn't seem to get that.

Blair was too slack for Sindee's liking; especially for this show.

Sindee had too much riding on this show to allow even the smallest item to be overlooked. She wasn't going to tolerate Blair's incompetence.

Sindee was too busy babysitting the director and the play-wright, and too busy trying to give this turkey of a play all the glitter and razzle dazzle she could muster.

Sindee was making every effort to save *Sorry I Missed Your Birthday* from a trip to the musical trash heap.

After years of attempted persuasion by several actors in the company, Sindee had been the one to finally convince Addison and Karson to stage their first musical and they were appre-hensive. The Taylors had built the reputation of their theater on classic comedies and dramas. After seven seasons, the the-ater was about to start showing a profit.

Now the production was way over the budget Sindee had projected, and they still had three weeks of rehearsals ahead of them.

The backers, many of whom were beginning to think that they were throwing their money into a bottomless pit, were cringing at the escalating extras, the most exorbitant being Sindee's insistence that Addison hire her old friend, Dale Mabrey to choreograph. It had been costly to bring him back from Florida, but he was the only one she could trust to give the dance a professional touch. Besides, Dale was desperate for work and Sindee could use that to her advantage.

Sindee finished her inspection of the stage, then walked to the rehearsal piano. She picked up her Zippo lighter with the masks of Comedy and Tragedy on it.

She let her fingers run over every inch of it. She lit a ciga-rette.

It was a good touch, she thought. Dale had given her this lighter years ago. He had it inscribed with the words "To my Bud, S from D." When he saw it, she hoped he would remem-ber and get sentimental.

Sindee tried to look casual as she watched Dale rehearse the finale.

It had been a while since they worked together. They would always be friends, but now Sindee had to be businesslike and completely objective. She wanted to make sure he was worth all the trouble it had taken to get him here.

Sindee had seen the earlier rehearsal. The second act was slow. Lines were dropped and it was obvious the actors didn't have a clue to what was going on. Sindee could only hope that Dale was doing his job and the songs and the dance numbers were coming together.

She looked at him as he rehearsed the chorus line. Since she'd last worked with Dale maybe a line here or there had appeared on his handsome face. Maybe he was a little gray at the temples, but other than that, he was the same friend she had known for over fifteen years.

"No! No! No! Unacceptable! Totally unacceptable! Those are not the steps I just did! You Tinkerbells are giving me a fucking President Kennedy memorial headache! Look! Half my scalp has been blown off! I've seen better arabesques from a line of 'Jerry's Kids'! What the fuck was that, anyway? 'Look at us, we're dancing'?"

One unfortunate young man made the mistake of laughing. Dale turned to him swiftly and without mercy. He got as close as possible to the hapless chorus boy without touching him.

"What are *you* laughing at, 'Lord of the Dance'? If you would spend more time concentrating on your movements and less time worrying about what the size of your package looks like in those tights, we might be able to get some work done here."

The young man felt his legs go rubbery.

"And take that sock out of there," Dale ordered, tapping his pointer on the young man's crotch. "We all know you're not Cockzilla."

The red-faced young man did as he was told.

Dale turned away from the chorus line ostensibly to take another sip of his Diet Coke.

Actually, he was replaying the last few moments in his mind. Inflicting shame and humiliation were talents he had honed to perfection.

He took a long, thirst-quenching drink. It went down well with his self-satisfaction. He was working on his third bottle.

God, he loved breaking balls. And to be able to break them on Christmas Eve! What a present he had been given! His joy was boundless.

He crossed his eyes and flashed a clownish grin at Sindee, who had witnessed everything. She returned his grin, then quickly tamped out her cigarette in an ashtray on the piano. She pretended to be absorbed in some sheet music to keep from giggling audibly.

By the time Dale turned back to face his scared and tired dancers, he had resumed his usual scowl. He spoke to them in a detached tone.

"If you want to dance, and I assume you do, then work with me. Follow me. I want you to reach beyond yourselves. Become the music. Become the dance."

The chorus line fell into place, hypnotized by him.

He lifted his pointer.

"Again, ladies. And this time thrill me."

He looked back at Sindee.

"Sindee, if you please . . ."

Sindee started the intro. Dale started his countdown.

"Focus . . . eyes front . . . and . . . 5,6,7,8."

The dancers went into motion. Dale walked among them watching their every step, calling out the dance combinations.

"Remember . . . together, unified, dancing as if you were one . . .

"And . . . kick, step, kick, step.

"Turn in, turn out.

"Back step, pivot step.

"Arabesque, arabesque.

"Double pirouette . . . and rest.

"Not bad. Again . . .

"And . . . kick, step, kick, step.

"Turn in, turn out.

"Back step, pivot step.

"Arabesque, arabesque.

"Double pirouette, and . . .

"Hold it . . . hold it . . . ," he said, drawing it out, making them strain. They had performed perfectly, but Dale wasn't going to let them know that.

No one moved. All arms and legs were extended with absolute precision. He searched their young faces. No one breathed. Not even an eyelash fluttered.

Dale looked slyly back at Sindee. His strategy had worked. Over the years he had learned that all he had to do was embarrass just one of the chorus boys, and their worst fears would drive them all to perfection. No one wanted to be singled out for ridicule.

They were all still young enough to dream of being the next Baryshnikov, the next Fosse, or a budding Alvin Ailey. Dale remembered being that young, and dreaming those dreams.

Actually, he was still a young man, but at 44, his time as a dancer was almost up. All the jumping, pounding, and demanding actions a dancer's body must endure had taken their toll. Now, all he dreamed of was inspiring a few of the ones he instructed to reach the heights he had never attained.

Well, that, and the new crop of boy toys each show offered up to him. He had a lot of sweet sticky dreams about them. Oh, yes. Life was still damn good.

". . . and rest," he said finally.

Bone-weary with fatigue, the chorus boys let their strained arm and leg muscles relax. They sagged and sighed with relief. They had put in about four hours of rehearsal time and they were beat.

Dale tapped his pointer on the floor.

"Okay, listen up, my little sugar plum fairies. Surprisingly, that last run-through was not as pathetic as all the previous ones. I suppose it really is the season for miracles. I've asked Santa for some real dancers, but I suppose you'll do until they come along.

"You are dismissed, but be back here January second at 7 P.M. Sharp. I don't give a damn how bad your New Year's hangover may be," he said sternly.

"Tonight is Christmas Eve. They tell me Christ is coming. I wish the same for all of you. Now be gone."

Sindee and Dale watched as the dancers bounded from the stage and changed into their street clothes. They watched and enjoyed as the hard young bodies were stripped of tights, leg warmers, and toe shoes and returned to jeans, sweaters, and Timberlands.

Dale hoped to fuck as many of them as possible. Sindee felt the sharp twinge of lust, too. She hoped to be fucked by as many of them as possible.

She lit a cigarette and tried to figure out which ones might be straight. Oh, but they were all so young and beautiful, she thought. Why set restrictions?

She would settle for the ones suffering from the delusion that they might be straight. The conflicted undecided ones were always good for a few laughs.

For some reason, there was always a lot of sexual energy around a theatrical production. Not that the theater itself is sexy, but performing can be a very sexual experience. All those raw naked emotions being played out, night after night under hot lights.

Gay or straight, almost everyone would be getting some action. And if you weren't getting some action or planning to get some, you were at least thinking about or hoping to get some.

It can't be proven that creativity causes horniness, but maybe it's a by-product.

No matter what the explanation, the theater turned those involved in it into Lust Bunnies.

Whatever the reason, sex was just a part of the experience of doing a show.

Attractions were felt, relationships were formed. The bonds frayed then broke. Partners changed, and it started all over again with the next show.

You couldn't do a show without some kind of sexual intrigue happening.

Drama and passion, a seductive combination. Some performers lived for it.

"God, I love the theater," Sindee said passionately as she watched the chorus boys leave.

She finished her smoke, blowing little smoke rings in the air, confident she had made suggestive eye contact with a few of the ones she wanted.

The last chorus boy to leave was Richard, the dancer with the sock stuffed in his tights. He was always the last to dress because he was so self-conscious about his abnormally small size. Some of the other dancers cruelly called him Little Richard to his face.

Richard believed that Dale was being so tough on him because Dale was trying to help him work through his shyness.

Richard had been so grateful when he found out that he had passed the dance audition and landed a spot in the chorus line.

Richard had big ambitions, but for the time being, this little community theater show boosted his self-confidence. He hadn't made it to the first string of the chorus line, but he had made it to the second, and he was thrilled. It was his confirmation that he had talent. His battered self-esteem needed the positive reinforcement.

Richard trusted that Dale had his best interests at heart.

Richard was stunningly mistaken in his perceptions.

As he walked out, Richard sheepishly wished Dale and Sindee a Merry Christmas.

When they were sure Richard couldn't hear them, Dale laughed, "Merry Christmas, Shrimp Dick."

"Happy New Year, Wee Willy," Sindee joined in.

Now that they were completely alone in the theater, Sindee lit another cigarette, walked over to Dale's Diet Coke and took a long drink.

"Aaaah. Mother's milk. Very refreshing," she said. "But next time add more rum."

"Will do," said Dale, smiling. He got serious for a moment. "Have I thanked you enough for getting me this job?"

"Yes, you have," Sindee reassured him. "But if you want to smother me with gratitude, I won't stop you. And, just so you know, I'm not offended by excessive flattery, either."

"Seriously, Sindee, I owe you. I haven't worked in a while."

Dale took the Diet Coke from Sindee, but avoided looking her in the eyes. He shook the bottle to mix the rum and coke then took a big swig. He wiped his mouth and gradually returned her gaze.

"I suppose you heard about the Disney thing."

"I heard. Why don't you tell me your side of it?"

Dale and Sindee had met years ago doing musicals in New Jersey community theaters. He was an extremely gifted dancer, and she was an exceptional singer and musician.

Dale made the rounds of auditions in New York City and

landed parts in a few off-Broadway productions. Frustrated by never dancing on the "Great White Way," he accepted an offer to choreograph a few shows on the Disney cruise ships. There he finally started getting the recognition he felt he deserved. His star began to rise.

Dale made his peace with not being the featured dancer in an elegantly mounted Broadway production and accepted his fate of teaching dance movement and technique to a bunch of cartoon characters.

Soon, he was promoted to head choreographer for Disney World in Orlando, Florida.

One day, after an afternoon performance of *Sleeping Beauty*, a seven-year-old boy wandered away from his vacationing Bible study group and found his way backstage.

He saw Dale with his pants down, while someone knelt in front of him, their head moving back and forth slowly. The face of this second person was obscured by Dale's well-toned buttocks.

The boy was speechless, but fascinated. He had accidentally witnessed his Mommy and Daddy playing the same silly game at home.

But when Dale pulled his fully erect and glistening cock out of his partner's mouth and started ramming it in and out of his ass, the boy gasped in horror. A man was on the receiving end of Dale's dick and now the man's face was completely unobstructed.

That man was "Prince Charming," still in full costume from the *Sleeping Beauty* show the boy had just seen.

The boy started to scream and continued to scream nonstop for a full hour and a half. After that, he did not speak or utter a sound for two years.

Disney made a substantial and quiet settlement out of court with the parents of the badly traumatized child. Oddly enough, as part of the settlement, the parents had demanded free lifetime passes to all the Disney theme parks, worldwide. After all, they had five other children.

The family agreed not to go public with their lawsuit, so it did not become a media disaster for Disney, but, of course, Dale was forever banished from The Magic Kingdom.

He wasn't even allowed at Disney's annual Gay Day festivities.

Since 1991, hundreds of thousands of gay men and lesbians from around the world get together one weekend in summer to celebrate a Pride event at Disney. Every gay person on the planet is welcome.

Every gay person except Dale.

His picture is posted conspicuously inside all the entrance booths for the ticket takers. Security guards are in constant surveillance of the park gates to guarantee he does not get through them.

There would be no more Gay Day breakfasts for Dale with Winnie the Pooh or Tigger, too.

The Mouse can be so unforgiving and vindictive.

After that, he was unable to get work at any of the other theme parks in Orlando, or at any of the Florida theaters.

When he went on job interviews, he was always asked why he left Disney. He would attempt to skirt the question by saying something about creative differences and his artistic integrity, but no one believed him. And no one called him back with a job offer.

Soon interest in him dried up completely.

Dale's career at Disney had soared brightly, then crashed and burned spectacularly. Now he couldn't get arrested.

When he got the call from Sindee asking him to help stage an original musical, he saw it as an opportunity to rebuild his reputation. He swallowed his pride, packed his bags, and returned to New Jersey.

"The screaming little bastard could have at least kept quiet until my Prince had cum," Dale concluded.

Sindee had just taken another drink from the bottle. She started laughing and spit the whole mouthful out, spraying rum and Coke all over both of them. They broke into fits of laughter. They wiped their faces and clothes as best they could.

"What happened to 'Prince Charming'?" Sindee asked.

"He was fired, too," answered Dale. "But with his considerable oral skills, he was able to blow his way into a job as Weatherman at one of the Florida TV stations."

Dale took another bottle of spiked Diet Coke out of his backpack and opened it. He became very serious.

"Do the Taylors know about it?" he asked nervously.

"No. No one here knows but you and me," Sindee replied.

"I'd like to work here again after this show is over. I'd hate for them to find out that I . . ."

"They won't find out," Sindee cut him off. "I'll make sure they won't. They're very trusting. Sometimes too much for their own good. I've never seen a theater where the owners let the actors and the crew have access to the accounts. I'll have to speak with them about that."

She laughed softly.

Dale smiled and nodded in agreement. His gaze drifted toward the theater's office. The Taylors were very trusting, indeed, he thought. The money in the office safe was available to everyone.

He returned his attention to Sindee. He drank some Coke.

Unlike Dale, Sindee's theater work had never taken her beyond New Jersey. It wasn't that she didn't have the talent to turn professional. She didn't have the temperament.

Sindee told Dale how she had auditioned for a part in the theater's production of *The Little Foxes* two seasons earlier. She would have taken anything just to get her foot in the door, but

luckily she landed the part of Regina Giddens, the female lead.
The Taylors thought Sindee had a very strong Bette Davis
quality. Davis had played that role in the movie adaptation.

After that, Sindee threw herself wholeheartedly into any production that was done at the theater, in any way that she was
needed, onstage or off.

Some of the regular members in the group who had been
there longer didn't like the way that Sindee had moved in and
gained the Taylors' trust, but Sindee didn't care. As long as the
Taylors were happy with her work, Sindee could weather any
backstage jealousy.

A number of the actors didn't want to do the necessary backstage work such as stage managing, assistant stage managing,
lights, or props, but Sindee performed these tasks as eagerly and
as skillfully as she did her acting assignments.

The Taylors were grateful.

So by the time Sindee approached them to do a musical, for
which she would write the musical score and hire the musicians and choreographer, she had earned their complete confidence. They were understandably unsure at first, having no
experience with musicals, but they had faith in Sindee.

Other members of the group were salivating to do a musical
as well, and even if they didn't share the Taylors' high regard for
Sindee, they climbed on board quickly.

So the Taylors nervously agreed to do a musical, and they
agreed to hire Dale Mabrey based upon Sindee's vigorous rec-
ommendation.

"You are so good to me," Dale said, when Sindee finished
her story. "Why is it that we never got together?"

Sindee chuckled. "You mean besides the fact that 'gayer than
laughter are you'?"

"Yes, besides that."

Sindee thought for a moment. "It's probably because I'd always be after your boyfriends, or because I'd leave you in a heartbeat if I met the woman of my dreams."

Dale smiled. Same old Sindee. "Still playing for both teams, eh?"

"What can I say," admitted Sindee. "I love men and I love women. I am intentionally and exuberantly ambivalent. I refuse to choose. And besides, it doubles my chances for getting laid on a Friday night. Any more prying questions?"

"Yes. You haven't seen me dance or stage anything since I went to Florida. And on top of that, God help me, I'm almost forty-four. Aging might be great for wine and Scotch, but it's just slow death for a dancer. What made you recommend me to the Taylors?"

Sindee took the Diet Coke bottle from him, and placed her almost finished cigarette in his mouth.

"Do the routine you just rehearsed with those kids. Go."

Sindee sang the musical accompaniment and clapped her hands to the beat.

Dale launched immediately into the demanding dance number and executed each move masterfully, and with great flourish.

When he was finished, Sindee went over to him and removed the cigarette from his mouth.

"That's why I recommended you," she said, pointing to the nearly finished smoke.

The long ash that had formed there before she first gave it to him had remained perfectly intact throughout the entire dance sequence.

"You were always as smooth and as graceful as a cat. I knew that if you were anything less, you wouldn't have taken the job. And like me, you're a fussy perfectionist. I knew you'd get every motion, every nuance you could out of these dancers. So, in the long run, if you're good, I look good to Addison and Karson. I simply made a smart business decision."

Dale did a deep *grand plié* acknowledging the compliment, then returned to the conversation.

"Well, your call came just at the right time," said Dale, as he began to pack up his gear. "I really needed to get out of Florida fast. I would have sprouted wings and flown here if I could. I owe everybody money; my agent, my lawyer, everybody. Hell, I owe God money. And no one I owe is being as patient as God."

Sindee began to gather her things, too. When they were both ready to leave, Dale turned to her.

"So, you're the only one here who knows my dirty little secret. I guess that means I have to do whatever you say to keep your silence. Who do you want killed?" asked Dale, laughing offhandedly at his own joke.

Intrigued, Sindee looked at him and asked, "Who do you have in mind?"

Dale stopped laughing. It took a few beats before he realized she was now joking with him. Then he laughed again when he was sure she had been toying with him.

"Maybe it won't come to that," she said, sounding cagey, "but I have figured out a way we can get some extra money out of this place."

She waited for his reaction. She watched him as she lit a cigarette using the lighter he had given her.

Sindee made sure he saw the masks. She took a long drag, then slowly released the smoke.

He didn't speak, but she knew he was interested.

Sindee stepped closer to him. Dale leaned in.

"I'm working on a personal project in addition to this show," she said. "I won't tell you how I got the start-up money, so don't ask me. You don't want to know. That's not your concern. I'm not proud of it, but sometimes you find yourself doing things you never thought yourself capable of doing. But, at any rate, I have the money now, and I'm ready to go. I need your help. It could mean a lot of money as a result if we do it right. Are you in?"

Dale took a long look at her. "You practically own me. Of course I'm in," he said.

"Good, we can talk about it over a drink. That is, of course, unless you have other plans for tonight?"

Sindee was fishing for information to see if he had met anyone special yet. She had tried to get Dale to go out for a drink after several of the rehearsals, but he had always rushed out immediately afterward, brushing her off, always with the excuse that he had to meet someone.

Sindee was dying to know who. Maybe she could get him to open up about it tonight.

Sindee was the theater's most accomplished gossip. She got all the tasty tidbits on everyone. It was killing her that Dale had a secret he wasn't sharing with her.

"No, no," Dale said. "I don't have any plans for tonight either. I was just going to go home, turn on the TV and watch *Lifetime*, the cable channel for women and gay men. It's their annual 'Twelve Days of Christmas Agony' marathon. Every movie is a 'My husband was a cheatin', lyin', wifebeatin' bastard, but I loved him anyway, right up until I killed him' extravaganza. But if we're going out for a drink, I really have to pee first."

"Well, the exit is right over here: closer than the men's room. Why don't you just do it in the parking lot?"

"Whip it out in the parking lot, in winter? I know what you're up to, my sexually schizophrenic friend," teased Dale. "You just want to see the cock that cost Disney millions."

Sindee returned his teasing. "Of course I want to see it. But, I am the most sexually clear person you will ever know. Being bisexual means I just want to fuck everyone."

Dale smiled and hugged Sindee and they began to laugh boisterously.

"Are you two ready to leave?"

Startled, Dale and Sindee looked up into the balcony in the direction of the voice.

"I'm getting ready to turn off the lights," called out Rachel.

"Yes, we're leaving now," Sindee replied, trying to sound as calm and nonchalant as possible.

She exchanged a worried look with Dale and they both wondered how long Rachel had been standing there and exactly how much she had overheard.

Again Rachel spoke, "Have you two seen Addison?"

"You might try the office, that's the last place I saw him," Sindee said.

"Thanks," said Rachel. "Good Night. Merry Christmas and Happy New Year."

Both Sindee and Dale smiled nervously up to her and waved.

As Rachel closed the balcony door Dale whispered, "Oh my God! Well, I don't have to go to the bathroom anymore. She just scared the piss out of me."

Dale took hold of Sindee's arm and pulled her in close. He stole a look over each of his shoulders. He spoke very softly, his eyes searching the theater. He wasn't going to chance being surprised again.

"How much do you think she heard . . . everything?"

"I don't know. Let's just get the hell out of here and go for that drink," Sindee whispered back.

"We've got a lot of planning to do."

The two friends quietly left the theater together, each confident they were spending the approaching Christmas with the one person they trusted without reservation.

3

Slick helped Laura onto the stair seat and walked down beside her.

Judson, head of the household staff, was standing at the bottom of the staircase holding a small tray with two Absolut martinis on it.

Typical Judson, thought Laura, when she saw him waiting there. He had an astonishing gift of anticipation; always the right thing at the right time. He always seemed to be ten steps ahead of those he served, knowing what they needed before they knew it themselves.

Judson was an anachronism, but he was the only other person in the world Laura trusted as much as Slick.

Judson came from a long tradition of English personal service. Before she'd been born, Judson had been her father's personal valet. When Laura was a little girl, and her parents were away, it was Judson who had taken care of her scraped knees, driven her to and from school and tennis lessons. It was Judson who had convinced her that it probably wasn't a good idea to eat a worm.

Laura remembered that when her parents were away, she had the run of the house. At least Judson had let her believe that for the few hours between finishing her homework and bedtime, she ran the house.

It was the rule that she had to finish her lessons first. There was never any backsliding on that. Laura had to earn her grades and not rely on her father's prestigious name.

Owen was very strict about that; so, in turn, was Judson.

But once her homework was done, Judson would let her into her father's study. It was a wondrous room to Laura, filled with her father's papers and books. Laura would climb into her father's big swivel chair behind his giant desk. She would sink into the cushions and look at the papers on his desk.

She was never allowed to touch anything on the desk, but she was fascinated.

Judson would stand by, silently watching in case she tumbled from the chair.

Laura never knew Judson was following her father's instructions. From this early age, Owen wanted Laura to be comfortable in his study and in his chair.

For the longest time, Laura believed Judson was a member of the family. She was too young then to recognize that delicate line of familiarity at which the rich and their servants separated themselves.

After her father died, Laura asked Judson to become head of staff. She offered him a suite of rooms in the southern end of the mansion and was grateful when he accepted. Often she wondered what he thought of the changes that had taken place from the days when her father owned the house until now.

Laura's father, Owen Charles, had made his fortune in the early 1950s in New Jersey's clamming industry. He started with a few small boats working out of the Atlantic Highlands. By the time he retired, he had built one of the largest clamming concerns on the Northeast Corridor. His company employed hundreds of fishermen and he owned several plants where the clams were processed. His holdings extended from Cape May, New Jersey, to Montauk, New York.

Owen built his home, a sixty-two-room mansion, on 30,000 acres in the sprawling Ramapo Mountains of New Jersey. It was built to resemble a Tudor castle, and because of this, he was often called "Owen the First, King of Clams." Owen loved it not only for its business connotations, but for its sexual ones as well.

Like many successful businessmen, he was always cunning and shrewd, but not always ethical, and not always faithful. Once Owen had the taste of success, he couldn't be held back by any restrictions. He chafed at the rules of convention.

His marriage to Laura's mother Vanessa was loveless; they stayed together only because they were totally devoted to Laura.

Laura's mother's family had their own money, old money that was inherited and passed down to the next generation. It was class-conscious money, not made from fishmongering the way Owen had made his. They felt that by marrying Owen she had married beneath her. Now she was a fishwife, wasn't she? They felt that common businesspeople like Owen were contributing to the disappearance of manners and good breeding.

After a while, Laura's mother began to believe it, too.

She went on performing her social duties as Owen's wife, graciously, but humorlessly. Eventually, she cared less and less about Owen's other women. She had no delusions about it. Owen liked women. He would never be satisfied with just one. So be it!

She only cared about her daughter.

Both parents doted on her. Laura was the only thing they agreed on.

They made sure Laura had the best of everything.

Owen was especially enchanted with her. Sometimes his face ached just from smiling at her. Laura was the one person Owen truly loved unconditionally. He was determined to be a better father than he was a husband. Owen knew what the rest of the world thought of him and he really didn't give a damn, but he wanted to see something else when he saw himself reflected in Laura's eyes. He wanted to see love in her eyes.

Growing up, Laura had been well aware of the rumors of her father's infidelities and unscrupulous business dealings, but she adored him.

As his fortune grew, Owen cultivated many influential friends in the world of politics and commerce. His office desk and walls proudly and conspicuously displayed dozens of photographs of himself flanked by the important people of the moment. These photographs were regularly updated or replaced with others, depending on the shifting celebrity status of those pictured.

The television industry had its infancy in New York, and Owen Charles accurately recognized the potential of this new medium early on. His company sponsored one of the first television game shows: *The Charles Clams Casino Hour.* Contestants would select to play blackjack, 5-card stud, or deuces wild. All games required spinning a big wheel with playing cards painted on it. Fortunes were made and lost, and audiences tuned in each week to watch the drama of winning or losing. Winners got as much as $10,000 and losers were sent to the Clam Dip Pit. But, win or lose, every contestant walked away with a three-month supply of Charles Minced Clams.

Owen was a marketing genius.

The television show and his company were becoming big successes.

Soon he had politicians, CEOs, and television and Broadway actors, directors, and producers welcoming his phone calls; they all would gladly stop what they were doing to talk to Owen Charles.

He threw lavish parties in his home, and worked his way into the better social circles.

And, of course, since he made his living from the ocean, he

bought an enormous yacht and entertained there as well. He named it *The Prince Caviar*. It was a floating paradise with a thoroughly stocked bar and a perpetual party buffet, specializing in seafood.

The food kept coming and the bar never ran dry on *The Prince Caviar*.

There was continuous music, perfect for dancing and swimming and drinking, and of course, for extramarital affairs. If Owen was going to be one slippery son of a bitch, he was going to be one slippery son of a bitch in style.

He was driven.

Laura was his only child; he never wanted any others. He worked hard to amass his fortune for her.

To some, it seemed that Owen Charles wanted to leave his daughter so much money, that she would never have to depend on a man like himself to care for her.

Ironically, he needn't have worried. Laura had never shown even the slightest romantic interest in men. She often joked, "Some of my best friends are men, but I wouldn't want my daughter to marry one."

When Laura's time came to run the company, she renamed it and restructured it to make it her own. Where Owen was only concerned with how much he could take from the waters off New Jersey and New York, Laura started to harvest shellfish. She set quantity restrictions on fishing and made sure the company adhered to the set limits.

Her dedication, hard work, and talent had reinvented every aspect of her father's company. Now Laura was the company.

She knew that if she spent her money extravagantly for three lifetimes, she would never spend all that he left her, so she set up charities and foundations in her father's name. Laura wanted history to treat her father more kindly than he deserved.

Now that her parents were dead, there was only Judson.

In this huge castle she had inherited, only he had known Laura as a little girl. Only Judson had been there to witness her maturation into a young woman and now president of the company her father had started.

Laura still entertained the rich and powerful in her home, but her relationship with Slick had introduced a more flamboyant, colorful element that hadn't existed before. If Judson disapproved of her life now, he didn't show it. He maintained the house in his usual devoted, polished, genteel but firm manner. He made sure he and the staff was always available when they were needed, and invisible when they were not.

After Slick moved in, he carefully and deliberately weeded out any staff members who had even whispered about the gay union of the white socialite and the black ex-detective.

Laura hoped he did have some genuine feeling for her as she did for him. She hoped that his loyalty to her came from something more than his sense of duty. She would have welcomed a more casual interaction with him but knew his code of conduct would not permit it.

So, her affection for him went unspoken. But she truly loved this faithful old gentleman who seemed to have removed all traces of the needs of his own life and dedicated himself to the needs of others.

And now Judson watched from below as the white lesbian socialite mermaid and her black ex-cop Sherlock Holmes lover descended the stairs.

He watched as they approached with the same everyday blasé expression one would watch the Weather Channel.

Slick helped Laura off the seat, then she looked up at the ceiling as if she were outside and pretended to study the atmospheric conditions.

"My senses are tingling. Yes . . . yes . . . It feels like it's going to martini."

Then turning to Judson and feigning surprise, she said, "Look I was right!" She took the martinis from the tray.

"Wonderful, Judson," she said. "Thank you." She took a long sip from one of the martinis, and handed the other to Laura.

"You're quite welcome, Miss Slick. I thought you might enjoy a quick one to catch up to your guests."

Slick never tired of hearing Judson's proper and efficient British accent.

Slick had a soft spot in her heart for Judson.

From the first day she met him, he had made her feel comfortable and welcome, like she belonged here.

He had worked for Laura's family for almost all her life, and when it was clear that Laura had chosen Slick for her life companion, Judson treated her as Laura's equal in the house, and in doing so, the rest of the staff did as well.

"How are the revelers doing?" asked Laura.

"They're eating heartily and the drink is flowing. Most are mingling in the Grand Assembly Hall. Those preferring a less raucous evening have gathered in the north sitting room, enjoying the stringed quartet and the Dickensian Carolers. A few are in the Billiard room. All are quite comfortable.

"I've instructed a few of the staff to remain on hand to answer the door for late arrivals, and to keep the food and beverages replenished."

"Thank you, Judson, for overseeing things until we arrived. I think we can manage from here," said Laura.

"Very well, Miss."

"Merry Christmas, Judson," said Laura and Slick together.

"Merry Christmas," he replied with a bow. He turned and was gone.

Slick and Laura were about to enter the assembly hall when they heard voices calling their names.

"Slick!" "Laura!" "Hi!" "Merry Christmas!"

They looked around and saw the "Three Little Pigs" rapidly approaching them. Slick and Laura looked at each other and smiled.

The three guests removed their masks.

It was Sam Billingsley, Cathy Simpson, and Paula Rafferty, three cops from Slick's old precinct.

Sam and Slick had attended the academy together. They liked each other instantly because they shared the same belief that police officers should be model citizens, good and true.

After the academy, they were assigned to different precincts but they stayed in touch.

The night they came out to one another, they knew they'd be friends for life.

They started a chapter of the Fraternal Order of Police for black and gay police officers in Newark. They called themselves "The Homey-sexuals."

They both applied for and entered plainclothes school at the same time and ended up as partners in the same precinct.

When Slick left the force to start her own detective agency, Sam had given her whatever support she needed; access to police leads, crime photos, witness statements.

The Department would have prohibited the sharing of such information, but in the end it benefited everyone. Many cases that had remained open or had been considered unsolvable were closed as a result.

The precinct's conviction rate had risen substantially with Sam working inside the law and Slick now free to chase down every lead and get into areas forbidden in the regulations.

Word quickly spread about Slick's success rate, and soon cops from other precincts were unofficially cooperating with her and she with them.

Cathy and Paula were partners on the job who had taken over the helm of "The Homey-Sexuals" after Slick left.

Cathy and Paula had instituted a big campy award cere-
mony every year in tribute to the best and bravest of the gay
and lesbian police officers. The recipients of these awards were
simultaneously honored and roasted at these events.

In recognition of Slick's outstanding contribution to the
force and the community, there was an award presented every
year in her name. Over the years this award came to be known
as the "Dyke" Tracy or "Dickless" Tracy award.

Laura and Slick exchanged hugs and kisses with all of them.

"Are you crazy, dressing up as pigs?" laughed Slick.

"Hey, it's Christmas time. Everyone has a sense of humor at
Christmas," said Sam. Paula put her arm around Laura and
asked, "When are you going to stop living off this woman's
money and get back to some real work, Slick, detective work?"

"Managing Laura's company is real work," she replied. "Do
you have any idea how many crooks are out there disguised as
businessmen?"

"Sounds pretty cushy to me," said Cathy. "You get paid to
do nothing. I never thought I'd see the day that you'd become
a 'kept woman,' Slick. If you moved to Vermont, you could
just marry Laura for her money."

"I keep proposing," Laura smiled. "She keeps turning me
down." They all laughed.

"Seriously, Slick, we miss you out there. We all sit around
sometimes and talk about those cases you solved that no one
else could. Remember that one about the nearsighted, suicidal
twin? She killed her sister by mistake. That was a thing of
beauty, Slick."

Sam took a long pause to make sure he had everyone's attention. Then he continued.

"But the best, the all-time best . . . was the earlobe."

Sam's demeanor changed from jovial to reverential.

He raised his glass in tribute to his former partner and

started to tell for the umpteenth time how Slick had reconstructed a crime scene where the only thing left of the murder victim was his right earlobe.

An anonymous untraceable phone call was made to the police station saying a murder had been committed. The caller gave the address where the murder was done.

By the time the police arrived at the scene, there were no witnesses, no fingerprints, no suspects, and more important, there was no body.

The blood evidence and DNA was inconclusive because so many police officers hadn't spotted the earlobe. It was stepped on repeatedly by everyone investigating the scene.

The newspapers were crawling all over this story, calling it a real-life whodunit. It was a reporter's wet dream. The press was giving the story all the attention of an international manhunt.

They thronged the police station every day asking hard questions of whatever spokesperson *du jour* was sent out to them as a sacrifice at press conferences.

All the major journalists were vying for an exclusive.

Words like *Mysterious* and *Puzzling* were used on the front page headlines everywhere. *"Baffled!"* read the *New York Post*.

It had been a particularly gruesome crime. After the initial discovery of the earlobe, the murderer left various body parts in various locations. And always, the locations were wiped clean.

Privately the police referred to the crime as the "Immaculate Dissection." Many were skeptical about ever catching the killer.

But Slick solved the crime in three days without causing embarrassment to the force, the coroner's office, or the DA.

When the press finally got hold of the break in the case, Slick shared the credit with everyone. She faulted no one and insisted that solving the case had been a joint and coordinated team effort.

She never told anyone that she alone was responsible for finding the rest of the victim's remains and capturing the murderer.

Years later the case was still being taught at the academy in the crime scene analysis course.

The cops never got tired of hearing these stories or telling them.

Cathy and Paula respectfully raised their glasses to toast Slick and then they all took a drink.

Slick tried to look modest but failed.

"Until I met Laura, my life was filled with daily run-ins with winos, freaks, degenerates, and other assorted lowlifes," Slick said, trying to change the subject.

"You miss it, don't you?" asked Sam

"Every day," said Slick. "But Laura wanted me off the street and managing her company. Laura has a way of being irresistible. We talked about it and we agreed it was time for me to quit."

"You are so whipped," laughed Paula.

"Every night," winked Slick.

"Okay," sighed Sam. "Since we can't change your mind, we're gonna go eat some more of your gourmet food and drink some more of your expensive liquor."

"Wait, before you go, we have to do it one more time. All together now . . . which is easier, being born black, or being born gay?" asked Slick.

"Black!" they shouted in unison.

"Why?" asked Slick.

"Because you don't have to come out to your parents," they all said.

Laura and Slick watched as their friends headed toward another part of the mansion.

When they were sure no one else was watching, Slick and

Sam looked back at each other, conspiratorially, and Slick gave him a "thumbs up" sign.

That meant she'd call him soon to see what cases he was working on. She wanted to get back to doing some kind of law enforcement work, and she wanted to see what was happening.

Slick's job at Laura's company, Clam-de-Monium, paid her well, but it wasn't very challenging.

She didn't like keeping things from Laura and was going to tell her as soon as possible, but not tonight. Tonight was the eve of their tenth Christmas together and not the time for such serious matters.

It could wait.

Slick and Laura finished their martinis and set the glasses down.

"Who did you get to be the house band this year? Did you get that kid? What's her name? Broccoli Spears?" asked Slick facetiously.

Slick really didn't care who was playing. She was looking forward to dancing to a few slow tunes when Laura would close her eyes, put her head on Slick's shoulder, and they would melt into one another.

"No," said Laura, laughing. "Bruce called and said he was going to be spending the holidays at his home here in New Jersey. He said he and the guys would love to play tonight. Plus, Melissa and kd are here, somewhere. They both told me they'd gladly do a few numbers when Bruce wanted to take a break. kd and Melissa are thinking of getting together and doing a remake of that Julio Iglesias and Willie Nelson song, 'To All the Girls I've Loved Before.' They may sing it here tonight."

Slick and Laura walked to the Grand Assembly Hall and looked inside.

The entire hall was decorated from floor to ceiling with

lights, garlands, and wreaths. Swags of rich red and green velvet were draped about. Overhead, the candelabra was entwined with holly, berries, and ivy, making it the mother of all mistletoe.

A colossal twenty-foot Christmas tree loomed above the guests. Decorated with hundreds of candy canes, presents, strings of popcorn, tinsel, and bows, it was the centerpiece of the room.

The air was filled with the sounds of laughter, happy conversation, and great music.

Bruce was wailing, and the place was rocking.

"Santa Claus is comin' to town . . .
Santa Claus is comin' to town . . .
Santa Claus is com-min' to-o town!"

Through it all was the sound of corks popping and ice tinkling in the cut-crystal glasses.

Jugglers and magicians strolled throughout the room, performing and entertaining. Above, acrobats did stunts in midair.

The serving staff, dressed up as Santa's helper elves and pixies, moved deftly and unobtrusively through the crowd with trays of canapés and cocktails.

A wildly diverse mix of people had been invited into their home to celebrate Christmas Eve. Most of those invited gladly accepted.

Here in the subdued lighting, behind the camouflage of their masks and costumes, politicians and CEOs danced and chatted with ex-hustlers and pimps.

Kings of industry sang Christmas carols with queens of drag.

Republicans toasted Democrats.

Reporters and celebrities peacefully suspended their usual hunter-versus-the-hunted maneuvering.

There were even a few members of some royal families on hand.

That had been the only requirement to get on the guest list of a Laura Charles and Cassandra Slick party; they had insisted that guests in their home treat each other with respect and courtesy.

With that came discretion.

Whatever happened at parties here remained known only to the partygoers.

Even those with nothing to lose, those who may have been tempted with large, fast, easy money into talking to the press, remained silent.

Slick still had powerful contacts and considerable influence at a lot of PDs. Everyone understood the greater value of keeping her as a friend, so they kept their mouths shut.

Slick and Laura gained the reputation of providing an atmosphere of fun and privacy.

Over the years the famous and infamous, the privileged and the less-than-privileged had socialized together in their home, confident that they wouldn't read about their adventures in the tabloids. Consequently, their guest list grew longer after every party.

Slick and Laura lingered at the entryway for a moment to see if they could recognize some of the masqueraders.

"Is that who I think it is?" asked Laura, looking in the direction of a handsome young man in a Zorro costume.

Slick looked. "I think it is. Yes, it's definitely him."

"Who's that cute cowboy he's playing kissy-face with?"

"That's Tony 'Ten Inches' Gillardo, former male prostitute."

They were about to continue with their name game, when they were spotted.

"Merry Christmas, Laura. Great Party. Slick, I need to talk

to you. Now." Slick turned to the man in the jester costume who was grabbing her arm and pulling her aside.

Laura stumbled momentarily when Slick let go of her arm, but soon felt someone else holding her up.

"This is wonderful, Laura. A lovely party. I love your mermaid costume. Your home is just beautiful. Thanks for inviting me."

Laura immediately recognized the voice behind the Abe Lincoln makeup.

She thought the Honest Abe costume was a brilliant idea.

"Senator, I'm so glad you could be here. Abe Lincoln looks good on you. There are some things I'd like to . . ."

"Excuse me, Miss Laura," interrupted Evelyn. Judson had assigned Evelyn to answer the door for the evening.

"There's a gentleman at the door who insists on speaking with Miss Slick."

Laura could see that the jester was still bending Slick's ear.

"I'll see to it, Evelyn. Thank you."

"Senator," she said, turning back to "Abe." "Please excuse me for one moment."

"Certainly." The senator walked away and struck up a conversation with "Lucky Numbers" Nussbaum.

As Laura took little baby steps out of the room, she saw Henry, who worked in the kitchen, pushing an empty food cart.

"Henry," she said. "How about a lift?"

"Of course, Miss," Henry obliged.

He helped Laura onto the food cart and wheeled her down the long hallway toward the front door.

Evelyn followed them, quietly amused at the sight. She couldn't help being reminded of a mermaid float she had once seen in a parade. She imagined Laura on the float, doing the queenly hand wave and nodding regally to the crowd.

"Thank you, Henry," said Laura when they reached the entryway. "Please continue to do whatever you were doing before I cart-jacked you."

"Yes, Miss."

Laura hopped off the cart and looked around. There was no one there.

"A man *was* here a moment ago, Miss. I let him in myself," said Evelyn nervously.

Judson had emphatically directed the staff to exhibit their most professional service for this party. He would not abide any mistakes. Evelyn did not want any bad reports about her work getting back to him

"Oh, I believe you, Evelyn," Laura reassured her.

Laura opened the door and peered outside into the snowy night. Eventually there was a rustling in the shrubbery.

"Hello. May I help you?" she called out.

Gradually a little man stepped into view.

"I'm here to see Slick," he called back eventually.

"She's a little busy right now. I'm Laura Charles. I'm sure Slick wouldn't mind if you talked to me. You must be cold out there and I'm tired of shouting. Please come in."

He looked around to make sure no one was watching. He climbed the steps, wiped his feet and stepped inside.

Evelyn stood by and watched him closely. He was short and sturdy and he looked confused and uncomfortable. He removed his hat.

Laura smiled and tried to put him at ease.

"How may I help you, Mr . . . ?"

"McDonough," said the little man. "Snatch McDonough."

"Pleased to meet you, Mr. McDonough," said Laura, extending her hand.

He wiped his hand on his faded brown coat, then shook hers. He let out a low whistle.

"This is some house," he said, looking around at the tapestries, the Greek vases, and the hand-carved ceiling.

Snatch was not an educated man, but he knew money when he smelled it. This place was marinating in it.

"Thank you." Laura smiled and patiently waited for him to continue.

"I got this invitation. There was a note inside from Slick." He pulled an invitation from his pocket. "I just wanted to stop by and say hello and thanks."

"Did you work with Slick?" asked Laura

"Oh, no ma'am," he answered. "She arrested me. I just got out three weeks ago. Twelve years, grand larceny. Slick was the only one to ever catch me. She promised me that if I cleaned up my act, she'd help me get a job. She kept her word. For that I am grateful every day. I just wanted to let her know that I'm workin' at Wal-Mart now and I'm doin' alright. She's a real nice woman, Slick is."

"Yes she is."

Snatch didn't know what to say next. He rocked back and forth on his heels and fiddled with his hat.

"Well, okay, then. Just tell her I stopped by. I'll be on my way now. Good night. Merry Christmas."

He put his hat on and turned to leave.

"Please stay, Mr. McDonough," Laura said. "You were invited, so you're welcome here."

"I don't think I'm dressed for it," he said, looking her up and down in her mermaid costume.

He'd been in jail a long time, he thought. The civilians sure were dressing funny these days.

"I didn't know this was such a fancy place. I haven't been around nice people in a long time. Well, to be honest, I ain't really ever been around nice people, unless I was robbin' 'em. I used to be a thief, ya know. I done my time, but the cops still pick me up now and again for questionin' when somethin' goes stolen.

"I know Slick hears stuff about me, but I wanted her to know I'm clean. I ain't lifted nothin' since I got out. I ain't even gotten a parkin' ticket, I swear."

Then Snatch raised his hand as if he were taking a solemn oath. It was a promise, strong and sincere.

"Well, I better go now, I wouldn't want to embarrass Slick or you by being here."

"Please stay," Laura said. Snatch had stolen her heart. "I know Slick would want to see you."

"Well . . . okay, Miss Charles, if you say so."

"Laura. Call me Laura, please."

"Call me 'Snatch,' or 'Snatch Mc D,' or 'Snatchmo.' You know, short for Snatch McDonough."

"Please forgive my bluntness, but if you're trying to distance yourself from your former life as a thief, maybe you should consider dropping your nickname," suggested Laura. "That might make your life a little easier. What's your first name, Mr. McDonough?"

"Adolf," he replied quietly, thoroughly embarrassed.

" 'Snatch' it is," said Laura quickly.

She tried to turn to lead Snatch back to the Assembly Hall, but her tail made it difficult to rotate.

"Snatch, I know you don't know me. We've just met, but would you please give me a hand? I could use all the help I can get." Laura didn't want to fall ungracefully on her backside in front of a friend of Slick's she was meeting for the first time.

Snatch handed his hat and coat to Evelyn, then grabbed hold of Laura's waist and started steering her back to the party.

He glanced again at all the tapestries and oil paintings that adorned the hall. He marveled at the exquisite taste of every-thing, the arrangement, the perfect matching of forms and colors. He knew that the artworks were originals, and momentarily wondered what he could get for them on the street.

Snatch took a deep breath, closed his eyes, and repeated to himself, "I am not a crook. I am not a crook."

As they were about to enter the party, Snatch suddenly stopped.

"I'm sorry, Miss Charles. I don't think I can do this. I'd be wonderin' all night if you and Slick felt like you could trust me here with all your fine things."

"Let me show you something, Snatch," said Laura. "Look over there. See Abe Lincoln over there? Do you know who that is?"

Snatch looked closely. Slowly he made recognition. His eyes widened. "Oh my God!" he gasped. "Is that who I think it is?"

"Yes, it is," said Laura. "The junior senator from New York, the former First Lady. She and her husband were accused of all kinds of mischief. If I can be comfortable with them here, I can certainly be comfortable with you."

Snatch straightened his tie, smoothed down his hair, and felt more relaxed. "I ain't got a costume," he said shyly.

"No one will notice."

"You got a lot of nice stuff here, Miss Char . . . Laura. I'll make sure no one cops any of it and then says it was a gift. Know what I mean?" he said protectively.

"Thank you, Snatch."

4

"That was not my line! My character would never say that line! It's stupid! I don't get it! This script is bullshit! This play is bullshit! You're the stage manager, you idiot, do your job! When I call for a line, give me the exact line, and give it to me immediately! How can I memorize it if you give me the wrong fucking line? I am an artist! I will not be compromised by your stupidity! Isn't it bad enough that I've got to rehearse this dreck on Christmas Eve?"

Randall picked up the heavy binder containing his copy of the script and hurled it angrily at the wall.

Blair, who was leaning against the target wall, moved slightly at the last second just before the binder sailed past and slammed into it. There was a loud thud and chunks of plaster fell to the floor.

The walls of the men's dressing room were pockmarked with craters made from Randall's fits of temper. The craters ranged in size from little knicks to fist sized cavities that Randall had punched in when angered.

Blair was so used to these outbursts that she was only vaguely aware that she had just barely missed being hit in the face.

She sat silently waiting for Randall to calm himself.

Blair did not look directly at him because he hated when people looked directly at him after he had a temper tantrum. She wouldn't speak until he spoke.

Even though she could hear him sobbing now as he sat at his dressing table, she would not look at him or speak to him until he gave her the sign that he was back to normal.

Now that he was crying Blair knew the worst was over. Nothing else would be thrown or broken, but she knew he wasn't ready to talk yet.

Randall had conditioned her to wait for him to make the first move after he had one of his episodes.

Blair busied herself by picking up the binder and gathering the pages that had scattered all over the dressing-room floor. She kept her head and eyes down, as he had instructed her to do. She put the pages of the script back in their proper order.

Randall grabbed a handful of tissues from the box in front of him and blew his nose. His sobbing had stopped. He stood up and checked his hair in the mirror. He took a step back and studied himself from head to toe. His ears were large and stuck out a little, but he told himself this made him look like a young Clark Gable.

He truly was a good-looking guy, but right now he looked bad. Real bad. Jesus, he thought, this stupid show was beginning to affect him physically. He was too thin. He needed to gain some weight, but he was working on it.

He sat down and began to retouch his makeup to cover the lines on his face made from his tears.

Randall caught sight of Blair's reflection in the mirror. She was busy doing something on the floor. He didn't know what. He didn't care.

He watched her for a few moments until he was sure she hadn't been watching him. No, she hadn't caught him primping in the mirror. He was certain of it.

Randall cleared his throat as he always did to signal that it was okay for her to resume talking again. Blair heard the signal, put the binder down, and gave Randall her full attention.

"How bad was I?" he asked self-consciously, trying to downplay the last few moments.

Blair, not sure yet what he wanted from her, chose her words carefully and spoke to him as gently as possible.

"First of all, are you all right? Your blood sugar, I mean. Do you need to check it? Should I get you something, some juice, or maybe a candy bar?" Blair asked cautiously. "Wait. I think you may have some medicine in the refrigerator." Blair walked quickly toward the refrigerator and opened the door.

Randall stood up, crossed to the refrigerator and cut her off. He slammed the door shut and turned to her angrily. He spoke gruffly and impatiently. He didn't want to have that particular conversation about his health with Blair.

"Forget about that right now, will you? Just tell me how I did."

Not wanting to set him off again, Blair did as she was told.

"You're playing the part wonderfully, considering that Karson keeps giving you a lot of script changes. Your character has been rewritten more than the others. And you're right, the script is bad. It's derivative. The dialogue is stilted. The plot is abysmal. Even the stage directions are unintelligible. But because you're such a skillful actor, Karson knows you can make any line work. You've always been able to breathe life into even the worst material. Karson and Addison expect too much from you. I don't think they realize how much pressure they put on you."

Blair finished talking hoping she had said the right things. She was still treading cautiously.

Randall was still lost in despair.

"Karson keeps cutting and changing my lines, making my part smaller and smaller. Why? Why? What does she want from me?"

Blair looked at Randall's face to make sure it was safe to continue. She wanted to encourage him without sounding patronizing. Randall hated to be patronized.

Blair kept her voice even and tried to keep any intonation, patronizing or otherwise, out of it.

"Even with all the changes she keeps throwing at you, you are off book with your lines more so than the others. Your singing and dancing is outstanding. I think Sindee and Dale pick on you sometimes because you have more talent than the rest of the cast."

"Really?"

Randall looked at her, needing to be reassured. Blair knew she had him under control now.

"Really," she continued. "You are the best thing on that stage, as usual."

Randall started to pace around the dressing room. Actually, he started to strut. His confidence was returning.

"I thought so," he said. "I just needed to hear it."

He felt better. He started to vent everything that had been building up inside him.

"I can't believe that Addison and Karson are spending all the money they've made these last seven seasons to do this stupid musical. I was the lead actor for all seven years and what thanks did I get? None. I never got paid. Now that they are about to make some money, they gamble everything on this piece of crap. Why? Because Sindee tells them they can reach a broader audience by doing more modern plays! Well, no shit! I've been telling them that for years, for free. But all Sindee has to do is talk Karson into writing a musical and then they practically give her their checkbook to mount the stupid thing, plus, they're paying her a salary! And she is such a pretentious bitch, spelling her name the way she does. Does she think we're all so stupid we don't know her name is spelled C-I-N-D-Y? She's up to something, I can tell."

Blair nodded but remained silent. She agreed with everything Randall was saying. She had taken every opportunity to point out those very facts to him in private. She wanted him to be angry, but sometimes he was too volatile, too unpredictable, especially when he missed his medication.

Blair wanted to be the one controlling his anger; she wanted to make sure it was directed at the right people. Sindee and Dale headed her list of people. There were others, of course, but at this moment Blair was happy to hear Randall voicing his hatred of them.

If it wasn't for Sindee, the company wouldn't be doing this insipid musical and Blair wouldn't have had to stage manage it. She was used to being cast as the lead opposite Randall.

Blair was tone deaf and couldn't sing at all. Addison and Karson had to bring a few new actors with musical experience into the company, and Blair didn't like it one bit. She saw these intruders as competition for the roles she and Randall would normally have filled. She wanted them out and she wanted Randall's help getting them out.

She decided to push him just a bit more.

"Did I tell you how much money they spent to bring Dale from Florida? At least five thousand dollars."

"Are you serious? How do you know that?"

Randall was more outraged by this revelation than he was disbelieving of it.

"I'm the stage manager," Blair explained. "I have to keep track of our budget for the show and the overall cost of the production."

Randall stopped walking around the dressing room and returned to his chair with absolute loathing. He pounded his fist on the dressing-room table.

"Five thousand dollars for that fucking faggot! I hate that dancing queen."

Just the reaction Blair had hoped for. She knew Randall's
hatred for Dale was especially strong.

"I didn't want to tell you about it. I knew it would upset
you," Blair said coyly.

Blair felt it was safe to approach him. He was angry, but
now they were on the same side again. She started to massage
his shoulders. Blair had great hands. Randall relaxed and let
himself be manipulated.

They had played this game many, many times before. They
both knew the rules.

Randall would erupt, treating her and everyone around him
horribly. Blair would comfort and soothe him. Make excuses
for him.

She would be whatever he needed her to be.

Blair wanted Randall angry and needy. That way she could
be his mother or his lover, very often both at the same time.

She suffered all his torments and humiliations.

Everyone in the show saw how cruelly he treated her. What
they didn't see was how later, alone in bed, they would feast on
each other.

Blair took Randall's hand and led him to the cot against the
wall. She sat down and lifted her sweater over her head and
threw it on the floor. There was nothing underneath but her
soft alluring skin.

Randall tried to keep himself from getting hard. Lately he
had wanted to end things with Blair for a variety of reasons.
First and foremost was that he thought of himself as an artist.

Everyone knows that attachments of any kind are fatal to an
artist. An artist needs his freedom. It had something to do,
Randall was almost certain, with the agony of being creative,
and artsy-fartsy stuff like that. Randall was looking forward to
suffering for his art.

He wasn't going to get stuck in these amateur theatricals forever like the rejects he was surrounded by here. This little theater was just a layover on his way to bigger and better places.

The offers were going to come rolling in fast as soon as Randall was discovered, and he was certain that he would be discovered soon.

It would have been so easy for him to trade on his good looks, but Randall was a serious actor. He didn't want to make it that way. He had too much integrity for that. He knew his talent would take him where he wanted to go. Broadway would find him and Hollywood would follow. William Morris would come knocking on his door to sign him up.

He had already done a few infomercials and some "extra" work in three movies, and he had a friend who was close to getting his own public access spot. This friend promised Randall a regular segment on the show where he could do monologues and soliloquies.

It was just a matter of time.

Randall was a star-in-waiting. He was going to explode on the acting scene, and it wouldn't be long before these people, these rank amateurs, were eating his stardust.

An actor of Randall's caliber had too much talent not to make it big. He wanted to be rid of Blair before he made it.

For the longest time, Blair had been his own personal audience of one, but Randall was tiring of her.

Sure she pampered him, but Randall felt she also stifled him.

Blair was too clinging, too high maintenance. She was becoming his shadow. It was difficult sometimes for him to remember where he began and Blair ended, like they were melding into something he didn't want to be a part of. Sardonically, he often thought of himself as Jeff Goldblum in

The Fly. Blair was the fly in his machine. He wanted to move on before Blair overtook him completely.

So Randall looked away from Blair's voluptuous, inviting breasts, trying to think only of his impending stardom, but it was too late. His penis was already straining to get out of his pants. By now it was just a conditioned response. Love had nothing to do with it. It wasn't even lust anymore. But then again, he reasoned, there was no point in wasting a perfectly good hard-on.

He gave in.

He lay across Blair's lap and eagerly sucked one breast while rubbing the other.

Blair smiled and put her head back against the wall. He would be hers again tonight. She moaned and sighed. She loved the sound of Randall's mouth as he sucked and bit her nipples.

She unzipped his pants and released him. It sprang up and twitched at her slightest touch. She couldn't decide if she was excited more by stroking him or by her fantasy that she was suckling him. She was aware that at this moment, with Randall spread across her lap, they must resemble some abhorrent version of the pietà.

Blair gently squeezed his balls then began to move his foreskin back and forth with exquisite, almost aching slowness as she whispered to him softly and seductively.

"Don't worry. Dale and Sindee won't last here long. This musical will be a disaster, and then Addison and Karson will come to their senses and go back to doing what they do best. You'll go back to playing the leading man as you always did, and I'll be your leading lady. If Addison and Karson insist on keeping Dale and Sindee, we'll start our own company. We'll find a place and open our own theater. All the years we've worked here, we've got a following. We don't need these losers.

Either way, Sindee and Dale will become a dismal memory. I promise."

Blair stopped stroking him and slid her hand toward his ass. She started rimming him gently with her fingertips.

Randall was as much aroused by the thought of Dale and Sindee being out of his life as he was by Blair's touch.

He buried his head in Blair's cleavage and roughly crushed a breast in each hand. It was such a delicious pain. Blair trembled and moaned.

"Oooooohhhh."

"Oh, my! Excuse me! I am so sorry."

It was Rachel and she was totally embarrassed.

Randall stood up, adjusted "little Randall," zipped up his pants, and acted as if nothing had happened.

Blair, her sweater in a heap on the floor, her nipples hard and exposed, didn't have that option. She simply crossed her arms over her chest and asked what Rachel wanted.

Randall laughed, trying to put Rachel at ease. She was so pretty. Not a bad actress either, he thought.

Rachel tried to smile at Randall and tried to avoid looking at the bulge in his pants or at Blair's breasts. Her eyes darted around trying to find something, anything, to look at.

She fixed her sights on a row of top hats and kept it there.

"I was just checking all the doors and windows and lights. I wanted to make sure everything was shut down for the holidays. Sometimes Addison forgets to lock up."

"No problem. Blair and I weren't doing anything."

Blair shot Randall a hurt sideways look.

Randall stepped closer to Rachel and asked, "What are you doing tonight?"

"Well, I'm going to a party later after I leave here. Come with me if you'd like, Randy."

Randall loved it when she called him Randy. Everyone else always called him Randall. He had insisted on it because he thought it sounded more theatrical. Rachel was the only one he would allow to call him Randy.

Blair was going to be sick. No one seemed to care at all that she was sitting there with her tits hanging out. So she made a large gesture of getting off the cot and putting her sweater back on. She wanted Rachel to see her breasts and know that Randall had just finished giving them a workout.

"We're going to be busy tonight, so we can't go to your little party," said Blair. "Besides, David told me a while ago that Addison is looking for you. Randall and I were just leaving."

Rachel looked at Randall and Randall looked at the floor.

"I'll walk you to the door," said Randall.

"So will I," said Blair.

Blair kept her eye on Randall and Rachel as they talked and preceded her to the dressing room door. Once there, Rachel kissed Randall on the cheek and Randall kissed her back. They exchanged whisperings that Blair couldn't overhear.

When Randall stepped back inside the door, Blair removed her sweater again. She saw he was still hard in his jeans and knew they were in for a great night of lovemaking.

Randall sighed and thought, what the hell! There were worse ways to spend Christmas Eve. It wouldn't be the first time he had banged Blair all night while fantasizing about others. He did that a lot these days.

But this time, as New Year's Eve approached, he had resolved that it would be his last.

Rachel watched as Randall closed the door of the men's dressing room. She knew that Blair was about to consume him as only Blair could, but there was nothing Rachel could do for him now.

She sighed and walked in the darkness toward the office.

The old convent was slowly quieting down now. The actors, dancers, and musicians were heading off in various directions to bring in the holidays, each in their own separate way.

The sound of talk and laughter originating inside the old building grew softer, then diminished until it mixed into the distant noises from the street.

This was Rachel's favorite time of night. This was when the theater stopped being the theater and the convent was returned to its rightful owners.

Rachel was convinced that spirits resided within these walls. She had never been afraid of that idea, she liked the thought of it. She hoped the old souls didn't mind having their home invaded by the theater troupe.

Rachel believed that sometimes they tried to express their feelings through the occasional odd creak and the sounds coming from the old organ.

A few of the actors had even claimed to see faces in the windows, only to have them disappear in the blink of an eye. Sometimes lights would go on and off mysteriously, but nothing bad had ever happened in all the years the theater was here, so Rachel assumed that the group had not offended their ghostly hosts.

She stood alone in the darkness trying to picture all the weddings, baptisms, funerals, and town meetings that must have taken place here.

The structure was over two hundred years old and had quite a history. It was originally built as a convent to house an order of the Ursuline nuns. The Ursulines originated in France. Twelve nuns journeyed from France to New Orleans in 1727. Of these twelve, six moved on to New Jersey.

These nuns were remarkably different from their counterparts in religious life. Traditionally, female religious orders lived apart from their communities, cloistered, and engaged only in prayer. The Ursulines, however, lived in the outside world and dedicated themselves to the education of girls. They established schools and boarding schools for women. Eventually, when the order died out in New Jersey, the convent was used as a chapel, a school, and then a town hall.

General George Washington had a few secret meetings here to plan battle strategies in the Revolution.

Alexander Hamilton had attended many of the Sunday services.

It had been a stop on the Underground Railroad.

Ghost stories and legends about the convent abounded. They ran from the horrible to the humorous.

One of the most popular and enduring ones concerned the first Mother Superior of the convent, Sister Deanna Sympathy, who, when she died, was buried in a vault under the convent. Sister Sympathy was often referred to as "Zit" by the other nuns, because of her very small head. This was, of course, done with great affection. The Ursulines were very devout and very dedicated to their mission, but they could also be a spirited, fun loving bunch of gals.

It was said that Sister Sympathy's apparition could be seen sometimes on Sunday mornings, walking outside on the path that was in later years called the "Nuns' Walk," calling her nuns inside to prayers before disappearing into one of the doors or walls.

A section of the convent had been used as a small classroom; in this area it was said that the ghost of Sister Lucianne Dessi, the convent's first catechism instructor, could be seen teaching her class of young women.

Another was supposedly the ghost of a soldier who was killed in an accident on the day he was to be married in the chapel. Legend had it that his uniformed spirit could be seen wandering inside, looking and waiting for his bride-to-be.

One truly horrific story was about two men who had worked on the building of the convent. The men did not get along. The story was that one night after working hard on the convent all day, they were drinking at a bar and had a terrible fight. One man pulled a knife. The other man left the bar swearing revenge.

The next day, the man who pulled the knife did not show up for work. He was never seen again.

The story was that the man who left the bar first waited outside for hours until the man with the knife left. After the long hours of drinking, the man with the knife was too drunk to start a fight or offer much resistance in his own defense.

It was believed he was bricked alive that night into the convent walls by the man he had threatened.

No ghosts are attributed to this story, but it is said that sometimes on a still night, scratching sounds inside the walls can be heard.

But the most repeated ghost story was the one about the chapel soloist.

The story was that there was an overly zealous choir director who wanted to make an impression on the parishioners at an Easter Sunday service he knew would be heavily attended.

He instructed the soloist to sing her part from the balcony in the chapel. The plan was to have the organ music swell, and the woman would appear high above the faithful, giving the hymn a grand special effect.

Sadly, the choir director had not considered the age of the building. When the soloist, a large woman weighing over three hundred pounds, stepped out onto the designated balcony, the rotted boards gave way, and she crashed twenty-five feet to her death.

Those gathered below watched this tragic accident, stunned and paralyzed.

She didn't get to sing one note.

It *was* over before the "fat lady" sang, the locals liked to joke. They say her ghost can be seen in the choir loft, in the balcony, by the organ, or falling through the air to the spot where she died.

When Addison and Karson took over the building, they had put their own identity on it by converting it into a theater. With just a minimum of reconstruction, they built a large proscenium stage, removed the pews and brought in spotlights and a soundboard.

They had wanted to maintain the original integrity of the building and worked tirelessly restoring it.

The backstage area had remained mostly untouched, and it was here that Rachel felt most at peace.

Addison wanted to see her before she left for the night. He said it was important, but she knew he'd forgive her for lingering in this spot. He knew it was her favorite place in the convent.

Rachel thought back to when she had first entered the convent.

She had been just another skinny black kid from the streets of Irvington.

Her mother had died.

Rachel and her father lived alone in a small apartment. Her dad worked long hours to support them both, leaving Rachel alone for extended periods of time. Being an only child, she was forced to find ways to entertain herself. She discovered at an early age that she had a talent for drawing. Often she would walk through Irvington and the surrounding areas with her sketch pad and charcoal pencils, drawing whatever struck her attention.

There was an abandoned convent in South Orange that she particularly liked. She would stand looking at it for hours. She had done a number of sketches of it, but was not satisfied with any of them. She had heard all the ghost stories while she was growing up and had gone to the library to do research on its history.

Rachel was sketching the convent again late one Saturday afternoon. The sun had set and the street lights were just beginning to flicker to life She stood up and looked all around her. The street had cleared.

She couldn't remember how long she had been sitting there drawing. She had been concentrating so deeply on her picture that the background street noises had vanished and she realized she was alone. Rachel became uncomfortably aware that she had been alone for a long time and now darkness was approaching rapidly.

In the fading daylight she saw the convent door slowly open.

A mist, a thick rolling mist, spilled out of the open doorway. It spread out in all directions, eerily engulfing everything in its path. It was moving toward Rachel. It was about to claim her, too.

Rachel was frozen, too frightened to move. Her stomach gave a nervous lurch.

Suddenly, there was a shadowy figure, barely visible in the dense, billowing white clouds, standing in the doorway. It looked to Rachel as if this apparition were beckoning to her. There was a dull clanging sound, too.

All the old ghost stories she had ever heard about the convent came rushing back to her.

In the next instant, Rachel heard a highly cultured baritone voice bellowing out.

"Cursed secondhand fog machine. How could I buy this damnable piece of rubbish?"

The irate man shook his fist angrily and was about to lunge at the dilapidated piece of machinery, when, in a last gasp for life, it coughed and choked and spewed one remaining glut of haze so intense that it enveloped him and knocked him down.

Addison Taylor came stumbling out of the fog waving his arms and coughing.

When he heard the sound of Rachel's relieved laughter, he promptly collected himself, lit his pipe, and introduced himself.

Rachel looked up at him and liked him at once.

Addison Taylor was an older man, still big and hearty with a merry twinkle in his eyes. He had a friendly, contagious smile that made anyone looking at him smile too.

He explained that he and his wife had taken over the convent and were going to convert it into a theater. So far he was doing all the carpentry and electrical work that needed to be done to get the theater ready. Rachel noticed his huge ring of keys. At the moment, though, he was looking for actors. He hoped that Rachel would audition.

When Rachel explained that she had never acted before, he shook his gray balding head as if that didn't matter.

"I'm a very good director, my dear, and therefore, a great judge of character. May I?" he asked, reaching for Rachel's sketch pad.

He studied each drawing intently, turned each page tenderly.

"Lovely, just lovely. You already have the soul of an artist."

Rachel was charmed by his playful dramatic flourish, but wasn't quite sure if he was teasing her or not.

That had been eight years ago and sometimes Rachel still

couldn't tell when Addison was teasing her. That was just his style.

The convent was completely silent now. The lights were off and the place was filled with shadows. Rachel stood in the dark and softly whispered "Merry Christmas" to any soul who might be listening in the shadows, then headed for the office.

5

Addison sat at his desk, staring at the ledger and bank statements. It was all there in black and white. Nothing in his thirty-six years in theater had been as disappointing as this. For the first time ever, he felt despair.

He looked around at the walls covered with reviews and head shots, mementos of the seven years of shows he directed at his theater. Nothing was pinned up in any particular order or preference It was all scattered, and haphazard, and beautiful.

Each show was special to him. It seemed that everything in his life had led him here.

As a young man, Addison wanted to be an actor. He'd been a big handsome leading man in his college productions. After college, he enjoyed some modest successes on the regional theater stage circuit.

He went to Tinsel Town and landed roles in a few low-budget movies. But soon he got bored with all the tinsel and headed home.

Then, like a lot of actors, he got the urge to direct. After he directed his first show, he gladly gave up being on the stage or in front of the camera. Directing opened up a new world of creative possibilities for him that acting didn't offer.

Addison loved the idea of bringing plays to life on the stage.

He liked standing in the lobby of the theater and listening to the audiences laugh and applaud.

He loved building the sets: creating scenery, moments in

time, images that lasted maybe only two or three hours for each audience, but in Addison's heart, these things remained intact and unfaded.

More than anything else, he loved working with the young actors and guiding them through the classic plays.

Sometimes the young actors were more willing and enthusiastic than they were talented when they showed up for auditions, but that was just fine with Addison. It showed they had the desire and the passion. He always saw their potential. He loved seeing their spark and energy, and witnessing that moment when it all came together for them.

He was not so old that he couldn't learn things from them, too.

Addison had no delusions that he was changing the world. He had chosen to become a director of community theater plays. To many, this was foolish and useless. But for Addison, it was almost as though there was no other choice for him.

When he was in his early forties, he met and fell in love with a kindred spirit, Karson Parker. She was a young and lovely aspiring playwright who was starting to gain recognition on college campuses and off-Broadway theaters because of her antiwar and feminist themes.

She wrote a show that Addison was hired to direct.

Karson shared Addison's love of bringing art to small communities. They had an ardor for theater and for each other. They fell in love almost instantly. More important, they understood each other almost instantly. Their twenty-plus-year marriage was a happy collaboration of heart and soul.

She and Addison never had children of their own, so Karson made a home for all the actors, stagehands, or crew who worked on their shows. They welcomed and accepted all the eccentric theater types who were often considered strange everywhere outside the theater.

Addison and Karson made the "Broad Street Players" a place where those who worked on their plays felt free and were encouraged to grow as artists.

They worked hard on their dream, and eight years ago they invested all their savings in this old convent in South Orange, New Jersey. They took a small section of the convent and turned it into an apartment for themselves. This place was not only where they worked, it was their home, and they cherished it.

They had gotten a few grants to help with the renovation and restoration of the old convent, but mostly they lived on whatever profits they made at the box office.

Finally, they started to make money. After seven seasons, Addison and Karson developed not only a talented troupe of actors, but cultivated enough interest in their shows in the community that each play was guaranteed large audiences.

To open their eighth season, they wanted to try something different. Addison had never directed a musical, but he wanted to do one. Many of his actors performed in musicals at other theaters, and they begged him for the chance to do one here.

His followers in the community indicated they would be supportive of such a production. Addison knew that investing money in the theater was notoriously risky, but a few of the subscribers were anxious to put up their money. They readily invested money thinking that the popular little theater would certainly yield them a nice little profit.

To keep from spending a huge sum of money obtaining the rights to do an established, popular musical, Karson wrote an original work, entitled *Sorry I Missed Your Birthday*. She and Addison were able to get a grant to mount the show, but mostly used the savings they accrued during their seven seasons.

Karson had written her script with a part for every member

of their theater family. Addison wanted everyone in his company to be a part of this project.

That's what made his discovery that $25,000 was missing from the theater's account so horrible.

Addison went over and over the books, refusing to believe it was true, but the truth was inescapable.

Like most small community theaters, all the participants had many different duties. An actor who had the lead in one show, might also work the lights or sound in the next.

Addison trusted everyone.

If money was needed for props, costumes, or any expenditure related to a show, all anyone had to do was make an entry in the ledger and get money out of the theater's safe.

Everyone had access to it.

Addison didn't know what saddened him most of all: that someone he knew and trusted had stolen money from him, or that for the first time in his long theatrical career, he might have to cancel a scheduled production.

"The show must go on" was more than just an old theater cliché to him. It was a time-honored tradition.

What was he going to tell his neighbors who had put up their own money? What would he say to the foundation that had approved the grant money for the show?

Addison reached into his desk drawer and took out the bottle of bourbon and the shot glass he kept there. He poured himself a drink. He needed an alcohol ameliorant to blur the memory of the look in Karson's eyes when he had told her the money was missing. It was still too fresh in his mind.

A few drinks would dull the image, take it out of focus for a while.

He had seen something in his wife that he didn't recognize, and it scared him.

Both Addison and Karson had been born and raised in the

South. They grew up with small town hospitality where you treated everyone like a friend even if you'd just met, where your word was your bond and a handshake sealed a deal.

Karson had often warned him that they were no longer in the South and the rules were different in New Jersey. But Addison hadn't listened. He had believed that everyone was as trustworthy as he.

As soon as he discovered the theft, Addison called Karson into the office. It wasn't easy for him to admit that he had been so recklessly trusting of others with their money, but he told her what he had found in the bank statements. He was visibly disappointed and disillusioned. He apologized to Karson repeatedly.

Addison looked at Karson expecting her to offer him encouragement and comfort. He wanted her to say that everything would be just fine like she always did, but she offered him nothing.

Always in the past when they faced hardships and he was discouraged, Karson would give him hope and solace. But this time, Karson just looked at him coldly detached and unsympathetic. She wasn't angry with him, or upset about the theft, or even concerned about the future of their theater.

Addison couldn't detect a trace of any emotion in her at all. There was no sign of love in her eyes. No hint of anything they had been through in all their years together.

The woman who owned his heart, who was the source of his inspiration, seemed suddenly hollow and vacant.

And that's what scared him the most, more than facing the backers and more than explaining to the Foundation the disappearance of their grant money.

He wondered if Karson had lost her faith in him and in their dream. She had sacrificed so much, made do with so little. Was it possible she was unable to gather her strength to lift him up one more time?

Addison felt a staggering rush of guilt.

It hadn't occurred to him until now just how preoccupied he had been in pursuing this dream of running his own theater.

They had had several others around the country before coming to New Jersey. The names of the towns were different, but it always ended the same. Each one had failed and each new try took them farther and farther north, away from Karson's home, and the things she knew and loved.

Addison had never once wondered about her happiness. He just assumed that if he was happy, then she was happy, too.

Addison was frightened to think that now he may have lost Karson somewhere along the way. He would be nothing without her. His purpose had always been clear because he had Karson to help him.

If Karson lost faith in him . . .

After they had sat in silence looking at each other for a while, Karson simply stood up and walked to the office door. Without turning around to face Addison, she stared straight ahead and said indifferently, "Tell Rachel about the theft. She's been with us longer than anyone. She should be the first to know what's happened."

With that Karson closed the door behind her and left Addison alone with his misery.

Seconds later, David Castrato, the persistently jubilant assistant stage manager, knocked on the door and shouted, "Hey, Addison, I got the balloons like you wanted." David spoke in his usual sing-song, sunshine and buttercups voice.

"Not now, David," Addison called back.

Normally Addison appreciated David's natural good cheer and buoyant attitude. Being assistant stage manager was usually a thankless task, and David was doing his job nobly with great humor. But Addison was not in the mood to endure David's unflinching merriment right now.

"If you or anyone sees Rachel, tell her I need to see her right away."

"Will do," David called out. Then he was gone. Addison imagined David with a dozen helium-filled balloons in assorted colors, giggling and skipping along like a little girl, a strange little girl with facial hair, on his way back into the theater.

That had been over an hour ago and Addison still hadn't found the words to tell Rachel, his favorite and most loyal member of his company, about the missing money. This was going to be almost as difficult as telling Karson. Rachel was like a daughter to him.

Addison poured more bourbon into the glass.

As he raised it to his lips, the old actor suddenly laughed in spite of himself. This was a familiar plot line, he mused: a man drinking and despairing over money missing on Christmas Eve.

Of course Jimmy Stewart played that part wonderfully, but Addison couldn't help thinking that if *he* had directed the movie, he would have given Stewart a few different acting choices.

Addison swallowed the bourbon and looked slowly around the office of the old convent.

Was this the part where his Guardian Angel showed up?

Addison was brought back to reality by a tapping on the office door.

"Addison? Are you in there?"

Addison recognized Rachel's voice.

"Come in," he said, wearily.

"David said you wanted to see me. All the doors and windows are locked. Everyone has left for . . ."

Rachel stopped in midsentence when she saw Addison's face. For the first time in all the years she'd known him, he looked old and tired. She knew immediately that something was horrendously wrong.

Addison could only manage to speak in sporadic bursts and incomplete sentences.

Rachel was able to piece together that money had been stolen; the show was cancelled, apologies would be made to the backers and to the foundations that had given them grants.

Addison said he never wanted to direct another play again; he was broken.

Rachel listened in silence, hearing the pain in his words.

When he finished, Rachel thought he looked even worse than when he started. It was like watching the life flow out of him from an open wound.

She continued to look at him, searching his face for signs of suspicion.

Is that why he called her into the office . . . to see her reaction, to look for some sign of deception?

Had he figured out what she had done?

Rachel had reasoned that with all the funding coming in from the backers and the grants, her crime would go undiscovered, at least until the show was up and running, and earning money.

She would have told Addison the whole story then.

She hoped the shame she was feeling didn't show on her face.

Rachel stood up and tried to avoid looking Addison in the eyes.

"Did you say you got a grant from The Owen Charles Foundation?" she asked faintly.

"Yes. Why?"

She needed to get help fast, but to do that she would have to call on the one man she had hated for most of her young life.

It would also mean that Addison would find out that she had stolen from the theater.

She fell back into her chair, motionless, almost numb with indecision.

It was so difficult to make that call after all these years had passed, and on Christmas Eve, no less.

But she loved Addison too dearly to see him lose everything, even at the risk of exposing her theft.

Rachel picked up the office phone and started to dial.

6

The old man sat alone in his spacious, comfortable rooms and looked into the fireplace.

He was warm and secure, and given his position and status, he should have been untroubled, yet something was missing from his life.

He never had the time to notice this fact until Christmas Eve.

He never felt the loneliness more than on Christmas Eve.

It was the same every year. It was the one night when he indulged his sentimentality and remembered the family he had lost and the family he had discarded.

He wondered how many more Christmas Eves were left to him, and if the memories of the mistakes he had made in his life would be his only companions at the end of each year and the start of the new.

He sipped his exquisite brandy from the smooth snifter and waited for these thoughts to ebb and leave him in peace as they always did.

He concentrated on the crackling and snapping sounds coming from the fireplace. They distracted him and quieted his mind.

After all, this was just another night he was alone.

He was jarred from his thoughts by the sudden ringing of his telephone. He slowly got up from his chair and walked over to answer it.

He was surprised to see that the call was placed from an outside line. Probably just a colleague calling to wish him happy holidays.

"Hello," he said into the receiver.

There was no sound at the other end. The old man waited and thought himself a fool for getting duped by a telemarketer on Christmas Eve.

He was about to hang up when he heard a very faint sound on the other end.

What was it? A rustling, a cough, maybe? It wasn't much.

He closed his eyes and strained to listen. He didn't know what it was, but somewhere in his heart he knew this was the phone call he had waited for for years.

In a rare unguarded moment, he felt his spirit soar. Then he quickly regained his composure. He didn't want to scare her away.

Finally she said, "I need you. We have to talk."

There was hesitation and uncertainty in her voice as she struggled to speak, but eventually she got out the whole story, the reason for her call.

He knew this was difficult for her so he listened silently, only speaking when she took a long pause.

There was so much he wanted to say to her, so many things he wanted to explain. But he kept those things inside. This was not the time to think of his own peace of mind. This was her time.

She opened up to him, reluctantly. She explained her problem.

"I have money. I can certainly . . . ," he interrupted. He would gladly give her what she needed. He practically begged her to take his money.

She wouldn't hear of taking his money. She would never take his money. She protested, and the old man heard anger in her voice. Then she seemed to calm down and went on with her story.

"I'll do whatever I can," he said gently when she finished.

Then she hung up.

He continued to listen a moment after hearing the receiver at the other end replaced, reluctant to let go of the connection, fearing it would be years before he would hear her voice again.

He stood still for a while, taking it all in, and then he started to tremble uncontrollably, his emotions overtaking him. He couldn't believe she had really called.

Finally, after all these years, the old man had been given a chance at redemption.

7

Slick and Laura stood outside their front door with an arm around each other's waist, waving good-bye, and watching as the last limousine filled with the last guests to leave the party wound its way around the plaza, passed the fountains, tennis courts, and gardens, then drove away into the dawn of the new Christmas Day.

They lingered there huddled together against the stone lions, enjoying the cool crisp air.

Thousands of lights blinked on and off, silently splashing the landscape with color for as far as they could see. A gentle wind stirred; bells tinkled softly in the distance.

They watched as the dark night began its gradual change to light gray.

"Let's go inside," said Laura. "I'm freezing my tail off. Literally."

"Good idea," said Slick, helping her inside. "I am not a morning person."

They went inside, closed the door and fell against it.

"Another great party," said Slick, loosening her tie and removing her Sherlock Holmes cap.

"Yes, it was, wasn't it!" Laura agreed, yawning.

"Why did Hillary leave so early," asked Slick. "She seemed to be having a good time. Everyone thought her Abe Lincoln costume was a riot."

"It was because of your friend Snatch. He was stalking her all night, making sure she didn't take anything. When she finally confronted him and asked him who he was supposed to be, he got so flustered he blurted out 'John Wilkes Booth.' Her Secret Service guys made her leave immediately. They didn't want to have to change the title of her book to *Re-Living History.*"

They both burst into that uncontrollable laughter that comes from alcohol and exhaustion.

"Oh my God . . . that's too funny," said Slick, laughing and wiping tears from her eyes. "Oh, and did you happen to catch Calista walking around, eating everything in sight? I swear, at one point I saw her in the corner chewing on a whole leg of lamb. If Garbo had been in the room, it could have gotten very ugly."

"Stop. Don't make me laugh. You'll make me have an accident. You know how long it takes me to get out of this thing," Laura said, wishing she could cross her legs. She was looking forward to the simple act of wriggling her toes again.

"Okay, my little 'Chicken of the Sea,' " said Slick, trying to get serious. "It's about 5:30 in the morning. Do you want to get some sleep before we open our presents?"

Laura pulled Slick closer and started to unbutton her shirt. She kissed Slick's exposed cleavage.

"Well, I want to go to bed, anyway." When she was done with the shirt, she reached for the wall switch and turned off the lights.

"Why, Miss Charles," said Slick, feigning a Southern accent. "I do believe you're trying to seduce me." She reached behind Laura's costume and unfastened the bra. It fell on the floor.

She ran her fingers around Laura's waist and started to pull down the fish suit.

Laura put her arms around Slick's neck and licked her ear. "Yes, I am trying to seduce you. Hopefully, it's working," she whispered.

In one swift downward tug, Slick had Laura stripped bare to her toes.

Laura took hold of Slick's pants, unfastened and unzipped them.

They were soon naked, touching and stroking each other in the dark expansive hallway.

"I've got to warn you, I'm not easy. I'm not passion's plaything. I don't go all the way on my first date." Slick grabbed hold of Laura's butt and pulled her close.

"We'll see," Laura said, jumping up and wrapping her legs around Slick's waist.

"Speaking as a former officer of the law, I must say this is a clear-cut case of entrapment, using your sultry charms on me. There are laws against this sort of thing. I'm doing this under protest," Slick said between kisses.

"Shut up. Take me upstairs," Laura said with rising urgency.

Slick was ready to drop the witty repartee and enjoy the beautiful woman she had in her arms.

She gently guided Laura to the long staircase. She reluctantly removed one of her hands from Laura, and groped around until she found the stair seat and the switch. Slick got on the seat, and then placed Laura in a sitting position onto her lap. She explored the back of Laura's neck with her mouth and took hold of her knees.

She spread them apart and slowly caressed the insides of her thighs.

She spread Laura's legs wider. Each caress went higher and higher, exploring and teasing.

As the seat chugged and bumped its way upward, Laura felt the cool night air on her wet pubic hair and her soft pink tissue. She responded by arching her back and grinding into Slick's lap.

Slick cupped Laura's breasts in her hands and eagerly fingered the taut nipples. Her hips started moving to meet Laura's grinding.

By the time the seat stopped at the top of the stairs, they were hurting for each other.

They opened the door to their bedroom, barely noticing the cozy fire in the fireplace, or the carefully chosen assortment of brandies, coffees, and other delicacies Judson had set out for them.

Opposite their bed were huge glass sliding doors that led out to a terrace. The drapes in front of the doors had been pulled back, letting in the panorama of the rising sun glistening down on the regal snow-covered mountains. The view was breathtaking, almost as if it had been prearranged just for them, but they didn't notice.

They didn't even notice that the linens they so roughly tore from the bed had been freshly changed.

They simply threw themselves onto the bed and sank into the satin sheets, and into each others' arms.

All through the dawning of their tenth Christmas together, they opened up to one another the way rose petals unfold to welcome the sun, petal by wondrous petal. Slick was as dark in the night as Laura was light.

They touched and tasted and savored one another, sometimes tenderly, sometimes hungrily. When their passion for one another receded, it would come back again with redoubled power.

While their neighbors unwrapped gifts and created mountains out of discarded paper and boxes and bows, Slick and Laura drifted into a serene and sated sleep, so sweet and still, locked in each other's arms, touching body to body, soul to soul, with one synchronized heartbeat.

*   *   *

Hours later, as Slick slowly awakened, she became aware of movement on the bed followed by a rustling under the sheet that covered her.

Without opening her eyes, she tried to make sense of what was happening. Someone was singing "The Twelve Days of Christmas" woefully off-key in the distance.

That, she knew at once, had to be Laura. Poor thing, she couldn't carry a tune to save her life. Her voice was indescribably bad.

The first time Slick heard Laura sing, she thought Laura was joking. She had to be joking, no one could sound that bad. Slick soon found out the hard way that Laura wasn't joking.

Slick could only liken experiencing Laura's singing to how it must feel to have your head run through a food processor.

And what Laura lacked in talent, she made up for in enthusiasm.

After all these years Slick still couldn't understand how such an atrocious noise could be made so joyfully. She always wondered how Laura herself could stand it. Where were her auricular nerves, anyway? In her feet?

Slick imagined that outside birds flying within hearing range of Laura's voice were falling dead from the sky.

She pictured frightened little kids running and screaming for their parents.

Dogs were probably howling, their eardrums ruptured, blood gushing from their brains.

Slick shook her head, driving away the horrible images. She knew then she had a moral obligation to end the pain and suffering of innocent animals and children.

Slick raised the sheet and looked underneath. Garbo, with eyes wide and haunted, shivered with fright and looked back at her.

"Don't worry. It will all be over soon," she reassured the little dog. Then she called out, "Good morning. Merry Christmas."

" 'Five golden rings' . . . oh, Merry Christmas to you." Laura stuck her head out the bathroom door and smiled lovingly at her. "And it's two in the afternoon."

Laura walked to the bed and kissed Slick.

She was dressed in only a fur coat which was open and revealed her naked body underneath.

Slick could smell the fresh soap and perfume on her. Her skin was still warm and moist from her shower. She wasn't wearing any makeup. She just glowed naturally, Slick thought.

"Can I get you anything, coffee or something," asked Laura. She walked toward the little kitchenette they had off their suite. They had added it on for those occasions when they didn't want to bother the staff for food.

"I could fix you some eggs, if you like. You never could resist my omelets," Laura said.

"No, thank you, baby. How long have you been up?"

"Just long enough to take a shower and start opening my gifts."

"So I see. Did I get you that coat?"

"Yes, you did, thank you very much. Do you like it?" Laura posed and modeled the Blackglama fur.

"I'm spoiling you," Slick said. "I'm amazed by my own generosity."

"What did I get you?" Laura asked.

"You got me a new Rolex," Slick answered. "It's beautiful, but you really shouldn't have."

Long ago they had decided they would buy for themselves what they really wanted, if they wanted anything. Several Christmases had passed without a single gift being purchased. But this was their tenth. It was special, a milestone.

Separately they had decided to splurge to celebrate the event, but here and now, they realized that, as usual, they shared the same thought, the decision wasn't separate at all.

"What's on the agenda for today?" asked Slick. She got up from the bed and put on her robe.

"I thought we'd watch some old black-and-white movies. *Miracle on 34th Street* has got to be on TV somewhere. Oh, did I tell you that Joss Whedon sent us the entire *Buffy the Vampire Slayer* series on DVD? Someone told him we were big fans. What a nice man! It's not even available to the public yet. We can watch it from the time Willow becomes a lesbian, or we can listen to some music and play 'You Don't Know Jack,' if you promise not to cheat like you usually do. It is Christmas, after all. No cheating."

Laura helped Slick into her robe and tied the belt at her waist.

"I really don't care what we do." Laura put her head on Slick's shoulder and closed her eyes. "I just want to be with you."

"Perfect," said Slick. "Being with you is the best present I ever gave myself." She kissed Laura's forehead. "I'll jump into the shower and then meet you in front of the television for a 'Buffy' marathon. What would Christmas be without some cheerful holiday slayage?"

There was a knock on their bedroom door.

Slick and Laura looked at each other in surprise.

They had thought they were alone. Most of the staff had been given time off for Christmas, and the few that remained normally worked downstairs, never coming to this part of the house.

Garbo, who had been resting on the bed, jumped off, ran to the door and started sniffing at it along the bottom.

Laura pulled her coat tightly around her.

Slick walked to the door.

On the other side, Judson wondered if he had made a mistake.

He hoped that when the door opened, he would find the right words. He had always been so precise and impassive in his speech and manner. He did not want to be overcome by emotion now.

It was all happening too fast. He needed more time to think and organize his thoughts.

But, it was too late to turn back. He had knocked, and the door was starting to open.

The only thing he was certain of was that in a matter of seconds, his life with Slick and Laura would be changed forever.

8

By the time the door fully opened, Judson had regained his composure and had willed his body into a rigid stand at attention; eyes focused straight ahead, heels together, and his arms tightly against his sides.

Slick smiled when she saw him. She felt a little foolish seeing him standing there so formal, dignified, and solemn, while she was in a bathrobe and unshowered, her eyes not yet fully opened, and her hair in a rabid state of confusion.

"Judson," she said. "Please tell me you're not working today of all days. If you've come here to check on us, we're fine. It's Christmas. Go relax and enjoy yourself."

Laura joined Slick at the door.

"It was a perfect evening, Judson. Everyone had a magnificent time. Please express our gratitude to the staff. They made the party a success, as always."

"I will certainly relay your appreciation, Miss Laura, but . . . beg pardon, that is not why I'm here. I apologize for the intrusion. I have a bit of a situation . . . very personal, that I need to discuss with you."

"Oh, certainly. Please, Judson. Come in, then," said Laura, very taken aback.

She had never envisioned a day when Judson would want to discuss anything "very personal" with her. It was an awkward moment for both of them.

Neither knew what to do next.

"Please sit down, Judson."

It was the only thing Laura could think to say.

"Actually, I'd prefer to stand, Miss."

"If you wish."

Laura looked at Slick, still in a state of surprise.

Slick, thinking that Judson would find it easier to talk to Laura alone, began to excuse herself and said, "Well, I was just about to go and take a shower, so I'll leave you two . . ."

"If you don't mind, Miss Slick, I'd rather you stay. What I have to say concerns you as well."

"All right, Judson," said Slick. She exchanged a brief look with Laura. Then she closed the bedroom door and sat next to Laura at the foot of the bed.

Judson entered the bedroom and stood perfectly still.

He cleared his throat and hoped for the best as he began to speak.

"As you know, my family has its roots in the tradition of English personal service. My father was a butler, as was his father before him. It was expected that everyone in my family would enter into service; the males would be butlers and the women would aspire to be head housekeepers. We became well known for our superior work ethic, and the well-to-do requested children of my family to work in their homes as footmen and under-butlers, knowing that the children were raised and groomed at home to serve.

"I can remember a time when my family held the top servant positions at all the best houses in England and here in the States. It was a different time then. To us, the most noble pursuit was to become a gentleman's gentleman and serve in the homes of the wealthy. As I said, this way of life was expected of everyone in my family. My younger sister, Alma, was the first ever that I know of to refuse it. She tried, but she could not exist in the strict rigidity of this life. She was possessed of an independent spirit. My father would scold and berate her, but it did no good. She simply was not suited for it. One day she announced that she was going to make her own way in the world by teaching music, or literature. She excelled at these things.

"She asked our father for his blessing. Of course he refused, but Alma left anyway. She was hurt but not discouraged and she and I stayed in touch over the years. I would visit her and write to her. One day I received a letter from her telling me she had met the man she loved and planned to marry. In this letter she asked me to come for a weekend visit. I accepted.

"When I arrived at her home, the man she introduced to me as her fiancé was black. I was startled at first, and frankly quite skeptical, but it didn't take me long to realize that they were deeply in love, and she was going to marry this man regardless of any objections I may have had. Alma was determined not to keep her upcoming marriage a secret from our father. She was not ashamed and she had nothing to hide. He was a very good man. I'm sure, however, you can guess my father's reaction. He not only refused to give them his blessing, he made me and the rest of the family cut all ties with them. I stand here, ashamed to admit that I was a very dutiful and obedient son, and a very inadequate brother. I never saw or spoke to my sister again."

Judson felt a momentary rush of emotion, that was barely discernible to Laura or Slick. His voice quavered only slightly, then he continued.

"Years later, after my father died, I tried to reestablish contact with Alma, but without any success. I told your father, Miss Laura, about my efforts to find her. He used all his resources to locate her for me. He would not give up until he found her."

Laura felt a sudden flush of love for her father to learn he had done what he could to help Judson. It was not often that she heard anyone say something kind about her father.

She looked at Slick, and Slick understood immediately what she was feeling.

Slick took hold of Laura's hand as Judson spoke.

"I learned Alma and her husband had a daughter, but I was too late. Alma was dead. I never got the chance to tell her how sorry I was for not standing up to our father for her; for not being there for her. She was gone. And her husband, quite understandably, did not want to hear my meager overdue apologies for all the time I had rejected her. Over the years, I've continued to write to him and my niece, but I never got a response. They live very modestly so I've sent money and gifts, but they are always returned to me. I had all but given up hope of ever hearing from them.

"So, imagine my shock, when last night, I finally received a call from my niece, Rachel." He paused and took a deep breath. Somehow he managed to stand even more erect. "She's in trouble and asked for my help. I've come to ask for your help."

"What can we do, Judson?" asked Laura.

"She's performing in a theater that has received a grant from the Owen Charles Foundation. The money has been stolen. Rachel admits that she took money from the theater's account, but swears she replaced it. She can't explain why the money is missing now."

"How much money was taken?" asked Slick.

"Twenty-five thousand dollars," Judson replied. He looked extremely uncomfortable.

Judson glanced briefly at Laura. Laura and Slick exchanged glances.

"I believe her," he continued firmly. "I offered to give her the money myself from my savings, but she refused. She's more concerned that the owners of the theater will be ruined and will face serious disciplinary actions from the foundation because of the misappropriation of the grant money. Miss Laura, I came here to ask you . . . to beg you . . . to please, take the money from me. Rachel needn't know. This one thing may be the only thing I can ever do to help her. I failed my sister when she needed me. I don't want to fail my niece. Please allow me to put right the theft of your grant money, and if you or Miss Slick feel I am not worthy to work here because of my failure to support my sister out of prejudice, I will understand and tender my resignation immediately. I would not want to continue if I no longer had your confidence."

Slick looked at him for a long moment, then said, "You can't blame yourself for the actions of your father, Judson. It was a different time then. Don't resign because you think you may have offended me. You haven't. I have just as much respect for you now as I did before you knocked on the door."

Laura approached Judson and touched his arm.

"After all the years you've been here, Judson, did you honestly believe I wouldn't do whatever I could to help you?"

Judson sighed in tremendous relief.

"I was hoping you'd say that, Miss Laura. I think I will sit down now."

Judson sank heavily into a large plush chair.

"Would you like something to drink?" asked Laura.

"Some water would be lovely," he said with hesitation, clearly not used to being the one waited on.

Slick went to the bar, opened a cold bottle of Perrier, poured some in a glass, and handed it to Judson.

As he drank, Laura began to speak.

"Let me worry about the money and board of directors at the foundation, Judson. I promise you that no charges will be brought against your niece or the theater. The owners will not have to shut down the show. I'll call the theater later today. Do you have their number?"

"I've got all the information written down here, Miss."

Judson pulled a piece of paper from his breast pocket, and handed it to Laura. Then he rose from the chair, his face showing both his gratitude and his uneasiness at displaying vulnerability.

"Thank you, Miss Laura and Miss Slick. I've taken up too much of your day, so I'll be going now."

He bowed to each of them separately. He walked to the door, opened it and bowed again.

Laura, who had followed him to the door, watched as he disappeared down the hallway.

Her heart ached for him.

"That poor dear man," she said as she closed the bedroom door, her voice cracking. "Isn't it amazing how you can share the same space with someone for years and not know them? I never knew he had a family of his own. My father never told me about it."

Laura's eyes started to tear up.

She turned to Slick just in time to see Slick wiping a smile off her face.

"What are you laughing at?"

"I wasn't laughing."

"You were practically twittering."

"Twittering? I was not twittering. I don't twitter. I have never twittered in my life. I was merely smiling."

"Why were you smiling, then?" asked Laura, totally recovered from her emotional moment.

"Because now I can finally be of some use around here," Slick answered. "I'll just take a few days off from the clam company—it practically runs itself anyway—and find out what's going on at this theater. I'm only looking out for you and Judson."

Laura took a long moment to study Slick's face.

"I don't believe it," Laura said.

"Believe what?"

"You're actually glad that money was stolen, aren't you?" asked Laura.

"No, of course I'm not glad, but this is a crime. This is what I do. It's what I'm good at. You may be able to convince the Board not to press any charges or bring any fines against Judson's niece or the theater, but they're still out $25,000. So, what happened to the money? Hell, I want to know, don't you? What if Rachel is lying to Judson? There is that possibility. I care for him, too. It was obvious he was suffering over this. I don't want to see him lied to and taken advantage of. And if Rachel did return the money like she told Judson, then where is it? What happened to it? I'm going to find out for you."

Slick kissed Laura's cheek, then walked into the bathroom and began running water for her shower.

Slick was getting psyched about having a crime to solve.

Laura hadn't seen her this enthused in a while. She started to feel guilty.

Slick had walked away from being a detective for her.

Laura knew it hadn't been easy for her to do that, but she did.

Slick had a talent for solving crimes, and Laura saw now that her talent was being wasted. No wonder Slick was so impassioned now.

It became very clear to Laura what she had to do.

"Okay, but I'm working with you on this," Laura shouted to her.

"What?" shouted Slick over the sound of the rushing water. She was still adjusting the water temperature for her shower.

"Don't try to talk me out of it. I know you're the hotshot detective and all. True, I don't have any experience at this. Most people think I'm just a rich socialite with nothing to do but fill my days indulging in whatever idle amusements satisfy my whims. But it's my foundation's money, and if I'm going to intercede for Judson, I'd like to give the Board some idea of what went on at this theater. Plus, if I'm with you, I know you won't do anything reckless or dangerous," Laura said loudly and emphatically.

"Laura, I don't think . . ." Slick was shouting over the sound of the water.

"You are not going to talk me out of this, Slick." Laura was adamant. "These are my terms and they are not negotiable. I could actually be of help to you, if you'd give me half a chance. I have great instincts. I took over the family business, and it has thrived under my leadership. Most people expected that after my father died, I would run it into the ground, but I have proved them wrong."

Laura started to pace around the room, her resolve intensifying.

"People always think that just because I'm wealthy and have had servants all my life, that I just want to be pampered, that I can't do anything for myself. They forget that I actually have a brain. And it doesn't help that I'm a blonde. Life isn't always easy for wealthy blonde women, you know," she said, folding her arms, and forgetting momentarily that she was wearing an extremely expensive fur coat and living in a mansion that could have passed as a castle. "I've never been afraid to get my hands dirty or afraid of taking risks, and you know it. Besides, it's just about stolen money from a little community theater. How dangerous can it be? It's not like someone was murdered."

Slick came bouncing out of the bathroom.

"I don't know if you heard me over the running water, because I couldn't hear you, baby. Sorry. But I've got a brilliant plan," said Slick. "I've thought it over and, Laura, I don't think

I can do this without you. We can pose as backers for the show. That will be easy because you really are a backer. And it's just a theft, so there's really no danger. What do you say? Will you work with me on this? Please? I hope you will."

Slick smiled at her sweetly.

"What! Uh . . . oh, sure I will . . . if you insist . . . if you think I could be helpful. I can rearrange a few things . . . maybe cancel an appointment or two . . . Um . . . yes, yes . . . I think I can clear my schedule if you really need me. I don't mind," Laura said, stupefied and sputtering to find the right words.

"Great! Anyway, I've got the water temperature just right, so I'm getting into the shower now."

Slick walked away happily into the bathroom.

Laura sat still for a few moments trying to make sense of what had just happened.

Her mind was swirling in confusion.

Did she win that argument? Had there even been an argument?

She looked suspiciously toward the bathroom.

Laura waited until she was sure Slick was in the shower.

She slipped out of her fur coat, tiptoed to the bathroom, then slowly and quietly, she opened the shower door.

There, in the thick steam stood Slick doing a victory dance under the shower nozzle. Her arms were extended over her head, and she was slapping her legs together to a rhythm only she could hear.

These were the moments that made life worth living, Laura thought.

She smiled mischievously, savoring the moment and anticipating the look on Slick's face when she realized she was being watched.

Laura was not disappointed.

Slick turned slowly, dancing and enjoying the pulsing water with total abandon.

She stopped abruptly, her eyes widened, and her jaw dropped when she saw Laura.

Laura took her time. Slick was frozen.

"And you were twittering, don't even try to deny it," said Laura, coolly.

Slick, looking like a drenched rabbit under a waterfall, suddenly caught in the headlights, started to stammer and splutter incoherently.

"No, no. Don't you say a word, you smooth talker, you," Laura interrupted her.

Laura stepped into the shower and closed the door behind her.

"Just hand me the soap," she said. "I've got your back."

9

The ride from Oakland, New Jersey, to South Orange, New Jersey, takes a little less than an hour.

Slick loved driving through the Ramapo Mountains, especially in the summer when she would wind the car down the curving roads while drifting cloudscapes moved slowly across the infinite powder blue sky, and everything on the ground was a sumptuous verdant green. It was a wondrous convergence of nature.

The mountains were so beautifully forested.

But it was winter, and the trees stood practically naked now, like pale ghostly gray sentinels, stiffly reconciled to losing their former lush covering to the winter cold.

Even though the colors of the sky and the landscape were dull and muted by the season, they still retained the rich promise of the natural glory that was to return again in the spring.

Slick loved seeing the hiking trails and the parks, the openness and the fresh air.

She had lived and worked in a depressed section of Newark for most of her life.

She wondered if Laura, who had grown up surrounded by all this grandeur, appreciated it every day as much as she did.

It was a crisp winter evening. The air was frosty with only a negligible sting to it. Most of the snow had melted after

Christmas. What was left was just enough to coat the ground without interfering with the road conditions. The landscape was filled with millions of sparkling ice diamonds that glinted under the moon and the street lights.

Winters in New Jersey were never predictable from year to year. It was either buried under tons of snow or lightly coated with a sprinkling of flakes. This winter was going to be one of the mildest on record.

On the drive, Slick and Laura playfully fought over which radio stations they would listen to, and then sang together whenever they agreed on one.

Garbo slept most of the way curled up in the backseat, the hum of the motor mercifully drowning out their singing.

They drove past the malls and shops that dominated Route 46. Then Slick took the exit for the Garden State Parkway South. She started to fumble through her pockets and the change holder for thirty-five cents.

"Do you have any change?" she frantically asked Laura as they approached a toll booth.

Laura, who had learned to prepare for Slick's lack of change, casually handed her the thirty-five cents.

Laura decided to have some fun. She cleared her throat and said innocently, "You know, all you have to do is buy an E-ZPass and you wouldn't have this problem."

"E-ZPass was a stupid, stupid idea and I will not validate it by supporting it," Slick exhorted. It was one of her hot button issues. "If they weren't going to do away with these toll booths like they said they were going to years ago, they could have at least left the Parkway the way it was. It was fine the way it was. It wasn't broken, so they fixed it. I love New Jersey! In spite of the pollution, the high property taxes and the most outrageous car insurance rates on the planet, I love New Jersey! But this E-

ZPass deal is ridiculous and I refuse to be sucked into it," Slick said with stubborn conviction, as she tossed the coins into the toll basket.

She continued to vilify the builders and proponents of the E-ZPass system and their mothers for several miles after the toll booth, and the next one, and the next.

Laura interjected the occasional "Yes, dear" or something similar, in that universal spousal tone when she thought it was appropriate.

She pretended to find positive things to say about E-ZPass when she felt Slick was winding down. Then, Slick would take the bait, which Laura knew she couldn't resist, and start up again.

Laura smiled to herself, knowing she had successfully pushed that button.

She shared Slick's views on the E-ZPass debacle, but getting Slick to rant and rave about it was just too entertaining to pass up whenever Laura got the chance.

Slick continued to sermonize on the evils of E-ZPass all the way to Exit 145.

"Did you find anything on the web?" Slick asked, as she turned the car off the Parkway exit ramp onto South Orange Avenue.

Laura had brought along her laptop and was online looking for information on the theater.

"Yes. They have their own site with all the pictures of the actors in their plays. I found a photo of Rachel and the rest of the cast. She's precious. Let's see . . . the building was originally an old convent. It says it may be haunted. The owners have had it checked out by clairvoyants, spiritualists, and a bunch of 'other world' sensitive types equipped with machines that detect and measure ectoplasm, auras, and psychokinetic energy."

Laura stopped reading, looked at Slick and did the "Doo-

Doo-Doo-Doo-Doo-Doo-Doo-Doo" from the *Twilight Zone* theme.

Slick rolled her eyes and looked at Laura askance.

"Try to keep an open mind about it if they mention it," advised Laura with diplomacy.

"My mind is open. But I haven't taken leave of it."

Slick continued up South Orange Avenue and found the convent.

It was impossible to miss.

It was an architectural masterpiece on a street filled with pizzerias, office buildings, and video stores.

The convent held a commanding position on the corner of the tree-lined street. Its high roof dwarfed the buildings closest to it. Its pious visage overlooked the center of the village of South Orange, adding to it the grace of times gone by.

The smaller more modern buildings near it made the convent look out of place, but clearly, none could pass by without admiring it.

Ivy climbed neatly about the red brick walls.

There were plenty of windows in the front and Laura pictured the windowsills packed with potted flowers in the summer.

Above it all was a huge tower that housed the convent bell.

The gates had been left open for them, and Slick pulled into the parking lot behind the building.

As they drove to the rear of the church, they noticed that the four windows on the street side of the church were cleverly boarded with large placards advertising all the shows from the previous season.

Slick and Laura stepped out of the car, and Slick let Garbo out of the backseat.

Addison and Karson were waiting for them at the rear entrance.

Addison smiled and held out his hand as they approached.

"Hello and welcome. I'm Addison Taylor and this is my wife and partner, Karson Parker Taylor."

Laura also smiled warmly and shook his hand.

"I'm Laura Charles and this is my partner and partner, Cassandra Slick."

"No one ever calls me by my first name. 'Slick' will do just fine," she said, shaking hands with Addison and Karson.

"And this is Garbo the Wonder Dog. She's a very crucial part of our investigative team," Laura said with mock seriousness. "She's very well-behaved. Do you mind if we bring her inside?"

"No, no, of course not. Let's all get inside, out of this chilly night," Addison said dramatically, as he held the door open with a display of grand courtliness.

Years of stage performing and a few speech coaches had all but eliminated Addison's southern dialect. But when Karson spoke, her rich southern accent dripped from her tongue like sweet molasses.

She took pride in the way she sounded and often spoke with southern witticisms and expressions. She knew that northern arrogance being what it was, many would think her simple and slow.

Karson used this to her advantage.

A few members of the South Orange City Council had tried to block her and Addison from buying the old convent. They felt that a community theater was fiscal folly.

The Council wanted to demolish the convent and replace it with a strip mall or a municipal parking lot. They had tried to discourage Addison and Karson by constantly losing their building permits or stalling tax relief programs that would benefit their renovation of the convent. They hadn't figured that the little woman with the thick southern drawl would be such a formidable opponent with a keen intellect.

Eight years later, Karson and Addison had their theater and everyone on the City Council who had tried to thwart them had been voted out of office, due in large part to Karson mailing out hundreds of flyers and leading rallies against them.

The reasons for Karson's fierce determination to acquire and keep the convent were far more personal than anyone on the Council could have imagined or fathomed.

She was tired of watching her husband start a new theater in a new town every few years or so, only to have it fail.

They hadn't had any children because their lives were too unstable for a child. Even now, years later, it still hurt them with a pain that hadn't diminished.

Karson was unwavering in her crusade to make this place their own. She felt it was time for them to belong somewhere.

Addison had big dreams and ambitions that he wanted to achieve, and he wasn't getting any younger.

Karson would see to it that at least one of his dreams came true.

Addison may have been the heart and soul of their theater, but Karson was the brains and the driving force. And she was smart enough to know that sounding like a little ol' southern yokel amongst these Yankees sometimes came in right handy like.

As they all entered, Karson said, "Sorry we have to meet under such unfortunate circumstances, but we can't thank you enough for your help. You have no idea how much this has upset us. Everything we have, everything we are, is tied to this theater. We appreciate your generous financial offer to keep us going, Miss Charles."

" 'Laura,' please. And we appreciate the fact that you're not going to press charges against Rachel."

"Why didn't you call the police? Rachel confessed to stealing money from you," Slick said. "You only have her word that she replaced it."

Addison and Karson looked at each other. A shared heartache seemed to pass between them.

"Rachel has been with us longer than anyone. We want to believe her. She says she put it back, but she still refuses to tell us why she took it in the first place," said Addison.

"Her uncle is very close to us. We're glad that you will allow us to help you sort through this," said Laura.

"Honestly, we didn't want to go to the police. People who have supported us for the last eight years have invested their own money in this show. A scandal right now could ruin us," said Addison.

"Is it possible that Rachel was in this with someone else at the theater and they took the money again after she replaced it?" asked Slick.

Addison was about to respond, but Karson cut in.

She stepped closer to Slick and looked her directly in the eyes. Her tone was very direct and matter-of-fact. Her eyes and her manner revealed no emotion whatsoever.

"We just don't know what to think. It's so hard for us to accept that anyone here would do this. We treat everyone like family. We are a family. I'd hate to single out anyone, but I have tried to tell Addison many, many times that something like this would happen if we let everyone have access to the money. Anyone, even a good Christian, could succumb to the temptation of thievery. But Addison . . . Lord love him, is a very trusting soul. He just can't imagine that anyone close to him would be capable of such a thing. But I have always known that the human heart has many chambers. None of us can ever truly know another's deepest secrets or their innermost feelings. We all have something we want to conceal.

"Poor Addison was in such a state of shock and disbelief following the theft that you could have buttered his butt and called him a biscuit. I'm sorry he had to learn this lesson the hard way, but I'm glad we have a professional investigator here to solve this quickly and quietly, in an honest and lawful way," said Karson.

"Let me give you the grand tour and then show you to the office," said Addison.

Karson and Addison led the way showing Slick and Laura the backstage area.

First, they showed them the prop room. It held a vast collection of items ranging from old style phones to new models, table settings, stemware, hand-held fans, lamps, and wall decorations. There was enough furniture to fill a small warehouse. The variety of its inventory was seemingly endless.

Karson explained how they had gathered these things over the years from yard sales and flea markets as well as gifts from individuals and other theaters.

She showed them many fake guns, knives, and swords and told little stories about them.

Laura held a few in her hands and pictured how many of the older props could have been used by the Barrymores or by Bernhardt.

Next came the enormous two-tiered costume room, with clothing on the bottom, and hats, shoes, capes, robes, and other accessories on the top.

There were two life-sized mannequins, one in a costume and the other undressed.

There was a counter to one side filled with pins and spools of thread and a large space with a full-length three sided mirror, a cutting table, and an ironing board.

There was a sewing machine for making alterations. The sewing machine couldn't be seen but it was heard whirring in the back, off in a little cubbyhole.

"That's Cheri Boone-Blume, the costumer. She keeps that sewing machine in a state of perpetual motion during a show," Karson said confidentially.

Then she called out in the direction of the sewing machine, "How's Beautee's costume for the third act coming along?"

"I'm working on it right now. I'll have it done in about fifteen minutes," came the harried reply from the cubbyhole.

The words came out a little mumbled, as if the mouth saying them was crammed with safety pins.

Slick noticed that there was a trail of chiffon leading into the cubbyhole as well as several baskets of clothing. It looked like a laundromat had exploded.

"She is a treasure," Karson said. "She can whip up a new costume in no time. What a difference a little lamé or fabric can do to change the look or style. She can even construct a pattern. Cheri has worked on all these costumes. Sewing them and sorting them. There's over a thousand articles of clothing in here. One day, we hope to have them all organized and on motorized racks for the hanging garments, just like a dry cleaner.

"Bye, Cheri," Karson called out before they left.

This time there was no response, but the whirring from the sewing machine was distinctively faster and louder.

The next stop was the men's and women's dressing rooms. They were practically identical.

"This is where the actors prepare themselves to make magic," Addison said as he opened the door to one and then the other.

Taped to the dressing room walls, there was a seating assignment giving each actor a designated spot in front of the mirrors that ran the length of the dressing room and across an adjoining wall in an "L" shape.

A row of lit makeup lights was above the mirror.

Underneath the mirror there was a shelf that matched it and ran in an L shape around the room.

There were personal makeup supplies strewn about in a riot in kits, bottles, tubes, and sticks, and a chair at each spot.

There were blow dryers, curling irons, cans of hairspray, tissue boxes, snack food, scripts, and street clothes everywhere.

There was a scene by scene breakdown of the play at each actor's spot as well as a detailed guide as to which costume was to be worn in which scene. There were also rules as to how the costumes were to be handled after they had been used.

Each dressing room had a full-length mirror, a refrigerator, and a microwave.

As they continued through the theater, Addison and Karson beamed with pride as they told favorite stories about donations of set pieces and costumes from PBS and various other television networks and movie companies. It was a collection of memories of all the previous shows.

Addison and Karson talked about several pieces individually and how they had been featured in their productions.

The pieces were stacked and lovingly lined up against the walls. Put away, but not forgotten, ready to be used again whenever needed.

The whole place smelled of scenery paint, varnish, cigarettes, and dust. It had the smell of age, of wood and bricks, and of chambers and corridors left untouched by the sun and air. It was stuffy from windows long unopened.

These were the musty perfumes of a community theater. Laura stood still for a moment, breathing it in.

She speculated that some of the dust dated back to the convent's original days.

"I visited your Web site. This must have been a magnificent

building in its time. You're doing a wonderful job of restoring it," Laura said, truly admiring the painstaking work that was done.

Laura could see that in its conversion from convent to theater, the Taylors had kept the majesty and stateliness of the building intact.

Slick walked behind with Garbo on a leash, listening to the conversation and making mental notes of every bit of information that Addison and Karson shared and the distinct characteristics of every room: entrances, exits, windows. Slick loved the details, loved getting a feel of the terrain.

"Well, we have a lot still that we want to do," Addison said with enthusiasm.

He told Slick and Laura about their plan to build a second, smaller stage in the back area for workshops, classes in directing, playwriting, acting, and costume design.

The workshops and classes wouldn't be just for this company. It would be open to anyone in the area who was interested.

They also had the vision of staging lunchtime theater. Busy business audiences could come in the noon hour and partake in a short forty- to fifty-minute production, as well as eat their lunch.

As they reached the front of the backstage area, sounds from the rehearsal in progress could be heard.

"And that's our theater," Addison concluded when they had seen the entire backstage section. "I think we can skip showing you the cellar. It's used mainly for storage and there's debris down there from the renovation. You can cut through this corridor here to get to the office without going into the theater," he said, indicating the direction they should go. "It's unlocked. If you'll excuse me, I'm going to go in and watch the rehearsal."

"And I've got to go work on some script changes," Karson said. "Playwriting is rewriting, I always say. I don't have time to cuss a cat. I'm busier than a stump-tailed cow at fly time. I've got to lock myself in with my old Smith-Corona. None of that new age computer stuff for me," Karson said as she headed for their apartment. "Please feel free to look around at the rest of the theater as you please. For obvious reasons, the books are no longer kept in the office. They're locked up in our apartment. If y'all want to see them, just knock on this door and I'll get them for you," she said as she walked toward their apartment.

Then she turned back to them.

"And don't be surprised that as you're looking around, you hear sounds or feel like there's someone standing right beside you and there's no one there. We have ghosts. They're friendly, but sometimes they do make their presence known. The place can be a little spooky to newcomers," she said.

"Have you ever seen a ghost?" Slick asked.

Laura was surprised that she had managed to ask the question with only a hint of incredulity.

"Not me personally, but members of the company have claimed they have. And there are things that happen that I can't explain. All the usual haunting stuff like strange noises, cold spots, objects missing or moved from where they were. This is an old building. Many a soul has passed through here. Addison and I are very respectful of that. We may own it now, but we realize we share it with those who came before us," Karson said.

Slick was about to comment, but Laura said, "Thank you. We'll be careful not to disturb them."

Then Karson unlocked the door and waved good-bye before stepping inside.

Slick turned to Addison and asked, "After we finish in the office, may we watch the rehearsal?"

"Certainly. I think they're ready for an audience. This show is one of the best shows we've done here. And I'm not saying that just because Karson wrote the script. We've got less than two weeks until we open and this thing is humming like a well-oiled machine. The first act is perfection, and I have a few surprises in store for act three. I have to admit I was a little hesitant about doing a musical. I'd never directed one before, but luckily, most of my actors and crew have experience in musical theater, so I think we were all up to the challenge," said Addison glowing with confidence.

He was eager to show off his new production. He thought it was pure theater magic. Addison felt it was the crowning jewel in this season's lineup of shows. He was already anticipating the ecstatic reviews this show was going to garner.

"Will everyone who had access to the money be at tonight's rehearsal?" asked Slick.

"Yes. Everyone. No one called out sick and no one is late."

"Have you told anyone else that money was stolen?" asked Slick.

"No. Karson, Rachel, and I are the only ones who know," said Addison.

"Well, if Rachel is to be believed, then at least one other person does know . . . the thief. And just out of curiosity, do you think anyone here would recognize Laura? She's had her picture in several magazines and in the newspapers many times for various social and charity events."

Addison chuckled a little as he lit his pipe. He spoke between draws on it.

"Not unless she's had her picture in *Backstage, Variety,* or the *Spotlight* section of *The Star Ledger.* Actors tend to be pretty self-absorbed. Their main focus is the play they're performing in now and auditioning for the play they'll be in next. Narcissism is just a natural by-product of the theater. Some actors have it more than others, but there's a touch of it in all of them. I think it's because their entire being, heart, soul, and body is the instrument they use to create art from the written word. There's a bit of romanticism in it as well as a bit of insanity. Forever giving in to an all-consuming passion to create and perform, the need for applause and recognition, in a discipline that never guarantees anyone success. And even if it causes the actors insomnia, rashes, ulcers, heartache, or diarrhea, God love them, they can't stay away."

Laura thought of the famous actors she had known personally. Most were somewhat egocentric. But she had never heard it explained quite so charitably or with such genuine affection.

"I haven't yet developed a theory as to why musicians are the way they are. I don't think anyone can explain them," Addison added with a wink.

Laura laughed at Addison's little joke. She liked him. But she could tell from the "I'm only laughing to be polite" look in Slick's eyes that Slick was not enthralled.

Addison noticed that, too, and got back to the subject.

"Seriously, I can say assuredly that no one from my little company travels in the same social circles as you do, Laura. No one will know who you really are. I think you'll be free to move about here as you like without fear of being recognized."

"Just one last question, please, before you leave us," said Slick. "Who else knows the real reason we're here?"

"Just me and Karson. Rachel thinks Laura is here as a favor to her uncle to help financially. No one knows that you're a private detective, Slick. You said on the phone that you were going to pose as a backer with Laura. When you're ready to watch the rehearsal, that's the way I'll introduce you."

"Fine. Thank you," said Slick.

Addison turned and walked into the theater.

Slick and Laura made their way to the office. As they walked, the noise of the music, singing, and the rhythmic stamping of feet from the theater diminished and receded until it was nothing more than the noise that seeps through from a neighbor's home late at night. Just enough sound to let you know there's life and activity going on nearby, but the sound is muffled and indistinguishable.

Once inside the office, Slick kept the door open to see if anyone would seemingly happen to stop by nonchalantly or linger in the hallway. She checked the proximity of the office to the Taylors' apartment.

She then made a cursory check of Addison's desk drawers and the papers on top of the desk. She made sure that everything was rearranged from its original position.

Laura watched for a while, and then questioned Slick why she was only going through the motions.

Slick checked the door and hallway to make sure no one was listening.

"Addison and Karson may be expecting me to look at all this stuff and I don't want to disappoint them. I've got the general idea of what is kept in this office. This is a little theater and this is the center of its operations. This is where the reservations are done, the records are kept, agreements with outside contractors are signed. And, up until the theft, all the banking and financial statements were here. Look. All the names, addresses, and phone numbers are listed here on the cast contact sheet. And you were able to read brief bios of everyone at this theater online. Everyone here has access at any time to all this information."

Slick picked up the cast contact sheet and made two copies on the office Xerox machine and put the copies in her pocket.

"I'll have Sam run background checks on all these names. Everyone in this place is a suspect," Slick said.

"Everyone but Addison and Karson, you mean," amended Laura.

"Everyone *including* Addison and Karson," corrected Slick

"Oh, no," Laura said in disbelief, trying to keep her voice at a whisper. "They're trying to bring art and a love of theater to this community. Why would they steal the money from themselves? That makes no sense."

"It makes perfect sense. You saw all the projects they have going on backstage; finishing the restoration of the convent, adding a second stage, teaching classes. Very ambitious. All that is going to cost money."

"Well $25,000 is not going to make much of a dent in that."

"Maybe not, but $50,000.00 would make a nice little niche, wouldn't it?"

Laura still looked skeptical.

Slick continued.

"Indulge me for a moment. Let's assume for now that Rachel is telling the truth; that she stole the money and replaced it. Let's say Addison and Karson, or one of them without the other, discovers that Rachel stole the money. One, or both of them, pockets the money after Rachel returns it. They confront Rachel with the theft. Rachel admits to stealing money. She says she returned it, but can't prove it. Maybe she won't say why she took it because that may implicate someone else here. I don't know yet.

"Now, what if Addison or Karson knows of Rachel's connection to Judson? They know that Rachel has been estranged from Judson for years and they know why. They also know that Judson has been trying to reconcile with Rachel and her father.

"Judson told us he would send Rachel money and gifts over the years only to have everything sent back to him. When

Rachel finally reaches out to Judson, it's a good gamble that Judson will do anything he can to help Rachel, and to keep her out of jail. So the Taylors pick up another $25,000 from him. A tidy little theft with a convenient confession from Rachel, and a bit of extortion thrown in. And maybe that's the real reason why they didn't want to call the police in, because an investigation could lead straight back to them."

Laura had to admit that the theory was plausible. Either of the Taylors could have known about Judson, but hadn't planned on Laura and Slick getting involved to help him.

She didn't want it to be true, but it was possible.

Slick could see that Laura was uncomfortable at the thought of including Addison and Karson as suspects.

"Welcome to 'Detective 101,' my pretty Blue Eyes," Slick said touching her cheek softly. "Lesson Number One: Everyone is a suspect until you no longer have a reason to suspect them. A good detective has to consider all possibilities. Leave no stone unturned. I'm not saying that Addison and/or Karson is guilty of anything. I'm only saying that you can't start crossing people off your list until you've had the chance to check everything out. Even the nicest, most well-intentioned people are capable of a crime under the right circumstances.

"Money does strange things to people. I've had cases where far worse things were done for much less money. All it takes is the right amount of despair and the belief that stealing is the last chance grab for a way out of it. A situation presents itself, a bad choice is made, then you're stuck with the mistake and its consequences. Maybe Addison or Karson felt that taking the money would be a way out. Now, let's go have a look at the rest of our would-be felons."

10

Slick and Laura found their way into the theater's lobby.

The walls of the lobby were covered with framed pictures of the cast and crew of past productions.

One wall was filled with the head shots of the current cast.

Several chairs and a couch were scattered about the room.

Against the far wall was an old bureau with a coffee urn on top. There was also another urn next to that filled only with hot water for those desiring hot tea or cocoa.

Next to the second urn were three stacks of styrofoam cups, and sweetners, packets of Earl Gray tea, Swiss Miss hot chocolate with marshmallows, and Coffee Mate.

There was also an assortment of cookies and candy. A glass jar was at the end of the bureau, stuffed with a few dollar bills and coins; presumably it was the coffee and cookie fund.

The garbage can next to the bureau was filled with greasy hamburger wrappers spotted with melted cheese and ketchup, French fry boxes, Chinese food containers, and a few half-eaten KFC biscuits.

All around there was the aroma of coffee, junk food, and cigarettes.

A few people were milling about, talking and laughing, drinking coffee and smoking, discussing the show, or running lines. A few were filling up their water bottles from the water fountain before going into the theater.

As Slick and Laura entered the theater itself, they felt as if they had stepped into another world.

They noticed everyone was working within a group. Each group seemed to be focused on something different.

There was an unmistakable energy to it all.

There was a cluster of dancers in oversized practice clothing stretching or massaging their leg muscles.

Two of the dancers were performing lifts. The one being lifted into the air was obviously unhappy with the execution of it. They took up one corner and the musicians took up another.

At least Slick presumed they were musicians. They were long-haired and scruffy looking. They stood at the stage door smoking suspicious-looking cigarettes and pointing and laughing at the dancers.

The stage was alive with the buzzing sound of volunteers using electric saws and the banging of hammers. Some were busy applying finishing touches of paint to the scenery. Others were running electrical lines from the stage to the tech booth and calling for checks on the connections. Still others were up high on ladders setting spotlights and placing gels while people on the theater floor looked up gesturing at them for the proper adjustment.

Addison was busy talking to some actors in full costume and stage makeup when Slick and Laura caught his eye. He signaled them to have a seat in the balcony.

He watched as they climbed the stairs and took their seats.

When he was sure they were seated comfortably, Addison clapped his hands to get everyone's attention before he spoke. He looked around the theater to make sure all were present. All activity stopped.

"Good. Everyone's here. I'm happy to say that we have two investors with us tonight who have stopped by to watch our rehearsal of *Sorry I Missed Your Birthday,*" Addison said as he indicated the balcony.

All heads turned momentarily toward the balcony, acknowledging Slick and Laura with nods and broad smiles, each hoping they'd be noticed. Some made a few remarks about the cute little dog. Everyone wanted to be at their best for the investors, or "Angels" as they were called in the theater.

"I'd like to run the last number for them, please, so they can see for themselves how wisely their money has been invested and show them what a talented team of people you are."

There was a ripple of laughs and a few suppressed private comments.

"Blair, would you and David set the stage for the last number, please."

Slick and Laura watched as a slender woman with short reddish-blonde hair wearing a headset with a microphone approached the stage. She was attractive in a no-nonsense, efficient way. She went to the groups of technicians who had been working on the set, the lights, and the electricity and dismissed them. They all seemed happy to take a break and let the performers take over. They all headed for the lobby for coffee and cookies.

She was followed every step of the way by a smiling young man, also wearing a headset and microphone, and carrying a clipboard.

She was speaking and pointing to the stage and he appeared to be writing down everything she said. She paced back and forth, apparently giving assignments and he circled around her, anticipating her every turn and move.

David nodded often and seemed to be mesmerized by everything Blair said. He eagerly took notes and gushed effusively when it was his turn to talk. He smiled almost nonstop and seemed to be enjoying himself immensely.

Blair would occasionally smile back at David, but they were faint, economical flashes, done woodenly and perfunctorily, as if to abate his smiling, and she seemed very self-conscious and uncomfortable doing it.

Then they both climbed the steps to the stage and began to rearrange it.

"Dale. Sindee. I'll give you both a few minutes to speak with your people, and we'll go in five," Addison said.

With that, Addison reached into his pocket, got his pipe, and walked out toward the lobby.

As soon as he was gone, they all burst into hyperactivity.

Slick and Laura saw a tall, long-legged man in leotards, wearing a red sweat band on his head and a "Queen" sweat shirt, a man with a tight sculpted body and chiseled good looks, rush to the group of dancers who had been doing warm-up exercises during Addison's instructions. He spoke to them rapidly for a few moments, and they began doing dance steps. He repeatedly took sips from a bottle of Diet Coke and walked around them anxiously as they practiced.

The woman who had been calmly seated at the piano nervously picked up a cigarette lighter from the piano top, lit a cigarette, and began shouting at the musicians. Then she frantically started leafing through a pile of sheet music.

Blair and David, who had been leisurely arranging the set, went into warp speed.

Slick and Laura felt like they were watching a movie on fast forward.

Blair left David on the stage to complete the setup. She climbed the stairs to the opposite end of the balcony and sat down at the sound and light console.

When Addison returned to the theater looking rested and refreshed, everyone reverted to their normal speed.

Slick and Laura turned to each other, puzzled.

Five minutes hadn't passed. They doubted if even three minutes had passed. No wonder the cast and crew had scrambled at such a pace.

"Okay, folks," Addison said as he entered. "Let's do this. You're in charge now, Ms. Stage Manager," he said looking up at Blair. "We go on your command. I'm going to go backstage and set up the balloon effect I've been working on."

"Balloon effect? What balloon effect?" asked Blair, anxiously looking through her script notes. "You never said anything about balloons. This is the first time you've ever mentioned anything to me about balloons."

Blair blanched. Her voice went up two octaves.

"David and I have never handled a run-through on our own before. I think you should stay and oversee this." Then she dropped her copy of the script. She was clearly flustered.

From below, Sindee witnessed Blair's panic attack and shook her head in disdain.

The voice in Sindee's head was screaming "Blair, you twit!" She cursed Blair out under her breath.

Sindee smirked and wondered if Blair had suffered a severe head trauma as a child. Maybe the reason she was so dimwitted was because she had a collision with an ice cream truck, or something.

The thought of little Blair in excruciating pain with her head heavily bandaged, her skin a deep purple and yellow from the bruising, and wearing a halo neck brace with screws boring into her cranium was immensely appealing. Sindee was momentarily giddy.

"Don't you worry about it, Blair," Addison reassured her. "I'll be in charge of the balloons. You and David will be just fine."

Blair, her face lined with worry, nodded skeptically to Addison, then watched him with uncertainty as he hurried backstage. She put the script pages in order.

Everyone in the theater looked to her for the signal to start.

Blair collected herself, stood up, and called down to the man in the leotards.

"Dale, are your dancers ready?"

Dale took a sip from his Diet Coke and gave her an "A-OK" sign.

Blair turned to the musicians. "Sindee, is the pit ready?"

Sindee also gave her an "A-OK" as she made sure the musicians were in place and all the herbal smokes had been extinguished.

"David, we are at 'places.' Is everyone ready backstage," Blair said into her headset.

From backstage Slick and Laura heard David call out, "Third Act finale! Everyone onstage!"

"Good," Blair said. "Here we go."

The house lights dimmed, flickered three times and then went out completely. The entire house was dark except for the lights on the tech board and the few lights in the orchestra pit.

The stage lights came up.

The lit portion of the set was that of a modern well-appointed living room. It was all beautifully painted. In the dark unlit sections of the stage could be seen portions of other settings.

There were walkways and struts, raked at different angles.

The sliced and diced stage must have been quite a nightmare for the actors and dancers to maneuver, but from the audience's perspective, it was visually spectacular.

The lighting suggested the scene was taking place at night.

A very pretty young black actress was alone on stage. She

was dressed very plainly in an oversized drab brown robe and large frayed fuzzy bedroom slippers. She shuffled around the set for a while conveying sadness and lethargy. She was clearly despondent.

She waddled to the set window, looked outside, and started to cry.

She pulled a Kleenex out of the robe pocket, dried her tears, then wiped her nose.

With an air of great melancholy and a heavy sigh, she finally sank listlessly onto the couch that was in the middle of the stage, facing the audience.

She took more Kleenex from her robe pocket and attempted to keep from sobbing.

All this agonizing and suffering was performed as if it were a Greek tragedy.

"That's Judson's niece," Laura leaned in and whispered to Slick.

Next, the musicians started to play.

Sindee started them up with a piano intro and then the key-boardist, guitar player, and drummer joined in. It was a lively up-tempo tune, in direct contrast to the mood that had been set.

A door on the right side of the stage flew open, and a very handsome man in a tuxedo and top hat entered with a stunningly attractive woman on his arm wearing a gorgeous evening gown.

Laura recognized them from the Web site photos as Rock Scherer and Beautee Holsom.

Rachel looked at Rock and Beautee with feigned astonishment as they began to sing.

"Birthday! Birthday! Today is your birthday!
You're thinking that we forgot your birthday!"

A second door, upstage center, opened and a younger man, closer to Rachel's age, entered. He was also wearing a tuxedo and top hat.

Laura recognized him, too. It was Randall Garret.

Randall started singing, adding a three-part harmony, and all three sang to Rachel together.

"Kidding! Kidding! We were only kidding!
We never really forgot your birthday!"

The three singing actors moved to the center of the stage and stood behind the couch. Rachel immediately cheered up and laughed and applauded as the trio sang to her.

A third door on the left opened and a line of dancers in sequined tuxedos carrying top hats entered with their arms linked at the elbow and doing high kicks.

Once they were all inside, they put on their top hats and started leaping and twirling around the entire stage, and they joined in the song.

"Gotcha! Gotcha! Oh, boy, we really gotcha!
How could you think that we'd forget your birthday?"

These verses were repeated with the harmonies and dance steps becoming more elaborate and detailed with each repetition.

Rachel, now all smiles and very ebullient, went to each of the three lead singers and hugged them. After that, she turned her back to the audience and pulled off her robe with great panache. Underneath she was wearing an elegant gown.

Beautee smiled beneficently at Rachel, then handed her a pair of heels she had hidden behind her back.

Rachel kicked off the floppy slippers, stepped into the high heels, then took a moment to walk toward the audience and display her party clothes. Then she began to dance with the others.

Next, a champagne bottle, approximately six feet long, was lowered from above. Its cork popped off and bubbles began spewing out of it.

A revolving filter was activated in front of one of the spotlights, and little specks of light descended all over the scene, simulating confetti.

Then, a huge ornate birthday cake was rolled in through the door where the dancers had entered.

The music swelled and the whole cast gathered around the cake singing and dancing.

All the men removed their top hats one at a time in succession and made a sweeping gesture with them, pointing toward the cake. It was executed much in the same way as toppling a row of dominoes or doing the "wave" at a ball game.

The set lights dimmed.

A spotlight lit the cake and everyone looked at it expectantly.

Nothing happened.

The actors exchanged a few worried glances.

Sindee hastily signaled the musicians to build to the crescendo again, this time at a quickened pace, as if they were playing against time.

Slick and Laura could tell from the balcony that something was wrong. Even Garbo could sense something was wrong. Her ears stood straight up and she cocked her head to one side trying to understand what was going on.

The verse was repeated, the music swelled, and, again all the men removed their hats and pointed them toward the cake.

The set lights dimmed. The spotlight lit the cake.

Everyone looked at it expectantly.

Again, nothing happened.

Suddenly, Blair jumped to her feet at the console and angrily started yelling into her headset.

"David! Where the hell are you? You said all the props had been checked. Get your ass out here and do something!"

David, no longer bubbly and perky, came running out from backstage, shrugging his shoulders, looking up at Blair trying to explain something, but Blair didn't give him a chance to explain anything. She just kept shouting into her microphone at him, even though he was standing directly below the balcony, clearly in her line of sight and could plainly hear her now without the aid of his headset.

"Shut up! I don't care! Figure it out and fix it!" Blair exploded.

From inside the cake came a frenzy of pounding noises and muffled cries excitedly relating that something inside the cake was stuck.

Two dancers closest to the cake stopped twirling and climbed onto the base of the cake, grabbed the top portion and tried to lift it up. Everyone else continued to sing and dance, and act like all was well, but it was obvious that all attention was focused on the uncooperative cake.

Without warning, the spring hinge mechanism inside the cake suddenly engaged and the top burst open forcefully. The two featherweight dancers who were standing on the base of it, trying to get it open, suddenly found themselves airborne, catapulted from the stage, and became human projectiles, as if they had been shot from a cannon.

One was hurled into the orchestra pit, landing on the drummer, breaking his snare drum and sending the cymbals crashing into the keyboardist. This caused the metal music stands to topple. The musicians lost their way as the sheet music fell to the ground. The music continued along briefly in a jarring discordant out-of-tune cacophony before it abruptly stopped.

The other dancer was thrown against the set wall. The set wall fell backward, knocking an overhead light off its track. It dangled precariously for a few perilous seconds. Everyone directly under it scattered away just in time before the light crashed upon the stage.

Without any music to dance to, and now fearing that the entire set was collapsing around them, the remaining dancers fled the stage in a panic, screaming and shrieking as they ran away. It was like seeing a gaggle of prissy effeminate rats scamper off a sinking ship.

Dale watched crestfallen as his beautiful choreography was unraveled and shredded.

Unfortunately, the popped bubbles from the six-foot champagne bottle had left puddles on the stage, and as the chorus boys ran away, they collided into, bounced off, and tripped over one another, until there was a pile of them on the stage floor embroiled in a hissing, bitch-slapping melee.

"Ouch! Get off me, you cow!"

"Who you calling a cow, Missy Thunder Thighs!"

"Excuse me! Are they still calling you by your Native American name . . . 'Dances Without Rhythm'?"

"Watch it, 'billy goat Elliott'! Your movements aren't exactly fraught with inner meaning and excitement!"

"I'll show you inner meaning and . . . Oh! Oh! . . . leg cramp! Leg cramp!"

Dale took a long swig from his Diet Coke and wondered if he would ever work again.

Sindee started to shout obscenities up at Blair.

"Blair, you stupid, no talent bitch! You have the IQ of a fucking spatula! You couldn't stage manage the opening of a ketchup bottle!"

When she realized Blair was still screaming at David and couldn't hear her righteous wrath, Sindee sat down and began to pound her head against the piano. A wave of nausea had overwhelmed her and pounding her head always prevented her from throwing up.

Always prevented it, that is, until tonight.

Sindee cupped her mouth with both hands, and made a mad dash for the ladies room.

Alicia Beavers, the actress who had been hiding in the huge birthday cake, simply followed Addison's first rule of acting, which was, whatever happened on stage became a part of the play.

With a bravura attitude that signified all the blunders were intentional and written in the script, she lifted up her arms, flashed her prettiest smile and shouted "Surprise! Surprise!" All this while wearing a pink tutu and balancing a weighty Carmen Miranda fruit bowl hat on her head.

From Slick and Laura's vantage point, all these disasters played out like a video game. Their attention ping-ponged around the theater, not knowing where the next calamity would strike, but knowing another one would.

Slick, who had been grinding her teeth together, trying unsuccessfully to fight back laughter as all the confusion unfolded, stopped fighting it and roared out loud.

She turned to Laura with her index fingers jammed into her ears, pretending not hear it all, and said, "The real mystery here is how this theater ever qualified for a grant in the first place. Someone at your foundation has perpetrated an unbelievably cruel crime against an unsuspecting public. We should be investigating them. People are going to pay good money to see this. This is the worst thing to happen to musical theater since ABBA."

"Shh!" Laura shot her an impatient glance, fearing Slick was talking too loudly. Laura did this knowing that in this chaos no one was paying attention to them or could possibly hear them.

Laura was holding Garbo in her lap and the dog had begun to bark and howl at the noise and confusion.

Their focus was returned to the stage when suddenly Randall, furious, stripped off his Velcroed tuxedo. He pulled off his top hat, threw it on the floor and started stomping it. The cast looked on horrified. Costumer Cheri Boone-Blume was not going to be happy about his trashing the wardrobe.

"That's it!" Randall shouted, continuing his outburst. "I've had it with this garbage! Dale's choreography is undanceable and the music Sindee wrote is horrible and we all know it. *'Gotcha! Gotcha! Oh, boy we really gotcha.'* Wow! Now there's a lyric Sondheim would envy! Is that a Tony I smell? No! It's just the stink from this lousy musical! Give me a break! I could eat a box of Alpha-Bits for breakfast, and shit better lyrics than that before lunch. With plenty of hard work, Sindee could become a third rate hack. We're all trying our best to make this crap work and for what? To make the two of them look good? They don't give a damn about anyone. Every time I make my entrance Sindee has the orchestra play louder. She shouldn't do that while I'm singing!"

Sindee, who was just returning from the ladies' room where she had chewed about eleven Altoids, snapped back at him.

"How many times do I have to explain to you that I bring the music up to subdue the sound of your voice? You can't sing. This is a musical, and you can't sing. You were cast only because there wasn't anybody else. The audience should be spared the sound of your voice as much as possible. The sound of two donkeys fucking is more melodious than your singing."

Sindee was exaggerating, of course. Randall's singing voice wasn't that bad, but after weeks of rehearsing and putting up with his temper tantrums and Blair, Queen of the Cretins, Idiot of the Village, Sindee had had enough. She didn't care anymore. This rehearsal was shot to hell anyway.

Blair brought the house lights up to full, then angrily threw off her headset and stormed down from the balcony. She could see things intensifying between Randall, Sindee, and Dale and she wanted to be there to support Randall.

She and Randall had starred together in most of the shows done in the theater's eight year history. All that had changed when Sindee talked the Taylors into doing this musical. Blair saw this as a power struggle with Sindee and Dale, and Blair wanted to win.

Winner take all.

"I was up in the lighting booth running things," Blair said angrily as she entered the fray. "David was supposed to be managing things down here. I can't do everything. It's not my fault that he doesn't know what the hell he's doing. I gave him detailed instructions on what to do. Any reasonably intelligent person could have followed the instructions. But not him. I'm not responsible for his incompetence. I had no way of knowing that he was such an unreliable imbecile."

Shell-shocked by the enormity of the rehearsal blunders, David had shrunk back into a dark far corner of the theater, trying to hide, trying to be little more than a silhouette, hoping that no one would look at him, but of course everyone did.

"And I am tired of you calling me stupid in front of the whole cast and crew. That is so unprofessional," Blair said.

Sindee just laughed and picked up her cigarette lighter. She fired up a cigarette, and blew smoke directly into Blair's face. Then she said, "You know what Blair, you're right. You're absolutely right. Calling you stupid is an insult to stupid people. You have to work your way up to stupid. Achieving stupidity should be a goal for you, a lifelong goal."

Dale started laughing and Blair turned to him furiously.

"We were doing just fine here before you two joined us. Doing a musical was Sindee's idea and it was a bad one. Just look at this mess. Randall is a sensitive artist and you and Sindee mistreat him."

"Shut up, Blair, I don't need you defending me," Randall said.

Dale stepped up and said, "Yes you do. She's got more balls than you have."

"What would you know about having balls, you big butt-fucking ballerina?" Randall said.

"Ohhh! Ouch! That hurt! You're such a manly man. I'm afraid of you," Dale returned, pretending to shudder with fear.

"I've had enough of your fairy bullshit. I am an artist . . ." Randall began.

"Oh, please. Just because you burst into hysterics and have anger management issues and no one understands you, doesn't make you an artist. There's a thin line between artist and loser, pal. Guess which side of the line you're on," Sindee snapped.

The other actors started to back away. This fight between Sindee, Dale, Blair, and Randall had been brewing for a while.

They were like dogs of war, straining against their leashes. It was about to get ugly and no one wanted to be an innocent bystander in the line of fire.

The four of them squared off. Tempers were hot. Their patience was gone.

Then, in a moment of comic relief, Rock Scherer approached the foursome. He was totally oblivious to the fact that he was walking into a battle zone.

"Is anyone going to fix the light that fell? It was my spotlight. I want to be sure the audience can see my best side."

"Oh, sure Eugene. It's right at the top of my 'To Do' list. I'll get right on it," said Blair sarcastically.

"My name is 'Rock,' " said Eugene. "I've told you people over and over again to call me 'Rock.' Get used to it. I'm having my name legally changed. That's the way I'm credited in the program, on the Web site, on my resume. Everywhere. So please call me 'Rock.' "

"Rock" was on a roll. He launched into his next complaint.

"And, Dale, one of your dancers is constantly stepping on my toes. I don't know his name, but he dances with all the elegance and subtlety of a cattle stampede. He gets in my way and obstructs my sight line. I can't see around him, and I'm sick and tired of being trampled by him. Please speak to him about it."

The corners of Dale's mouth moved upward into a smirk.

"I did speak to him about it, Eugene. He says he can't see because he is constantly blinded by the glare from your bald spot."

Eugene gasped and reflexively ran his hand through his thinning hair.

He stared dumbstruck at Dale, his jaw hanging slackly.

Eugene, or "Rock" as he like to be called, did not see himself as vain, although he knew he had every reason to be conceited. He exemplified what every gay man wanted to be.

He was tall, buff, and he still had the skinny hips of a teenage boy.

He was extremely talented, with the looks of a rugged uber model. He had closely cropped strawberry blonde hair with just a hint of gray at the temples, inviting blue eyes, a straight and narrow nose, and generously full sensuous lips. He carried himself with an air that had "Leading Man" stamped all over it.

And, oh yes, Eugene was great in bed.

Every straight woman and every gay man fell in love with him as soon as he stepped onto a stage. The straight men in the audience thought he was good-looking, too, but not to the extent that they were intimidated by him. Eugene could toss back a few beers and talk sports and politics with the best of them after a performance.

Even hard-edged militant lesbians secretly thought he was attractive and sexy, although they would never admit it out loud, but Eugene knew it.

It took a tremendous effort for Eugene to keep his ego under control. It was a constant struggle. Good looks and talent were sometimes a burden.

Eugene's only flaw as far as he was concerned was that he was losing his hair. Rapidly. His beautiful hairline was moving backward. He kept it cut short to try to conceal it. Any reference to this fact immediately set him off.

Eugene may have been an innocent passerby before, but now he was involved.

He had been bloodied and now he was out for blood.

"I'm so sorry, Dale. I didn't quite catch what you said. Perhaps there's too much rum in your Diet Coke. I don't speak Alcoholic."

The jittery onlookers gulped collectively. The room fell into pin-dropping silence.

Dale's face went crimson red, swiftly changing to purple. The veins in his neck bulged and throbbed. He was unable to catch his breath as if his throat was closing. He was practically vibrating with anger.

He had assumed that Sindee was the only one who knew about his drinking during rehearsals. He was very glad neither Addison nor Karson were present.

Eugene continued.

"Oh please don't act so surprised, Dale. Do you think we can't smell the rum on your breath? Don't get your adult diapers in a knot, Liver Spots. Jesus, the elderly can be so sensitive and bitter! You're a little long in the tooth to be choreographing, aren't you? Are you trying to recapture your youth, or working your way through a midlife crisis? I see a walker in your near future.

"We heard you were a big deal in Florida, with Disney. Why is it that you're working here in this little theater in New Jersey? It must be profoundly frustrating for you to have gone so far just to end up back here. What happened? Did you hit the skids, and now you drink to forget everything that you lost in Florida?" Eugene asked sarcastically.

Dale stared Eugene in the eyes and spoke slowly, with venomous restraint. He was feeling enough violent anger to stomp Eugene and then attack Tokyo just for fun.

"I need to drink to endure your limited acting range. You have all of two emotions and you endlessly convey them the same way every time you're onstage. Shouting and grunting and hand-wringing for drama, and smirking and posturing for comedy. That's as far as you go. That's all you've got. That's your complete repertoire. You're not an actor, you're a poser. Your mannerisms are predictable and endless. I can't drink enough to dull the sight of you onstage. Hell, we should have an open bar before each show to anesthetize the audience."

Eugene moved closer to Dale until they were practically toe to toe, angry eyeball to angry eyeball.

Eugene was about to respond, but Blair cut him off.

"If you had cast Randall in the lead you wouldn't have had that problem. Randall was always cast as the leading man before you talked Addison and Karson into doing this piece of junk," Blair said viciously to Sindee.

"Shut up, Blair! I can speak for myself!" Randall yelled. He turned to Sindee. "I was always cast as the leading man before you talked Addison and Karson into doing this piece of junk!"

Sindee ignored Randall and went after Blair.

"Maybe Eugene can't act, but he can sing. Randall isn't even in the same zip code with the right notes. It's a musical, you genius. The emphasis is on singing. I'd explain the concept to you, Blair, but it has too many syllables and I'm afraid your almost-human brain would explode. Eugene can sing so he got the lead. Please warn me if you ever get close to understanding this simple fact. I don't want to die from shock," Sindee hissed.

"It's 'Rock,' damn it, 'Rock'! What do you mean I can't act?" demanded Eugene urgently, turning to face Sindee and sounding mortally offended.

Dale had rebounded. He was poised to strike another blow.

"All right, all right! I'll tell you what she means. Keep your hair on! Oops! Too late! Another tragic Rogaine failure!"

Dale was just getting started.

"Read my lips! *You can't act*. You don't have the talent. You walk on the stage and everyone feels a vacuum. You suck the life out of every scene you're in. You give nothing. You're like a big hole in the air," Dale said slowly, enjoying himself again. He was clearly savoring Eugene's indignation.

"It's not that my voice is bad," Randall said, ignoring Dale and Eugene and taking aim at Sindee. "The music is so poorly written. You should have your fingers broken if you even threaten to go near a piano again"

That did it. Sindee had taken all she was going to take from this moody, marginally talented bastard. And his little bitch, too.

She summoned up her fiercest "drop dead" glare. She was about to take a swing at Randall when suddenly, from overhead, there came a buzzing, crackling sound.

Almost as if on cue, one of the few cues that had been followed correctly on this wretched night, every eye in the theater turned upward to witness the lights flicker, then dim. They flickered and dimmed again and then everything went black.

There was the unmistakable sound of a generator, far off in the recesses of the convent, shuddering and failing for the last time, followed by a coppery electrical smell.

There was approximately fifteen seconds of startled silence before the place erupted into angry accusations, cursing, and name calling.

Now everyone was fighting. All the frustrations that had built up during the long weeks of rehearsal ripped through the worn tissue-thin membrane of everyone's self-restraint.

The hostility was tangible. Arguments broke out everywhere.

"You only have two entrances and you missed both of them."

"I was in the bathroom. I had to piss like a race horse."

"I wasn't in costume because I couldn't find my costume. What did you want me to do, come onstage naked!"

"Well, it is a comedy, isn't it?"

"You spit with every line you say. It's like being at Sea World. We should give the audience a warning: 'The first five rows will get wet.' "

"If you'd return your props to the prop table . . ."

"Who did your makeup? Stevie Wonder??!!"

"Where did you learn how to play keyboard? A correspondence school?"

"Have you ever considered switching to air guitar?"

"You were miscast. Think of Carol Channing playing 'Evita'— that's how wrong you are for this part!"

"Drama Queen!"

"You call yourself a dancer! I've never seen a dancer who didn't know how to do jazz hands!"

"You're too short for this role. If you wore lifts, 'Mini Me' would still tower over you. You could represent the Lollipop Guild . . . this is all going right over your head, isn't it?"

"What did you get on your IQ test, besides drool?"

Slick and Laura sat in the darkened balcony listening to the tumult below them.

"Well, Karson said they were like a family. She didn't say she meant the Manson family, or worse, the Osbourne family. Perhaps she meant the Soprano family And, you know what, the fighting is actually more entertaining than the play," Slick commented.

Slick stood up and was about to make her way down to the first row in the balcony. She wanted to get a better view of what was going on and hear what was being said.

She stopped short.

"Excuse me. Excuse me, everybody."

Beautee Holsom was standing on stage alone in the darkness trying to speak above the ruckus.

A light behind her inexplicably came to life and backlit her in a way that made it seem that the light was emanating from inside her.

Outside, the cold winter night had been an endless and un- broken dark gray. Not a star could be seen. But at this instant, the clouds parted and revealed a spectacular full moon. Now the stars had taken ownership of the sky.

A single beam of moonlight broke through a crack in one of the convent's highest windows and perfectly encircled Beautee's face in illumination.

It was an arresting face. Heart-shaped, with enormous brown soulful eyes, it held purity and character, strength and delicacy.

All the fighting stopped suddenly, the combatants having been hushed into silence by this ethereal vision.

Beautee spoke softly but fervently.

"I know everything looks bad right now. But we have been given this moment of possibilities, this moment of grace for a reason. This is a clarion call. We can go on attacking one an- other in the darkness or we can move forward from here.

"We have a second chance. What are we going to do with it? Aren't we all responsible to one another? With talent comes re- sponsibility. We have the power to make people laugh and cry and think beyond their day-to-day existence. They come here to be entertained and uplifted, enlightened and challenged.

"Every time we step into character, we are given the chance to invent a new persona, weave a new story of reality or fiction, spin a new illusion. That's what theater is about. That's why we're all here.

"Every night when those lights go down and that curtain comes up, a miracle occurs. A piece of theater is born, and we are its creators. Be proud of that. Now. We have a show to get up. There are a lot of people depending on us. Can't we all pull together?"

There was utter silence.

Beautee was a supremely accomplished actress. She could deliver a line and recite a monologue that had been performed by hundreds of leading ladies, hundreds of times, on a hundred different stages, and convince even the harshest of critics or the most knowledgeable theatergoer that her interpretation was what the playwright had intended all along.

There was a velvety texture to her voice, as if she were caressing every sound.

She found all the subtle nuances and poetry in the characters she played, found all their notes and pacings and cadences, all their colors and shadings. Her technique was so smooth, it seemed effortless, the result of countless years of practice.

No one could believe she wasn't a professional actress.

But no one believed she was acting now. They were all moved by her simple sincerity and poignancy. Such genuine emotion couldn't be faked. It had to come from her heart.

Everyone looked at each other sheepishly.

Beautee was right.

This was community theater and everyone lived by its code. There were no contracts. No understudies.

If you agreed to do the show, you showed up and did the

show. No matter what happened, no matter how god-awful the show may have been or what petty differences existed. You did the show.

Beautee took them back to their greater selves.

Slowly there came the sounds of agreement and embarrassed laughter at how hot tempers had flared.

A few apologies were exchanged, a few handshakes and a few slaps on the back.

All the unforgivable words spoken in anger would be forgotten.

The storm was over. Soon, all the tension was gone.

Peace and order descended.

Miraculously, from out of the darkness boomed Handel's *Messiah*.

> *"Hallelujah!*
> *Hallelujah!*
> *Hallelujah, Hallelujah!*
> *Hallelujah!"*

There were audible gasps from the floor.

"Oh, that's my pager with the sound turned all the way up," Beautee said sweetly.

When she left the stage, everyone heard the sound of the old generator coming back to life, and all the lights came on as powerful as before.

There were sighs of relief as everyone assumed the generator hadn't died at all. It was just a power failure.

"Did you see that?" Slick excitedly asked Laura. She was rubbing her eyes and blinking, trying to focus.

"See what?" Laura asked. She hadn't been watching what was going on. She was still trying to calm Garbo down.

"Oh . . . nothing. Never mind. My eyes are playing tricks

on me, going from dark to light like that. Who knows? Maybe this place is haunted after all," Slick said, shrugging it off, trying to change the subject.

Slick decided to keep her mouth shut.

There would be no end to Laura's teasing if she told her that for a few seconds, she swore she saw little cartoon bluebirds circling around Beautee.

Suddenly, dozens of balloons drifted down onto the stage and Addison came running in excitedly.

"It worked! It worked! What do you think about . . ."

He stopped in midsentence when he saw that his entire company was laughing. But not because his planned balloon effect had worked. It was something else. He looked from them to the stage.

When he saw the fallen spotlight, the overturned set wall, the wet stage floor, and the busted-up orchestra pit, he could only imagine the havoc that had occurred during his absence.

They were laughing at the sheer ridiculousness of the moment. The balloons must have been the last straw.

Addison sized up the situation from the looks on the faces before him, and being a wise and experienced director, he did the only thing left to do.

"Ladies and gentlemen, boys and girls, go home and get a good night's rest. You've all worked very hard and you deserve it. Anyone can have a disastrous rehearsal and, apparently, tonight you've had yours. I know your nerves are frayed. We have some problems to solve, but we'll get through them. That is why we have rehearsals, to find and work through the problems. The problems on the technical side will dispel. The production will come shining through. And when it all comes together it will be wonderful. I'll get the set back up and we'll run it again tomorrow night. The reason I was drawn to directing at small theaters was because I wanted to work with folks like you. You give all you've got and then some. I rarely saw that kind of dedication in the professional theaters I worked in."

He took a deep breath, pulled his pipe from his pocket, and settled in to tell them another one of his many theater anecdotes.

"Did I ever tell you about the time, many years ago, when I was still a young actor, I worked at a small theater in North Carolina with . . ."

Everyone started to groan good-naturedly.

Addison got the message.

His troupe was acting as an ensemble again. They were all united about wanting him to shut up.

"Okay," he said laughing at himself. He tucked his pipe back inside his pocket.

"We'll save that story for another time. Good night."

Slick and Laura and Garbo made their way down from the balcony. Laura wanted to speak to Rachel and Slick wanted to observe as much as she could.

She and Garbo lingered at the backstage door and walked around the parking lot as the cast and crew left for the night.

Garbo was relieved as only a dog could be for this opportunity to finally walk around outside.

Eugene and Beautee were the first to leave. They walked out together, happily discussing their plans for the rest of the night.

Eugene seemed to have totally forgotten about the hateful verbal exchange he had been embroiled in earlier. He said that he was glad to have the chance to leave early. He joked that he was up for a night of short-lived, but meaningful relationships. As many as he could fit in before dawn.

Beautee gently chided him. She loved him but couldn't change him. He was irrevocably gay. She had given up on the idea that there could ever be anything romantic between them years ago.

Onstage, they were the perfect lovers. Each felt the other's rhythm and timing.

They complemented and completed one another. Their love scenes were filled with fire and symphony. The chemistry between them was undeniable. At times they were community theater's Tracy and Hepburn, Bogey and Bacall, Astaire and Rogers.

But, only onstage. Only onstage.

Offstage, they were *Will & Grace*.

But Beautee did care for him, and they shared an unshakable friendship.

Beautee said that she planned to go to the homeless shelter where she was a volunteer, and since she was out early from rehearsal she could give a pint of blood, or some other act of charity and kindness before reporting to the shelter. She reminded Eugene that if he overindulged in his night of fun to call her. She would gladly pick him up and give him a ride home, no matter how late.

Slick watched as Eugene walked her to her car, kissed her on the cheek, then got into his own car.

Then David rushed out the door without a word to anyone. He seemed to be making an escape, or attempting an inconspicuous retreat at the very least, more than just merely leaving. His hat was pulled down and his coat collar was raised up. He was trying to be invisible. He didn't want to talk to anyone.

Slick assumed he was still embarrassed by all the things that had gone wrong.

David got into his car and was gone.

Randall was the next to exit, still in a horrible mood. He was parked at the far end of the lot and as he crossed it he muttered and cursed aloud.

Slick could make out that he was angry, but couldn't hear what he was saying.

Seconds later Blair rushed out the door and ran over to where Randall was standing. She seemed to be trying to placate him, but Randall wasn't responding.

Randall continued to speak to her harshly, his voice rising heatedly. Blair spoke softly and reached out to touch him, but he pushed her hand away forcefully.

Slick started to walk and pull on Garbo's leash, making her way over to them, but before she could get close enough to hear their conversation, Randall opened his car door, got in and sped away.

Blair hurried to her own car and took off after Randall.

Laura came out of the theater door next, talking to Rachel.

Slick could tell from Laura's demeanor that she had already taken Rachel under her wing. Apparently the "everyone is a suspect" lecture had done no good. Laura's heart was twice the size of her mansion and she was always taking in human "strays." She gave of herself freely to anyone who might need her. She always had room.

Slick loved her for it, but sometimes she felt Laura set herself up to be used.

Laura was very wealthy and she was always a target for those who hoped to get some money from her.

Her father had been a ruthless businessman. The clam company was his one legit operation, and he had left that to Laura. But Owen Charles had other operations that were illegal and unsavory.

Over the years former partners of her father and heirs of these partners had sought to collect what money or revenge they felt was due them. Laura's father had cheated a lot of people. Now that he was dead, sometimes they came after Laura.

The threats were few and infrequent, but every now and

then one was real. Slick rarely mentioned them to Laura anymore because she had always been able to handle them with the help of her contacts at the police department.

The fact that Laura lived in a castle that was practically impenetrable was a deterrent to most of these plots, but even so, after Slick moved in she installed security systems in the mansion and in Laura's offices at Clam-de-Monium and at the foundation.

The one other possibility that Slick purposely had not mentioned while searching the theater's office was that perhaps someone was using Judson and Rachel to get to Laura.

Slick wanted to be sure this was nothing more than a theft, and not a plot to get at Laura.

"Rachel, can we give you a ride?" Slick asked when Laura and Rachel approached her.

Slick had wanted to stay to hear what Sindee and Dale said as they left, but they stayed behind to have a few words with the dancers and musicians.

She decided that a ride with Rachel could be useful, too.

They all got into the car and headed back down South Orange Avenue.

Laura was trying to talk to Rachel, but Rachel was being very close-mouthed.

Impenetrable.

Slick watched Rachel's face as she was driving. She watched her reactions in the rearview mirror as Rachel politely but reservedly chatted with Laura, without giving many details of her life.

If Rachel had any secrets, she wasn't giving them up.

Slick's thoughts returned to driving. Then she saw the flashing red lights from two police cars in the distance.

She drove by slowly and recognized Snatch McDonough

sprawled out on the hood. He was handcuffed and the police officers were frisking him.

Slick parked the car and ran over to see what was going on. She flashed her PI badge as she passed several of the officers. They all knew who she was.

"What's going on here?" Slick asked the officer in charge.

"Nothing much, Slick," he said. "Just checking to make sure this guy is seeing his PO and shit."

Slick played the game with them and said, "Good for you. Is he obeying the rules?"

"Yeah, he's clean."

"Why don't you guys let me talk to him for a while. I was the one who sent him up and I vouched for him when he got out. I want him to know that he better not make me look bad, you know what I mean."

The officers all laughed knowingly.

"Sure, Slick, anything you say."

"Get those cuffs off him, will you? I don't want any charges of brutality."

Snatch was uncuffed, and he started to rub his wrists as soon as they were removed.

The police officers walked away and let Slick have her talk in private with Snatch.

"Thanks, Slick," Snatch whispered, still massaging his wrists, "I always hated wearin' the bracelets."

Then Snatch looked her straight in the eyes.

"I know this looks bad right now, Slick, but you gotta believe me, I'm keepin' my word to ya. I ain't done nothin'. I done less than nothin' since I'm out, ya know."

"I know."

Snatch seemed very relieved.

"I had a swell time at your place. Thanks again for the invite."

Snatch looked over at Slick's car.

"Who's the girl in the backseat? Is she an ex-con like me that you're tryin' to help? I've seen her around."

"You have? But you just got out of jail."

"Yeah. Jail. That's one of the places I seen her."

Slick spun around and looked into the car.

Laura was still trying to get Rachel to talk. Even though it was night and Slick was several feet from the car, she could tell from Laura's body language that Laura was beginning to care for her.

She quickly turned back to Snatch.

"Okay, Snatch. Tell me everything you know about her. Everything."

Slick listened carefully to every word he said. When he finished she looked back into the car at Laura and Rachel. Her eyes never left them as she spoke.

"I need a favor from you, Snatch."

11

Alicia made a slow deliberate study of Sindee's mouth. It was perfect. Gorgeous. The lips were full and a little pouty.

Sindee always wore an overstated red lipstick that made them look luscious, ripe, and juicy like cherries.

So Alicia leaned in and, at first, lightly brushed against them with soft butterfly kisses, then tugged at them more purposefully with quick and titillating nibbles and bites, then kissed them deeply, taking her time.

Wonderful.

Almost simultaneously their lips parted and their tongues started to explore one another. Alicia shivered. It was the sweetest sensation. She loved doing the Tongue Tango, especially with someone who had a great mouth and knew how to use it.

Sindee had a great mouth. If it had been a violin, it would have been a Stradivarius. If it had been a piano, it would have been a Steinway. If it had been a harmonica . . . Alicia couldn't think of a world class harmonica maker just now, but Sindee's mouth would have been made by them.

She enjoyed the taste of Sindee. There was the faintest bit of cigarettes and breath mints, but mostly it was the taste of a woman. A woman who knew how to give and receive pleasure. A woman who had been around the block a few times, and being bisexual, had learned a few tricks from both sides of the street.

Alicia kissed her ears, so small and so soft, then her neck, then started to work her way down to Sindee's breasts. She kissed and tugged at her nipples until they were in full bloom and almost as red as her cherry lipstick.

Alicia continued to fondle Sindee's breasts, but she moved back to her mouth. She couldn't stay away. She kissed her again and again. Her hands made ever widening circles on Sindee's stomach. She touched the inside of her thigh, then stopped. She touched the other thigh, then stopped.

Alicia wasn't sure she could hold out much longer. Her passion was running wild. She could almost feel the spasms of pleasure. She hoped Sindee was as wet as she was, and there was only one way to find out.

Alicia was going in . . .

Sindee lifted her martini glass and said to Dale, "Take it from someone who knows. Martinis are like tits and balls; one is not enough and three is too many."

Sindee laughed loudly, slapped the table for emphasis, then took a drink from her glass.

Startled by the noise from the smacked table, Alicia's sex fantasy dissolved and evaporated.

She returned to reality.

Sindee was making jokes in an effort to cheer up Dale.

Alicia, Sindee, and Dale had decided to go to Ryan's Pub in South Orange, not far from the theater, for a drink after the catastrophic rehearsal.

Alicia couldn't have cared less about what had happened at the theater. She hadn't enjoyed being trapped in the big birthday cake, of course. She was claustrophobic. But she wasn't sitting around, moping about it, bringing everybody down like Dale was.

He drank heavily all night. He had drunk enough to fill an

entire lake by Alicia's estimation. Oh, yeah, Dale was working on a six-aspirin, washed-down-with-tomato-juice hangover.

He mumbled things about his age, Florida, and Disney, and he kept droning on and on about his hatred for Eugene.

Fucking Eugene. Goddamn, fucking Eugene. Motherfucking, goddamn, fucking Eugene.

Blah, blah, blah.

Yadda, yadda, yadda.

Alicia was drowning in waves of boredom over the subject of Eugene. She kept trying not to hear Dale. What was the big deal anyway? The rehearsal was over. It had been a nightmare for everyone, but it was over. Big boo fucking hoo, now move on!

It was all so ten minutes ago, she thought.

Alicia had more pressing problems on her mind. She hadn't had sex in two weeks, and she was extremely horny.

Alicia was a very sexual creature. She oozed sex. She couldn't help it. She seemed to secrete carnal pheromones the same way most people perspired. Sex dripped nonstop from Alicia's every pore.

Alicia Beavers had left her home in Seattle three years earlier to pursue her dream of becoming an actress on Broadway. She made it as far as New Jersey.

She went to as many auditions in New York as she could, and got a few parts off-Broadway, but they didn't pay the rent. Without any family or friends here, she soon had to come to terms with the financial truth of her situation. She needed to make money.

She put her dreams of Broadway on the shelf. She was still young. She had time. The dreams would keep for now.

Alicia decided it was time to tap into what she was good at.

During the day, Alicia worked as an operator at a twenty-four-hour telephone call-in sex line called "Lip Service."

When she went to audition for the job, she walked in wearing nothing but a raincoat. Even though the job was purely audio work and the callers would never see her, when she went into the booth to do the voice audition, she stripped naked. She was an actress and it helped her create the mood, she explained to the sound guy. She was hired on the spot.

From the day she started, Alicia performed her duties very enthusiastically. She spoke fluently the language of the kinky freaky deaky.

Whether she was speaking to those who were into cross-dressing, bondage, or fetishes, or even those who were into battery operated toys, vegetables, and condiments, she satisfied her customers. She had a way with dirty words. Whatever the guilty pleasure, Alicia delivered.

She became the most popular and the most frequently requested operator at the service. So much so that she was given her own office.

Management had been forced to do this out of necessity.

Normally, the phone sex operators worked in the same room, sitting next to and across from one another, in full view of each other, at a long bank of telephones.

Alicia kept distracting the other operators. They would became so turned on by her that they would neglect the paying call-in clients.

The owners gave Alicia her own soundproof office with tinted one-way windows. She could see out, but the other operators couldn't see in.

Alicia was free to do whatever she wanted to do to get herself in the mood.

The owners were happy, their customers were happy, and a good time was had by all.

Alicia decided never to tell anyone what she did for a living.

Whenever she was asked what she did, she said she was a public relations consultant.

She wasn't ashamed of what she did, but she never wanted to run the risk of meeting any of her customers face to face.

Alicia felt that people needed a fantasy from time to time, if only to get them through the very real problems of life.

She was a very attractive young girl, but she was afraid that if her customers knew what she looked like, it would destroy their fantasy image of her and end her lucrative career.

Alicia made a lot of money working as many shifts as she could. She still acted from time to time on the stage, but it never paid as well as her phone job.

Now she only accepted parts in plays when she could fit it into her busy work schedule.

She had taken this nonpaying job as the maid in *Sorry I Missed Your Birthday* because she had done shows at the Broad Street Players theater before and knew many of the cast members, and also because there was no sign of a paying acting job in her immediate future.

She wanted to keep busy. What was the difference, really? Her job at the phone service was a form of acting, wasn't it? Alicia told herself it was.

Alicia had her fill of fantasy sex every day and got well paid for it.

Tonight Alicia wanted the real deal. No fantasy. She was tired of doing the "wet work" for everyone else. She wanted her own trip to happy land. If Alicia didn't rub up against someone very soon she was certain she would experience some sort of sexual nuclear meltdown.

But Sindee was too busy with Dale.

Alicia wasn't going to get any release from her tonight.

She glumly took a sip from her 7&7.

Nothing came through the little cocktail straw.

She picked up her glass and inspected her drink. She was surprised to see the straw was completely chewed and tied in a knot. She realized that she must have done this unconsciously while lost in her reverie about tonguing Sindee. She wondered if Sindee or Dale had witnessed her oral manipulations of the cocktail straw.

They didn't seem to be paying any more attention to her than she was to them.

Alicia took a long glance around the bar, looking for possible candidates to take home. Somebody. Anybody.

No one looked promising.

Unlike Sindee, Alicia did not consider herself bisexual. She definitely had a preference for women, but in a pinch, a man would do. To Alicia, who provided the breathy, captivating voice hundreds of men and women got off to weekly, sex was all just a matter of a well-turned salacious phrase and friction.

Alicia wanted to get some steamy, pillow talking, one-on-one friction with any warm and willing attractive body. And she wanted it all night long until she was good and chafed.

Discouraged, Alicia slouched back into her seat, threw the ruined straw to the floor, lifted her drink and tossed it back. Her situation was becoming desperate. She was a walking libidinous Chernobyl, on sexual overload, on the verge of spewing her radioactive hormones in one great explosion.

Alicia knew she wasn't going to get any action here with Dale and Sindee, so she decided to go into the dance area of the club.

The music was blaring and the dance floor was packed.

There were a few tables inside along the walls and in the corners, but the tables were kept at a minimum for the dance floor.

There were bodies pressed together and some dancing all alone, but not seeming to care.

The DJ was spinning some extended mindless techno crap.

You could meet someone, fall in love, break up, and the same goddamn song would be playing all throughout in the background.

Alicia was about to sashay into her best dance moves when she saw Richard, one of the chorus boys dancing on the dance floor. She caught Sindee's attention and beckoned her over.

Sindee had put on her coat and was ready to leave. After three martinis, Sindee was always ready to leave.

Alicia pointed to Richard and asked Sindee's opinion.

Sindee smiled mischievously and said, "Excellent choice. Go for it. Richard may be the only straight man in the chorus line. He can scratch your itch."

Alicia looked at her distrustfully for a moment. Alicia was only in the final scene of the play so she hadn't had to attend every rehearsal and hadn't heard all the backstage gossip, but she seemed to remember something about Richard being teased and humiliated for his small penis.

"Oh that's because all the guys are so jealous of him." Sindee tried her best to be persuasive and sound sincere. "He is *huge*. A real cherry popper. He is packing a crotch rocket. He may be called 'Little Richard' behind his back, but those of us lucky enough to know the truth call him the big D.O.D., Dick of Death."

Alicia became more interested. And aroused.

"You've done Richard?" she asked.

"My God, yes! He's a sex machine. I couldn't walk for almost a week afterward."

Sindee was lying through her teeth, but she was very proud that after three martinis she was able to lie with a straight face and so convincingly.

She could see Alicia was falling for it and knew she was about to make a move on Richard.

Sindee was looking forward to hearing the story of their sexual encounter. She was going to enjoy the hell out of it.

"I'll tell you what. If you get Richard into bed tonight, and you're not completely satisfied, I'll take care of you tomorrow night."

Then Sindee gave Alicia a long kiss on the lips.

Alicia was euphoric. She almost swooned. The kiss was better than she had imagined it would be.

"Dale and I are going to leave. He says he has to meet someone in a few hours. I'm going to pour about two gallons of black coffee into him and send him on his way, plus I've got to go home and give Staccato her evening insulin shot."

Staccato was Sindee's fourteen-year-old diabetic cat, and she was totally devoted to her.

No matter where she was, no matter how busy she was, she always made it home in time to give her cat its two daily insulin shots. Her friends sometimes razzed her about it, calling her "Claws Von Bülow."

Back at the table, Dale staggered drunkenly to his feet and attempted to get into his coat. He managed to get one arm into a sleeve, but then he whirled round and round trying to get the other arm in.

Dizzy and unsuccessful, he fell backward into the booth.

The waitress who had served them was standing nearby looking at Dale with obvious displeasure. She was thinking she wasn't going to get a decent tip from this group.

Alicia saw Dale fall into the booth and commented, "Thank God you're getting him out of here. That's the most fun and entertaining he's been all night. If I had to listen to any more of his bitching and moaning about Eugene, my ears would have thrown up."

Just then Richard saw them from the dance floor and started

approaching. Sindee waved back at Richard, then ribbed Alicia with an elbow and said, "Details, I want details."

She walked away toward Dale and then helped him toward the door. He tried to mutter something to her, but all he did was spray her with the alcohol fumes on his breath.

"You're drunk," Sindee said.

He rested an arm on her shoulder, leaned into her, and let himself be guided by her.

"You bet your ass I am," he said. "How can you take me away from all this?" His words were slurred. Then Dale laughed as they walked out the door.

Alicia watched them leave and she didn't envy Sindee at all.

Richard was out of breath from dancing and suggested that he and Alicia sit down. They sat facing one another in the now empty booth.

"I saw Sindee and Dale leave," Richard said. "Dale was sort of drunk."

"Dale was lots of drunk," Alicia replied. "But I'm not, and I am ready for another."

Richard waved the waitress over and ordered drinks.

He started talking about the play and the rehearsal, but Alicia wasn't really listening. She was planning on how she was going to seduce him. And even if she didn't, she would come up with some erotic story to tell Sindee that she did.

After all, Alicia specialized in erotic stories. Either way, her sex life was about to improve. It was a win-win situation.

Alicia glanced at the clock behind the bar.

Ten fifteen.

The night was still young. There was plenty of time to get this man into her bed.

Alicia smiled and nodded in agreement with everything

Richard said and made a slow deliberate study of his mouth. It was perfect. Gorgeous. The lips were full and a little pouty . . .

Karson was busy writing when Addison opened the door to their apartment.

It was late.

Every night he was coming in later and later after the rehearsals. That was not unusual as the opening of a show approached. Each show came with its own set of problems that had to be worked out.

Karson listened as Addison sat down in his favorite chair and said he had to get up early and reset a spotlight and fix a set wall that had toppled over. He was looking forward to doing the work He was enthused about the show.

It seemed to Karson that he had forgotten all about the theft of the money. She knew he hadn't forgotten really, but he was content to put it aside for now and let others worry about it.

He had a show to direct and it filled him. He took out his pipe, smoked it for a while and came up with some ideas for staging.

Karson heard him but her mind was elsewhere.

The money.

Addison got up from his chair and started for the bedroom. Karson said she'd be right behind him.

When Karson was sure Addison was asleep she took the lock box from the back of the closet and counted the money inside. Soon she would tell him why she had done what she had done.

She put the box back on the closet shelf and turned out the light. She decided to make a phone call before going into the bedroom and joining her sleeping husband.

But Addison wasn't asleep. He was watching, and he had see everything.

Sindee drove along, singing with the original cast recording of *Hairspray* that was playing in the car's CD player.

She looked over at Dale's sleeping body in the passenger seat. He wasn't much company.

She was about to replay the song that had finished, when her cell phone rang. She didn't like talking on her phone and driving at the same time, but she decided she should take this call.

"Hello," she said. "Yes, everything is going smoothly. Addison doesn't suspect a thing. And I've got Dale just where I want him. Trust me, it's going to be just fine."

The caller seemed satisfied and said goodbye.

Sindee looked at Dale's passed-out body again and smiled. She wondered if it would take the "Jaws of Life" to get him out of the car.

She started singing again with the CD and drove on.

Rachel opened the door to the apartment as quietly as she could, then closed it softly behind her. She carefully inched her way into the darkened living room.

The only illumination in the room was the muted light coming off the television set. The sound of the TV Guide cable channel filled the room. The program guide was doing a slow steady crawl up the television screen.

Her father was asleep on the couch. He had been working a lot of overtime lately.

He was a tour supervisor at Garwood Paperboard on North Avenue in Garwood, New Jersey.

The company was a paper recycling mill, in operation twenty-four hours a day, seven days a week.

They purchased used paper from the Garwood and Scotch Plains Departments of Public Works and processed the paper into rolls of paperboard.

From there it was used for the cardboard rolls in paper towels and toilet tissue, and for dividers in liquor boxes and shoe boxes.

Her father had worked there for fifteen years, operating the big machines that made vats of paper, fixing the machines when they broke down, and then rolling the processed paper into logs to be sold locally and internationally.

It was hard work, and most nights he came home and fell asleep on the couch in front of the television after dinner and a couple beers and catching up on all the sports news about the Knicks and Tiger Woods.

Rachel knew exactly what had happened.

Her father had watched the game and the news, then put on the TV Guide Channel to see what was on. It had lulled him to sleep instead.

Rachel tiptoed into the kitchen. She found a place setting there with a note on it that read, "Dad's Famous Chili in microwave. Eat something."

Rachel smiled. He still treated her like a little girl. He thought she was far too skinny.

She hadn't had a chance to eat anything before the rehearsal and she had to admit she was hungry.

She tapped heating instructions onto the microwave door and went to the refrigerator to get a soda.

"That you, Ray-Ray?"

"Yes, Daddy. Sorry I woke you up."

"I wasn't asleep. I was just watching television."

"It was more like the television was watching you. Why didn't you just go to bed? You didn't have to wait up for me."

Jon Brougham shambled sleepily into the kitchen and kissed his daughter's forehead.

"Can't a father wait up for his daughter, the actress? How was rehearsal? Do you want me to help you with your lines again?" He didn't bother trying to stifle a yawn. He looked like he could barely keep his eyes open.

"No, Daddy. Go to bed. I'm going to go to sleep myself after I eat."

He was too tired to press the issue.

"Okay," he said, through another yawn.

Rachel watched as he slowly walked to his room and closed the door.

She took her chili out of the microwave and sat at the kitchen table.

She looked around their small apartment with the threadbare furniture and the ratty carpet and wondered what it was like to be rich and live in a mansion.

The two women who had given her the ride home were rich.

She wasn't sure if the handcrafted customized car she was in was a Lexus or a Benz. But she knew it wasn't a dented twelve-year-old Saturn like her father drove.

So. Her uncle worked for them.

She hadn't wanted to ask about him. She didn't want to seem too curious. He had disowned her parents years ago, like they weren't good enough for him.

After Rachel's mother died, it was just her and her Dad.

He never remarried, and it had been a struggle for him to raise a daughter alone. He had been on the wrong side of the law twice in his life, and Rachel ended up living with her aunt for a short time when she was very young. But that was years ago. He'd never been in trouble again.

Until recently.

Rachel knew he did the best he could and she loved him. So much that she had stolen $25,000 from the theater's account for him. She was sorry, but she would do it all over again if she had to.

Rachel wasn't ready to tell anyone about that yet. Least of all the man who had turned his back on her family.

Rachel looked at the bowl of chili and decided she wasn't hungry after all.

It was late, the rehearsal had gone from bad to abominable, and she had had to ask for help from someone she never wanted to meet.

She wanted this day to be over.

Rachel turned off the television set, turned off the kitchen light, and walked down the dark hallway to her room.

The door to her bedroom was open. Just a crack but it made her pause. She always left it closed. It was possible, of course, that her father had been in there earlier looking for something, but he never went in her bedroom. He respected her privacy.

It was also possible that she hadn't closed it fully before she left for rehearsal.

Not very likely.

Her father had been sound asleep on the couch. It would have been very easy for a prowler to get in.

Her mind was racing now.

She couldn't remember if she had used her key to open the apartment door or not.

Had it been unlocked?

She could scream for her father now, but decided not to. If someone had broken in, they had not hurt her or her father, perhaps a scream would startle the prowler and lead to violence.

Then Rachel had another thought. She hated herself for it, but the thought came anyway. What if this had something to do with her father? What kind of trouble was he in this time?

She decided to handle this without him.

Rachel put her hand on the door and pushed it slightly. She

heard the faintest movement on the other side. Then she heard her bedroom window being pushed up. She threw open the door, and flipped up the wall light switch just in time to see a figure go out her bedroom widow.

Her eyes made a quick study of the room. Not much was out of place.

Her dresser drawers were open, but they hadn't been pulled out and dumped on the floor.

Some papers had been rearranged on her nightstand, and the covers on her bed were disheveled.

There had definitely been an intruder and he had searched her room.

Rachel kept still just long enough to calm herself down. Then, very cautiously, she looked under her bed, then checked her closet. When she was sure no one else was there, she looked toward the open window.

The curtains fluttered soundlessly in the breeze.

David Castrato stood before the full-length mirror in his home, wearing a Velcroed tuxedo and top hat. He was in full stage makeup. He inspected his face closely with a very critical eye. He had applied the makeup a little too heavily tonight. It looked garish, he thought. More like something from a Fellini movie than a musical.

The track lighting in the room had been rearranged to shine down directly on him. He did his best to recreate stage lighting and to use the right amount of makeup that could be seen even from the balcony of the theater, but up close he had to admit it did look a little frightening.

He was smiling, of course, and basking in the imaginary applause of thousands of his loyal, loving imaginary fans who had been eagerly awaiting his curtain call.

He toasted his reflection in the mirror with a glass of champagne and drank it down. He poured himself another. He deserved another after that brilliant performance.

There was a clicking sound in the dark background of his apartment. The cassette recording he had secretly made of an earlier *Sorry I Missed Your Birthday* run-through, came to a stop in the tape player. It was the third time he had played it since he left the rehearsal that night.

David knew all the songs and dance routines by heart. He knew the complete dialogue for each of the male leads. He knew the whole show backwards and forwards.

This is what David did to relax.

Every night he would sneak a costume out of the theater under his coat, put it on at home and perform the whole show in his living room.

He really needed it tonight after the fiasco at the theater. Everyone had stared at him, silently accusing him of being responsible for everything that had gone wrong.

No one said anything directly to him about it, but he knew what they had been thinking. He was in charge of the props, after all. He shuddered at the memory of it. He couldn't bear it. He loved this show.

David wanted to be in this show so bad he could taste it.

Theater was enchantment to him. It was his life. It was a living breathing thing. A thing to be worshipped. A god.

The rehearsal had gotten so unseemly and hostile earlier. How could those ingrates have let that happen? It was disgraceful.

Normally David was a happy, easygoing man, but he could become very angry. Nothing made him angrier than disrespect inside the hallowed walls of a theater. He got very angry about that.

Eugene and Randall were so lucky to have been cast in the show and they didn't appreciate it. They weren't worthy of the gift they had been given.

David watched every rehearsal from the wings, enraptured. He wanted to feel that lurch in his stomach that every actor feels. That sensation that's somewhere between joy and nausea, in anticipation of walking onto the stage. That exquisite fear.

David spent every rehearsal wishing he could be on that stage, and every night, he performed it at home as if he were.

He memorized all the blocking, all the songs, all the dialogue just in case one of the actors dropped out. Or worse; something unfortunate happened to them.

He dreamed of hearing that line said to him that was said in *42nd Street:* "You're going out there a youngster, but you've got to come back a star."

David sighed, and did one more bow before his mirror. He drank some more champagne.

It was late, a little after one thirty in the morning, but David didn't want to go to bed. He was too jazzed.

He decided to go for a ride. Maybe he could find some hot guy to spend the rest of the night with. He knew a great pickup spot.

David took the car keys from their hook on the wall and started out the door. He caught a glimpse of himself in the full-length mirror and smiled.

Perhaps he should take off the tuxedo and get out of the makeup, he thought. You never know who you might run into.

At 2 A.M., in the parking lot of a rest stop off the Garden State Parkway, Eugene Scherer was flying high and feeling no pain.

He sat in his car sipping a beer and watching to see who went inside.

Men would watch from their cars to see what was going on and who was going in.

When a man wanted sex, he would flash his car lights twice, then head inside.

Once inside, they would pair off in one of the stalls in the men's room.

Eugene had made the rounds twice before, having sex with four different men, and now he was ready to go again.

Fifteen minutes ago he had popped another Viagra, washed it down with a beer, and now he was up for more sex.

Lights were flashing all around the parking lot, and several hot-looking men were heading inside.

Eugene took a second to touch himself, to be sure. His penis was rock hard.

Eugene rides again, he thought. Let's go in and see what the boys in the bathroom will have.

He squirted some Binaca into his mouth and stepped out of his car.

He opened the door to the men's room. Inside, he could hear the sounds of sex all around him. The acoustics of the place amplified them.

He walked over to the corner stall and opened the door. He saw a familiar face.

Eugene was glad to see him.

Eugene closed and locked the door, then turned to him and pulled him close.

"I didn't see you come in. I'm surprised you're here. I didn't think you'd show up after the fight we had."

Eugene waited for a reply.

There was no response. He said nothing. He started touching Eugene roughly.

Eugene studied every detail, every move of his face. Eugene could tell he was still a little petulant from the fight. Eugene could also tell that he had quite a lot to drink and he was not in the mood for a lot of conversation or foreplay.

Eugene knew what would make him happy. He started kissing him and started moving down his chest, down his tight stomach.

Eugene knelt in front of him and just before he took his cock into his mouth, Eugene said, "I have to admit, that was a very funny comment about my bald spot."

There was a small laugh and he ran his hands through Eugene's hair, then guided Eugene's head back and forth.

Later, when Eugene was fully dressed, he looked for him, but he was gone.

Eugene waited for a while to see if anyone else was coming in. No one did. Eugene looked in the mirror and splashed some water on his face. Not a bad night, all in all. He took his cell phone out of his pocket and dialed a friend, then he stumbled outside to wait for his ride home.

Dale woke up screaming into his pillow. Actually, he was glad to be awake. It had been a fitful sleep.

He sat straight up in bed breathing rapidly with his heart pounding like it was going to punch its way out of his chest.

At first he didn't remember where he was. He didn't recognize the room. Where was he? Florida? No, New Jersey. That's right.

He watched his digital clock radio roll over to 7 A.M.

He tried to clear his head.

He had the same recurring nightmare again last night.

Mickey Mouse was chasing him. And it wasn't Mickey in color. It was black-and-white Mickey; the stark colorless Mickey, wearing the bloated oversized gloves.

Mickey Mouse was chasing Dale in his little boxcar with the herky jerky movements and the tinny music.

He chased Dale up one side of a black pointy cartoon mountain, and then down the other side, over and over. It was an endless pointy mountain range in a black-and-white cartoon nightmare.

For the longest time Dale managed to keep ahead of Mickey, always dancing just ahead of him, out of his reach. Then Dale couldn't dance anymore. His legs gave out on him and he stumbled and fell.

Dale looked back, and just before Mickey overtook him, Dale heard him singing, *"Gotcha, Gotcha, Oh Boy, We Really Gotcha."*

Dale forced himself to calm down. His head was throbbing. He messaged his temples with his fingertips and tried to figure out what happened last night.

Incongruous fragments of memories were crashing and tumbling around in his head. He remembered bits of the rehearsal. The cake. The fallen spotlight. The choreography.

Oh Christ, let's skip that shit, he thought.

Next subject.

He remembered going out drinking with Sindee and Alicia. And something about Eugene.

Dale couldn't remember driving home. He didn't know how long he'd been in his bed. Pieces of his memory were missing. His mind was a confusion of images.

Dale carefully swung his legs out from under the covers, gingerly found his balance, and started walking slowly toward the bathroom.

He didn't want to risk making his headache worse by making any sudden movements. Evil demons with mallets were already banging on the inside of his skull in protest to his slightest action.

Normally when Dale got out of bed in the morning, the first thing he would do was put his foot on the dresser, lean his body over it, and do stretches. He would do twenty-five stretches and then change feet. The stretches were followed by sit-ups and push-ups. He did this every day because long ago he had promised himself that he would still be in shape to dance *The Nutcracker Suite* when he was eighty.

The exercise regimen was so not going to happen today.

As if in punishment for missing his daily routine, as he walked, a cramp shot through his right leg. In pain he hobbled to the bathroom.

On the way he passed his telephone answering machine. It was flashing, loaded with messages for him. To his bloodshot eyes, it seemed to flash with the intensity of a searchlight.

Please make it stop!

He pushed "Play" just to make the light stop flashing; he already knew what the messages were about. He played a few seconds of each one.

Just as he thought, they were all about money he owed to people in Florida. All wanting to know when they were going to get paid.

Dale couldn't think about that just now. He had tapped everyone he could for money, sent back all the money he could get his hands on, every cent he could beg, borrow, or steal. He would think about that later.

All he could think of right now was that this hangover was bearing down on him with the force of a runaway train.

He was about to shut off the answering machine when one last message played.

"I know what you did. I saw you."

Dale was momentarily startled. He rewound the tape, turned up the volume, and replayed the message.

"I KNOW WHAT YOU DID. I SAW YOU."

Dale couldn't tell if the voice belonged to a male or female. It was a hoarse whisper, menacing and cryptic.

Oh great, he thought. He had survived a cartoon nightmare only to wake up in the middle of a teenage slasher movie.

Just a crank call. He turned off the machine.

He limped into the bathroom and ran some water into the tub and massaged the cramp away. Then he ran some water into the glass he kept there on the sink. He opened the medicine bureau and reached for a little blue packet, tore one open and heard the comforting plop plop fizz fizz.

Speedy Alka-Seltzer. Now there was an animated character who would always be his friend.

Dale wanted to laugh, started to laugh, but stopped. It hurt too much.

Blair stood looking out her window waiting for the sunrise. She hadn't slept all night. She needed to see the sun come up. Morning couldn't come fast enough. She wanted distance from the night before, a confirmation that it was over.

She looked at the horizon. Just a few more minutes to go. The new day was in that lull between the last dregs of the night and the start of day. Blair wanted the promise of a new day, a chance to begin again. She needed it

The rehearsal had left her shaken and confused. She was the stage manager. She was supposed to be in control. Everything had gone wrong. She must have looked like a fool to everyone. It had been a major fuck-up of Biblical proportions.

Then there was the fight with Randall in the parking lot; the hurtful things he had said to her. He was so angry when he drove away. Her self-esteem gone, she followed him. She couldn't lose him.

She couldn't lose him on the worst night of her life.

Blair picked up his shirt and held it to her face. She closed her eyes and inhaled deeply. She wanted to fill herself with his scent. It helped her get through the night while he slept.

The sun was coming up now and it was all behind her.

She looked toward her bedroom door. Randall would be awake soon and she wanted to start the day right.

Blair picked up his script and started comparing it to her stage manager's script. She wanted Randall's to be perfect. She wanted to make sure he was up-to-date on all the script changes Karson had made.

She frowned when she found a page missing. She sighed. Her purpose for living was reaffirmed.

Blair took the page from her own script and ran it through the copy mode of her fax machine, punched three holes in it, and put it in Randall's binder. Randall would be pleased that she had done this, he would realize how much he depended on her. She was so attuned to his needs. Where would he ever again find a partner so willing to give their life to him so completely? It was so very clear to Blair. She would see to it that it was clear to Randall, too.

The sun started to rise above the treetops. It was like seeing the light at the end of a tunnel.

Blair felt good again.

It was a new day with new beginnings.

Randall adjusted his pillow one more time, punched it and laid his head down and waited to fall asleep. It was useless. He had been trying to sleep all night unsuccessfully. He had tossed and turned so much, the sheets were coming undone from the bed. He finally gave up. He wasn't sure he'd ever be able to fall asleep again. Every time he closed his eyes, and got to the brink of sleep, his mind conjured up frightening images.

So now Randall stared straight up at the ceiling with unseeing eyes. His body was rigid; his breathing shallow. His mind was numb. He wasn't really consciously aware of anything around him at the moment. But the memory was beginning to filter through to him like headlights through a fog. His world started spinning again. He fought back the wave of nausea that was threatening his body. After a few minutes it subsided.

He looked outside the window. It was getting light out. He wondered what would happen next.

It was amazing to him just how much things stayed the same. The normalcy was surprising. Maybe it hadn't happened. Maybe he had dreamt the whole thing because he didn't feel at all different.

Yes, denial was an option. He had already barricaded himself behind a wall of it.

He listened to the sounds around him. He heard all the same noises, all the normal early morning sounds he always heard. Yet nothing seemed familiar. And there was something else, too. Something whispering at him through his wall.

Panic? Randall was miles beyond panic.

He refused to listen. He would not give in.

Life goes on. No matter what. Life goes on.

The police were at the rest stop, combing it for clues. Now it was a crime scene. The entire place was marked off with police tape. It would stay that way until the next evidence collection team finished its examination of the area.

The body found there had been positively identified. And even though it was obvious to everyone present that the victim was dead, it wouldn't be official until the evidence technicians and the coroner went about their routines.

The body was tagged, zip locked into a black body bag, placed on a stretcher, and taken away

So far, with the evidence gathered at the scene the cops were certain that the cause of Eugene, a.k.a. "Rock," Scherer's death was vehicular homicide. The multiple fractures of the skull and ribs, the bodily injuries, were all consistent with a hit and run. His stomach contents indicated the hit and run had occurred between 3 and 4 A.M.

Hours later, vehicular homicide would be the official cause of death given by the coroner.

12

Slick was awakened by the sound of her private phone ringing. Still sleepy, she reached over to the night table and picked it up.

"Hello? Hey, Sam! Thanks for getting back to me so soon. What did you find out from the background checks?" She yawned and stretched.

What she heard next startled her into sudden attentiveness. She looked around the room.

Laura was not in bed and she was nowhere in sight.

"Okay. Thanks, Sam. I'll be right there." She pressed "End." Then she made another call.

"Hi. It's me. I know you haven't had much time, but did you find out anything?" She listened intently.

"You did *what*? I didn't mean for you to . . . okay, okay . . . let's not get into that right now . . . just tell me what you know."

She hung up and made one last phone call.

Then Slick went into the bathroom, showered and dressed quickly, and went downstairs to the library. Just as she had expected, Laura was there with Judson.

Laura had gotten up early and wanted to share news with him about Rachel. She was online, showing him pictures of Rachel and the theater, and sharing her perceptions of his niece with him.

Judson had never seen a photograph of Rachel before. Laura had wanted to show him how pretty she was and tell him how nice the Taylors were. Laura wanted Judson to know that his niece was in a good place with caring people. She carefully left out the parts about the huge fight that had broken out at the rehearsal and the fact that the Taylors were still on Slick's list of possible suspects for the theft. Laura wanted Judson to have a little peace of mind about the niece into whose life he hadn't been granted admission.

"Laura, may I speak with you, please?"

Both Laura and Judson turned to see Slick standing there at the door to the library. She was dressed and wearing her coat.

Judson began to rise and leave to give them privacy.

"No, Judson, you stay here. Keep searching through the theater Web site. There are more pictures of Rachel from all the shows she's done there."

Laura rose and walked over to Slick.

Judson couldn't take his eyes from the screen. He was amazed at how much Rachel resembled his sister Alma. The similarities between them jumped out at him from every picture. Photograph after photograph, it was as if he were seeing Alma again as a young girl.

Slick told Laura what she had just learned from Sam about Eugene Scherer.

"*Murdered?*" Laura asked, startled. She was aghast and afraid she had reacted too loudly. She hastily turned back to Judson to see if he had overheard her.

He hadn't. He was too engrossed by the pictures of Rachel.

Turning back to Slick she said, "That's terrible about Mr. Scherer. I hope he didn't suffer."

"No one seems to think so. It was all over rather quickly."

"What am I going to say to Judson?" asked Laura plaintively. "All morning I've been telling him about the theater and showing him pictures online. First there's a theft and now someone involved there is murdered."

"It could be a coincidence. I'm going to go down to the station now to see what I can find out there, then go to the scene and take a look around. Maybe Eugene was murdered by someone from the theater and maybe not."

"What can I do?" Laura asked.

"Well, I've already spoken to the Taylors. They said they got word of Eugene's death earlier this morning. Addison said he's going to have everyone meet at the theater early today to discuss what to do about the show. Why don't you meet me at the theater at two this afternoon?"

Laura nodded and turned to look at Judson.

Slick kissed her on the cheek and started walking down the hallway to the door. As she walked she called out, "Come on, Garbo. Let's go."

The dog came scampering after her and followed her out the door.

Laura watched as the door closed behind Slick. She would meet Slick at the theater as they had planned, but Laura had a few things she wanted to take care of first. She had a little sleuthing of her own to do.

13

In order to get to the Homicide division, you first had to pass through the lobby of the jail. Even though Slick hadn't been here in a while, it remained unchanged. It was never going to change.

It was always in a state of unceasing, mind-numbing chaos, peopled by hookers looking bored and cheap in skintight spandex and stiletto heels, gangbangers in their gang colors, fresh from their latest drive-by, pimps, crooks, rapists, murderers, child molesters, arsonists, and drug dealers.

With them all were their frustrated, bewildered, and usually innocent family members or friends, who were always unwillingly dragged into the messy fray the accused was facing.

There were mothers, fathers, brothers, sisters, cousins, ex-wives, girlfriends, lovers, even children, all of them confused and all of them clamoring for information and answers, and none of them were ever satisfied with the answers they got from the police officers, lawyers, parole officers, and bail bondsmen who were also ever-present.

So, of course, the mothers, fathers, brothers, sisters, cousins, ex-wives, girlfriends, lovers, and children were angry, bitter, and ill-tempered, and mostly foulmouthed.

Shouting matches broke out regularly, but it was the constant thrum of all the yapping and yammering at a monotonous pitch that was maddening.

Nothing could dispel the sullen grimness that clung to every inch, to every corner, of the place. It clung to the walls and the ceiling, right down to the uncomfortable ugly old benches.

Placed throughout the lobby were floor-standing ashtrays, which no one bothered to use anymore, filled with filthy sand and the butts of long-dead cigarettes. The ashtrays were so nasty looking, the smokers preferred to let their ashes drop to the grimy floor.

And to top it all off, in the background was the endless sound of the jail cell doors clanking shut on the suspects. That sound brought everyone who heard it to the harsh reality that, guilty or innocent, they had just been swept up into the system.

Slick walked into and through this bedlam and approached the desk sergeant on duty.

"Hello, Sergeant Ames."

Sergeant Ames barely acknowledged her. He wanted as little interaction with these people as possible. Every day he tried hard to stay within the limited sanctuary the boundaries of his desk provided him. He wanted to keep his head down and avoid being hit by the shit storm swirling around him. He chose to hide his anger and his grief for them. He couldn't let his compassion show because they would take advantage.

He didn't want to hear their personal problems anymore. He didn't want to know their pain anymore. He decided just to process their paperwork, and let that be the end of it. It was getting harder and harder to maintain his humanity. He was losing ground. He had been steadily sliding downhill for as long as he could remember. A deep dark desolation was pulling him down, consuming him, swallowing him alive.

Stanley Ames had joined the force for all the right reasons. He felt he had something positive to offer his community. He wanted to protect and serve. He was tough, but he had a heart.

He was a good man and he had been able to see the goodness in every other man.

That all seemed like "once upon a time" now. His noble dream had taken a severe beating.

Little by little, time had had a corrosive effect on his once untainted robust heart.

Sergeant Ames had given up years ago trying to bring any kind of structure or organization to this seething quagmire. He just wanted to complete his tour of duty with the few crumbs of sanity he had left to him, go home, and crawl into the most recent bottle he had moved into and hide there, drunk and unfeeling until the comfortable numbness wore off and he had to report back to this hellhole again. He was convinced that if he just drank enough, one night he'd get lucky and manage to die.

"Just sign in and have a seat," he grunted without looking up. He had mastered the fine art of avoiding looking directly at them, of staying disengaged.

"I need a Visitor's pass and I need it now. My taxes pay your salary, you useless SOB. Why don't you get a real job?"

The overworked sergeant shot to his feet, ready for confrontation. Why couldn't this idiot just leave him the fuck alone. Now he'd have to deal with one of them. This was not going to be a good day.

"You'd better step down, you piece of . . . Slick! Hey, how you doin'? It's good to see you."

They shook hands.

"That was good, Detective. You got me good that time."

Even though Slick had left the job years ago, the Sergeant still called her "Detective" out of respect.

He smiled unconvincingly, without the faintest bit of humor, and opened his arms.

"Welcome back to the chamber of living horrors."

Slick stepped back and took in the whole spectacle of the place.

All around people were crying and arguing and cursing. Some people just sat and stared straight ahead, hopeless, without any expression at all. She realized at this moment how glad she was that she didn't spend every day here.

"It ain't exactly *Mr. Rogers' Neighborhood*, is it?" asked the Sergeant, sensing her thoughts.

"No it isn't," Slick agreed.

Then Sergeant Ames leaned forward.

"Say, you didn't by any chance bring my little buddy with you, did you?" he asked hopefully.

"I sure did," Slick answered.

She reached down and put Garbo on the Sergeant's desk.

Garbo danced and jumped around excitedly, butt wiggling and tail wagging, her nails tapping rapidly on the wooden desk. She slipped and tumbled and begged to be picked up. She stood up on her hind legs and started licking the Sergeant's face, giving it a good washing.

He scooped her up, then buried his face in the little dog's fur. She nuzzled him with her cold wet nose, tickling him.

Then Sergeant Ames laughed like he hadn't laughed in a long time. He laughed like he had needed to laugh for a long time. He laughed like maybe he could make it through one more day.

Then he sat Garbo down on the desk and began stroking her ears. The dog stopped squirming and wilted with love.

"I've got to go upstairs for a while," Slick said. "Can I leave her here with you?"

"Sure thing, Detective. She'll be just fine. If anybody says anything, I'll say she's with the K-9 Unit. Here's your pass. I'm sure you remember the way."

He tossed the pass across the desk to Slick, then went back

to cuddling the dog and letting her cover his face with wet kisses.

"Thank you, Sergeant."

Slick clipped on her laminated visitor's pass and started to walk up the three flights of stairs to Homicide.

She looked back at Sergeant Ames and felt a tremendous tidal wave of guilt. She hadn't stayed in touch with him like she had intended to after she left the force. She told herself that it was hard to stay in touch with everyone, but she knew that was just an excuse she used to assuage her conscience.

She wondered how Sergeant Ames was doing now.

Eight years ago Stanley Ames had been an excellent patrol officer with a promising career in front of him. In his rookie year, he had stopped more fights, spotted more stolen cars, and turned around more kids than anyone else on the force.

One night he and his partner responded to a domestic violence call. The police dispatcher told them that the neighbors had heard gunshots.

When they got to the scene, Stanley's partner went around to the back of the house to secure the area.

Stanley, gun drawn, went inside.

What he found inside was a gruesome nightmare.

Three small children and an adult female had been shot at close range.

Stanley heard a noise, a muffled whimpering coming from a corner of the living room. When he went to investigate, he found a little Yorkie puppy, not more than a few weeks old.

Not thinking, or perhaps just thankful to find something unharmed in this carnage, he holstered his gun to get the dog. At least he could save one life.

He heard a gun being cocked behind him, then fired. He felt something cut through and explode within him. He felt his insides get molten like someone had ignited a furnace within him, and then the whole world suddenly seemed to have been bleached white.

Officer Ames knew he had been shot. Drifting in and out of consciousness, he heard another gun go off. This, he learned later, was his partner taking out the man who shot him.

Stanley's partner called for backup.

Sam and Slick were the first on the scene.

Before the ambulance carried Stanley away, Slick promised she would look after the dog. She had a spontaneous case of puppy love.

Slick kept her promise to him.

After two years of therapy and rehab, Stanley Ames came back to the force. He was given a desk job, and that's where he'd been ever since.

Slick hoped he was doing well and vowed she'd reach out to him soon.

She began to climb up the stairway.

As she was about to take her first step, there came a thundering noise from the front of the jail lobby which resonated through the halls. A vibration came with the sound and it shook the whole building with the same intensity as a tyrannosaurus rex tramping through Jurassic Park.

The place was suddenly filled with screams of terror and people trying to run, trying to find cover in the overcrowded lobby.

Before Slick could get her bearings, and without warning, she felt two muscular arms surround her waist. Next she was being lifted up like a rag doll, as if her weight were of no consequence. Higher and higher she went until her head almost touched the ceiling.

"Detective Cassandra Slick! Girlfriend, where have you been?"

Slick looked down at the mountain of a man who held her captive in a great bear hug near the heavens and gave him a wan smile.

"Put me down, Lady. You're squeezing the air out of me."

"Wait, me too! Me too!"

Slick was then passed to his equally large twin.

"Really, Sheleeta, I think I'm starting to get a nosebleed up here"

"Oh, sorry, sugar," he apologized, then gently set Slick back down on terra firma. "We were just so excited to see you. We had to rush over and give you a big ol' hug."

He stepped back, put his hands on his hips, and looked at Slick appraisingly.

"My, my, don't you look fabulous. Just *fabulous,* sweetie! How long has it been?"

Before Slick could answer, two uniformed officers came running up to Slick to make sure she was uninjured. They apologized profusely to her for letting their prisoners get away from them.

When Slick assured them she was all right and wanted to talk to the prisoners, the officers left and set about reassuring the cowering masses in the lobby that everything was under control.

Slick took a moment to check herself for broken ribs. All were intact.

Then she looked up affectionately at the twin six-foot-seven, 350-pound, black transvestites standing in front of her who went by the street names of "Lady Dijonnaise and Sheleeta Buffet." It was always a little strange standing between them. It was like talking to both images in a mirror.

Lady Dijonnaise and Sheleeta Buffet had started life as Cleavis and Cleotis Stubbs.

According to urban legend, Cleavis and Cleotis had once been pro wrestlers turned bodyguards turned cross-dressing hookers.

Sam and Slick had arrested them regularly back when they were patrol officers.

Between them Cleavis and Cleotis had twenty-seven arrests, no convictions.

Sam and Slick had tried to get the twins off the street, but eventually gave up. Some people seemed to thrive there. The streets were dark and dangerous, but the streets had an undeniable current of energy that some found addictive. Cleavis and Cleotis belonged in this category. They could have left the life if they wanted to. They didn't want to. And as big as they were, no one messed with them.

People on the street naturally assumed they could take care of themselves, they were built like linebackers, after all. They had never once been ripped off by a john or beat up by a pimp. They had quite a devoted clientele that kept them in money, so Cleavis and Cleotis Stubbs were gone. They had disappeared into Lady Dijonnaise and Sheleeta Buffet.

When the Lady first started working on the street and was deciding on a title, she considered using the usual "Ladies" that came to mind like Godiva, Marmalade, or Chablis, but decided they had been used to death. But she did like the idea of naming herself for something edible. So she went with "Dijonnaise", feeling it was a much underappreciated condiment and hoping that one day a song or a story would be written about her.

Following in his older brother's footsteps (older by five minutes), Cleotis continued with the food theme and started calling himself "Sheleeta Buffet."

Today the twins wore matching pink halter tops, black

speedos, and pink "fuck-me pumps"—men's size sixteen—all topped off with blonde wigs.

Slick wondered briefly where they shopped.

Apparently the twins hadn't had a chance to shave yet, because their faces were still stubbly with last night's six o'clock shadow.

When Lady Dijonnaise spoke and tried to sound demure, her best falsetto was in Barry White's register. Sheleeta carried herself with the comportment of Michael Jackson, but without Jackson's raging machismo.

"It's been a long time, Lady D, Sheleeta. I see you're both still up to your old tricks," Slick said.

Lady Dijonnaise tossed her huge blonde head back and laughed loudly.

"Honey, I have missed you. You were one of the few around here who knew how to talk to the Lady. Listen, sugar, you still got some pull here? You need to speak to the powers that be. This place is nasty, you hear me? Look at it! It's depressing! You need to tell the folks in charge that they got to get some serious Christopher Lowell going on up in here. The Lady can't be sitting around in this squalor, on these raggedy old benches with these skanky-ass people."

Some in the crowd started to look around the lobby and at one another as if seeing themselves and their surroundings for the very first time.

Sheleeta joined in saying, "I'm sure you could get a better class of criminals in here if you just put in a nice area rug or two, some throw pillows, a splash of color, you know, a touch of whimsy, a touch of funsy. People need to feel good in their space, even if it is a jail."

Suddenly everyone in the lobby was shouting and applauding in agreement.

Slick looked over at Sergeant Ames who had uncharacteristically looked up from his desk and had witnessed everything. They both shrugged.

The jail lobby wasn't a portal to Hell after all. It just needed a makeover. It was a design challenge that could be fixed with a new paint job, some warm inviting fabrics, and a few well-placed accessories.

Lady Dijonnaise and Sheleeta Buffet bowed and vamped to their appreciative onlookers, said good-bye to Slick, then stepped to the desk and awaited booking.

Slick started up the stairs again.

She ran into some old coworkers who were happy to see her. They shook her hand, or gave her a high five. They made plans to get together.

When she got to the third floor, she opened the door. The air was gray and heavy with cigarette smoke and the pervasive aroma of strong coffee.

Just like old times.

All of a sudden, walking in, Slick missed the weight and the feel of her gun holstered beneath her armpit.

There were plainclothes detectives sitting at their desks with their shirt sleeves rolled up, taking statements, staring at computer monitor screens, or doing paperwork. On the walls there were overflowing bulletin boards filled with photographs and notices.

Slick walked through the division and met more former coworkers.

She thought it might be fun to see who was occupying her former desk. She turned the corner, and to her dismay she found Tom Brandeal sitting at her old desk talking into a phone, feet up, smoking a cigarette.

Slick and Brandeal had competed twice for promotions. Slick got them both. Brandeal eventually made detective, but he still harbored bad feelings toward Slick. He wasn't a bad cop, but Slick had no patience for his open and well-known Mark Fuhrmanesque contempt for blacks and gays.

As soon as he saw her he ended his phone conversation, put out his cigarette, and strolled over to her. Slick could tell he hadn't lost any of his arrogant swagger.

"Well, well, well. Look who's back for a visit. The great Detective Slick. How's the gay life with your rich white girl friend?" He grinned broadly, condescendingly.

"Her name is Laura, and life is just fine, thank you. I'm deeply touched by your concern for me, Brandeal. How thoughtful."

"That's just great. Glad to hear it," Brandeal said, stepping closer, getting in Slick's face. "I'm very happy for you, Slick. It must be real nice for you to finally live someplace that hasn't been targeted for urban renewal. Looks like that affirmative action thing works for you off the job as well."

Slick's internal defenses kicked in. She was about to ask him if he was still into racial profiling and planting evidence, but she let his insults go.

She didn't know just yet who had been assigned to the Scherer murder investigation, and if it was Brandeal, at some point she would have to get some information from this asshole.

"Hey, partner. Come on over and have a seat."

It was Sam, and he was pulling her over to his desk and away from Tom Brandeal.

"Let me fill you in on what's happening on the case," Sam continued, but Slick was still shooting looks back at Brandeal.

"You'll be happy to know that Simpson and Rafferty are assigned to the case."

Slick turned to face Sam.

"Really? Cathy and Paula?" Slick laughed ironically. "I

should have known. A 'queer' is found murdered at a popular 'queer' pickup spot, so they send in the 'queer' cops to solve it. The 'Odd Squad.' That's so typical. They think that's all we're good for. Some things never change, do they?"

Sam took a long look at his former partner.

"No, you're wrong, Slick. Plenty has changed. For example, I can't remember the last time I found "Fag" written on my locker, or heard anyone in here tell a joke about "faggots." When I radio in for backup, I get it right away; no question, no hesitation. And the straight cops don't have a problem with me, Simpson, or Rafferty being called upon to provide the backup for them. No one refers to us as the "queer" cops, or the Odd Squad. Simpson and Rafferty caught the Scherer case for no other reason than it was their turn. You've been away from here for a while, Slick. Attitudes have changed. Progress has been made. Things have improved," Sam said, with sober dignity.

It had all been stated flatly, but it sounded almost like a reprimand. Slick felt Sam's disapproval as powerfully as if her old friend had shouted at her.

She felt like she had been soundly chastised. And rightly so.

"I'm sorry, Sam." Her apology was sincere and from the heart. "Brandeal really got to me, I guess. He brought back memories of the bad old days. I left years ago. You and Paula and Cathy stayed here and fought the good fight. You're all excellent cops. You've shown by example that gays and lesbians are as capable as anyone of doing the job. You have earned the respect of every officer here because you deserve it. I didn't mean to trivialize what you've accomplished."

Sam noted the contrite tone of Slick's voice.

"Yes, there is all that, of course. We are good cops, and I like to think that we have had a positive impact on perceptions about gays and lesbians," he said, stiff-faced. "And it doesn't hurt that the Captain's son came out to him about three years ago."

Then Sam smiled and winked at Slick. She knew she had been played.

They both laughed heartily.

Getting serious, Slick pointed her thumb over her shoulder and said, "I see Brandeal hasn't changed at all."

"I said things had improved, Slick. I didn't say things were perfect. Cops like Brandeal will be around for a long time. But even he has dialed his attitude back a bit. He still has the same prejudices he always had, but at least he keeps them in check now, because of the Captain's son and all."

"Where's Joe?" Slick asked. She was referring to Joe Markowitz, Sam's new partner. He had replaced Slick when she left. Markowitz was a very good cop, and he had become a friend to Sam. Sam considered himself fortunate to have been teamed with another polished and competent partner.

"He had to be in court today. I'm in here catching up on some paperwork. The department started a 'reduction in paperwork' program which of course meant even more forms than before and more complicated ones, too. I'm now up to my hips in paperwork. It's a little like simplifying the tax code."

Slick smiled and nodded. She understood completely. Bureaucracy.

"Where are Cathy and Paula?" she asked "I'd like to talk with them."

"They're in Interrogation Room One."

"They have a suspect already? Great!"

Sam shook his head and said, "I don't think she's a suspect. She's just here for questioning right now. But she was on the list of names you asked me to run background checks on. Here's the information you wanted on the owners and the cast and crew at that theater."

Sam slid a large mustard-colored envelope across the desk to Slick.

Slick opened the envelope and made a quick look at its contents. Her eyes widened. There with the usual background information on the cast and crew was their personal financial data, too.

Slick closed the envelope and looked at Sam.

"You didn't have time to get the court orders necessary to access these bank statements. How did you get them?" Slick was talking very softly. She didn't want anyone, especially Brandeal, to overhear her conversation with Sam.

Sam's face was inscrutable.

"Let's play a game of 'Don't Ask/Don't Tell,' " he answered. "You don't ask and I won't tell. You said you were looking into a theft and wanted background checks on the folks at this theater. You still have friends here who feel they owe you. They felt the financial records could be helpful to you. Every bank is on the internet. A lot of people do their banking online. The Department has some very talented computer people working for them now. Some of them used to work on the wrong side of the law. Hackers. And that's as far as I'm willing to go to answer your question. Okay?"

"Okay," Slick said.

The subject would never be brought up again.

"Who are Cathy and Paula questioning?" she asked casually.

Sam looked at the notes he had taken for Slick.

"I wrote it down right here. Yeah, here it is . . . her name is Beautee Holsom."

14

"Beautee Holsom!"

Slick was unable to hide her surprise.

"Yes," Sam answered. "She's been in interrogation for a while now. Is there a problem?"

"No, no problem. She's just the last person I expected to see here."

Slick was not about to tell Sam, a fifteen-year veteran of the police force, about seeing little blue birds and the strange timing of the Hallelujah Chorus playing at the theater. Besides, Slick mused, Beautee's winged entourage probably took one look at the tragic souls in the jail lobby, packed up their musical accompaniment, and flew south for the winter.

"I would love to listen in," Slick said.

"Sure. Let's go."

They walked to the interrogation room. An officer stood outside the door, arms folded over his chest to make sure no one brought a weapon inside. Slick submitted to a search. No one wanted the suspects getting hold of a gun and shooting their way out.

The officer nodded to Sam and Sam opened the door for Slick.

"I've got to do some work on my own cases. I'm sure that Cathy and Paula will give you whatever info you need from now on," he said.

"Thanks for everything, Sam. I'll be in touch." Slick patted his arm with the envelope he had given her, and watched him walk away.

She stepped inside the room and closed the door behind her.

Inside, Detective Paula Rafferty stood drinking a cup of coffee, watching her partner through a one-way window.

On the other side of the glass sat Beautee Holsom at a small table.

Detective Cathy Simpson was inside with her, pacing back and forth and shouting questions at her.

Slick took a moment to observe.

"All right, Holsom. One more time from the top. Account for your whereabouts last night," Simpson demanded, practically barking at her. Then she kicked a chair in a menacing way. The scraping noise the chair made as it slid backwards was momentarily startling. Beautee was jolted from her weariness for a few seconds, then it pulled her back in again.

Exhausted, wiped out, lacking the energy to protest, Beautee swallowed quietly, took a deep breath and retold her story. Her hands were together with her fingers steepled in front of her on the table as if she were praying. Slick thought she looked positively evangelical.

"I left the rehearsal at the theater a little after eight. I stopped at my local Red Cross and gave blood. I had a cookie and some juice. From there I went to the Salvation Army to help serve meals and pass out cots and blankets for the needy. I was home in time to watch *It's a Miracle* on the PAX family entertainment network at eleven. I said my evening prayers and went to bed. Between two thirty and two forty, Eugene called me and asked me to pick him up at the rest stop. I drove there and I found him lying dead in the snow."

Beautee looked sad and tired, her eyes red and puffy from crying. She was dabbing them with tissues. She seemed to be preoccupied with her own thoughts. She answered the questions put to her in a detached robotic way, almost unmindful of or at least not reacting to the browbeating Detective Simpson was laying on her.

Slick took this all in then walked over to Paula and shook her hand.

"Hey, Rafferty. What's going on?" Slick asked.

"Hi, Slick." Paula smiled at her, then returned her attention to what was happening on the other side of the glass window.

"We're doing the 'good cop/bad cop' routine. It's my turn to be the 'good cop' today. I've already done my sympathetic ear and confidante bit. Cathy is in there yelling, pounding the table, and generally acting like she's in desperate need of professional help, or at least some serious industrial strength mood swing medication. It looks like something from an episode of *Law & Order: PMS*. Cathy really loves playing 'bad cop.' "

"Who doesn't?" Slick asked softly. Then she sighed heavily.

She felt a surge of homesickness overtake her. She almost became misty looking into the little room with the uncomfortable battered straight-back chairs, the worn hardwood floor, the scarred abused table, the harsh overhead lighting, the heavy don't-even-think-about-escaping razor-edged grill on the window, and the crumbling plaster on the dirty green walls that hadn't seen new paint in over twenty years.

Slick loved everything about the place.

She felt a little like a small child gazing longingly into a toy store window.

She kissed her fingertips then placed her hand lovingly against the glass, remembering some of the scumbags she had broken in this room and sent on their way to conviction, and ultimately to imprisonment, and sometimes, to their execution.

She had heard more sick and twisted confessions in her time here than most priests heard in church.

They were such happy memories. Good times. Sweet justice.

Paula smiled to herself at witnessing Slick's candid lapse into wistful nostalgia. Then she became very professional.

"So far all we've got is this Holsom woman saying that she got a call from Scherer at approximately two forty a.m. She said Scherer told her he was too messed up to drive himself home. We traced Scherer's cell phone records and it checks out. The last call he made was to her. She says she drove her car to the rest stop and discovered his dead body there. She called the police and an ambulance, and waited there with Scherer until help arrived."

"You think there's more to it than that? That she may have been the driver of the hit-and-run car?" Slick asked.

"I doubt it. She seems like such a goody-goody. Cathy's in there doing her best psycho cop impersonation, and she hasn't been able to shake her up one bit. But we can't rule out that she might have done it. Not yet. We also can't rule out that the driver of the hit-and-run vehicle had absolutely no connection to Scherer whatsoever. Lots of drinking and drugging goes on at that stop. Maybe the driver was DUI, hit him by accident, panicked, then drove away. We don't have any other suspects. There were no other cars at the scene when the patrol car arrived and no witnesses that we know of.

"If there were any witnesses, they haven't come forward so far. You know how that goes. If there were witnesses, they may be afraid to get involved. Who wants to admit that they were at a public rest stop engaging in illegal sexual activity? This morning we went to Scherer's home and confiscated his computer to see what his e-mail would turn up. He had his own Web page. His screen name was *1HandsumDVL*. It took our guys about one hour to figure out his password: 'Adonis.'

"His Web page was entitled 'Rock Scherer Presents an

Eclectic Cavalcade Celebrating the Theatrical Genius of Rock Scherer.' It had pictures and trivia of him from plays he had been in, plus info on upcoming productions. The Web page featured a soundtrack of him singing his favorite show tunes. An audio cassette copy of the soundtrack could be purchased for a few bucks, plus shipping and handling, of course.

"We couldn't find anything threatening that had been mailed to him. Actually, he had quite a few love letters from men and women posted there, as well as requests for nude photographs, also from men and women. We didn't find any nude photographs of him or anything to suggest that he responded to those requests. So, for right now, anyway, all we're looking at is Ms. Holsom," Paula said, looking through the glass.

"Well, it's called 'hit-and-run' for a reason. It's not called 'hit, then call the cops and an ambulance, then wait around at the scene, and then cooperate fully with the police.' Maybe you haven't been able to shake her up because she's innocent. I was at that theater last night. For what it's worth, what she's saying in there about giving blood and going to the homeless shelter is exactly what I overheard her say she was going to do after the rehearsal," Slick said.

Slick opened the envelope Sam had given her and leafed through the pages until she got to the information on Beautee Holsom. She started reading what was there.

"Okay," Paula continued. "But she admits to having had deep feelings for him. Romantic feelings. Maybe she saw Scherer doing something with a man at the rest stop that she didn't want to see, she snapped, and killed him. Forensics found evidence of Scherer having been inside her car. But that could have been there for a long time. There doesn't seem to be any damage to her car, but that doesn't prove anything. None of Scherer's DNA was found on the grill or the front of her car. But remember, she stayed at the rest stop all alone with the body. She had time to go into the rest stop, take some towels or tissue from the bathroom, wipe the grill and hood clean, then flush it all. She's a straight, Christian, conservative Republican. Sometimes that's a lethal combination to a gay man. We don't have any other possible motive yet. You know the drill. It's a possibility. Remote, yes, but we still have to check it out.

"Honestly, though, I have to admit, her story's pretty tight. We haven't found anything yet that's inconsistent with what she's told us, and we don't have enough evidence from the scene to charge her with anything now, so we're probably going to let her go soon. Cathy and I have a few informants we can check with. We're going to see if maybe Scherer had a problem with any of the regulars at the rest stop. Sometimes things can get a little rough there."

Paula looked away from the window and faced Slick.

"Sam says you're interested in this case because there was a theft at the theater where the deceased Mr. Scherer and Ms Holsom were starring in a play together."

"That's right," Slick answered, glancing only momentarily at Detective Rafferty. She was drawn to Beautee's background check. It was very interesting.

"Well this theater theft must be pretty important to you to get you away from your nine-to-five desk job at Laura's clam company."

"It's very important to me," Slick responded, remembering the sight of Laura and Judson sitting together looking at photos of Rachel.

"Are you thinking that maybe there's a connection between the theft and the murder?"

"I'm going to nose around the theater and see if I can turn up anything, see if there is a connection. And I want to go to the scene, okay?"

"Fine. Actually we could use the help. Cathy and I have our

plate full right now with other ongoing investigations. So, she's an actress, huh, this Beautee Holsom? She any good?" Paula asked.

"Yes," Slick answered, finally looking up from her reading, and looking past Paula.

She stared intently at Beautee sobbing on the other side of the glass.

"As a matter of fact, she's a damn good actress."

15

Laura eased her car into her designated parking spot and turned off the ignition. She exited the car and walked to the elevator.

As the elevator made its way down to her, Laura could hear the sounds of laughter and spirited conversation coming from within.

When the elevator car came to a complete stop and the doors opened fully and she could be seen by all the passengers in the car, the laughter and conversation suddenly ended.

There was a somber chorus of "Good morning, Miss Charles" as everyone in the elevator skittered past her, looking very professional and businesslike, afraid to let the boss see them sharing a joke or having a good time.

Laura had never gotten used to that.

She entered the elevator and pushed the button for floor number seventeen. The door slid closed, and the elevator whined slightly as it began to rise.

When the doors opened again on the seventeenth floor, she saw the huge glass entryway with the name "The Owen Charles Foundation" written across it in gold.

She stepped out into the carpeted hall, walked through the heavy doors, passed the security guard and the cameras, and walked to the receptionist's desk.

"Good morning, Sara."

"Good morning, Miss Charles." Sara had stood at her desk to greet Laura the instant she walked in.

"Sara, I'm going to be in my office for a little while, going through some files."

"Shall I have some coffee or something sent in for you?"

"No, thank you. I'll buzz you if I need anything."

"Yes, Miss Charles."

As Laura walked to her office, everyone working nearby noticed her.

Phone conversations stopped. Heads turned. Eyes popped, and jaws dropped.

Keyboards that had been clacking along rapidly, froze in midstroke. Meanwhile, Sara telephoned all the appropriate staff members to alert them that Miss Charles was present.

Laura punched in her access code on the lock, opened the door to her office, and stepped inside. She was greeted by a huge oil painting of her father on the far wall. She had to admit to feeling somewhat hypocritical every time she saw it.

In the painting her father was smiling philanthropically. He had never smiled like that in public in his life. Laura wasn't even sure that her mother had ever seen him smile like that.

In photographs he always seemed to be leering or beaming with capitalistic greed.

When Laura commissioned the painting, she had the artist take a few liberties with his face. Old friends of the family who stopped by her office for a visit got a kick out of wondering what Owen would think of the painting. She would explain to them that it was a charitable foundation, and that her father should look the part, not frighten people away who were in need of money.

A little part of it was vanity. Everyone said Laura looked like her father. In the painting she had given him some of her softer features.

Laura's office was always meticulously maintained, in anticipation of her possible arrival at any time.

There were freshly cut flowers and the cherrywood furniture was polished to a glossy shine. The windows, which took up two of the four walls, were spotless and gleaming, offering a fantastic streakless view. The chairs, sofa, and carpet had been recently cleaned.

Laura crossed to her desk and sat down. She powered up her computer and did a search of the files for The Broad Street Players. She scanned all the documents in the computer and didn't find anything unusual about Addison and Karson's grant request.

She buzzed Sara.

"Sara, would you please bring me the file on The Broad Street Players, and all relating files. They're a community theater located in South Orange. The owners are Addison Taylor and Karson Parker Taylor."

"Right away, Miss Charles."

Laura continued to read what was on the monitor. There was the usual information on Addison and Karson; their income and profit from the theater, the grant request, and their detailed account on how the grant money would be used.

After a few minutes Sara buzzed her back.

"Yes, Sara?"

"You have a visitor, Miss Charles." Laura noted that Sara sounded a little stressed.

"Who is it?"

"It's Mr. Addison Taylor, Miss Charles. He says it's very important."

Laura was completely taken aback. The idea that the subject of her little investigation was now standing just outside her door was a bit disconcerting.

She hesitated for a moment, then said into the intercom, "Send him in, and hold all my calls. I'm not available for anyone. I don't want to be disturbed for any reason, Sara. Understood?"

Laura didn't want Addison to see Sara walking in with the files on the theater grant under her arm. That would be uncomfortable for both of them.

"Yes, Miss Charles," Sara answered.

Laura stood up and walked to the front of her desk. The door opened and in walked Addison. He looked distracted. His eyes lacked the warm sparkle she had seen there when he spoke of his theater just a few hours ago.

They looked tired, as if years had passed, as if they had seen too much in that very short time since she last looked into them.

"I'm so very sorry about Eugene," Laura said. "Is there anything I can do?"

Addison looked at her as if she had just reminded him of something.

"Yes, that was terrible. Very tragic. But that's not why I'm here."

"Please sit down, Addison." Laura offered him the chair directly in front of her desk.

He sat down and forced himself to talk.

"I called your home earlier and spoke with a Mr. Judson. After I identified myself, he said you had come here to your office. I hope I'm not imposing too much on your time."

"Not at all." Laura went back to her desk and sat down.

Addison leaned forward and spoke very directly.

"I'm here about the grant money. I think I know who stole it."

Laura saw pain overtake him. She saw how difficult this was for him.

"God forgive me. I think it was Karson. I think Karson took the money."

Laura felt like she had just had the wind knocked out of her.

"Are you sure? What makes you think that?" Laura was full of questions.

"I found some money hidden away in the back of a closet. Thousands of dollars. I didn't have time to count it all."

"Did you ask her about it?"

"No. This horrible thing happened with Eugene. We've been scrambling around all morning trying to figure out if we should go on with the show, contacting backers. I haven't wanted to confront her with it. I feel like it's all my fault. I think she gave up on me. I think she took the money as some sort of security in case the show didn't do well."

Addison felt so small and weak. Laura could sense his despair. He was looking to Laura, a stranger whose money was stolen, for help.

Laura felt nothing but compassion for him.

"Addison, thank you for coming here and telling me your concerns. It may look suspicious that Karson has all that money hidden away, but you really have no proof that it's the grant money. I'll tell Slick what you think, but let's just keep this between us for now. You've got so much to deal with right now, Eugene's death and the show. So many people are looking to you for direction. I promise you we will sort this out."

Addison rose to his feet. He looked a bit stronger.

"Thank you, Laura. See you later at the theater?"

"We'll be there at two."

Laura walked him to the door and watched as he walked past the receptionist's desk, then out the main doors.

Laura, still somewhat stunned from Addison's visit, walked back to her desk and sat down. She barely had time to collect her thoughts when Sara buzzed her again.

"Yes, Sara."

"You have another visitor. It's Miss O'Hare. She wanted to bring the files you requested to you personally."

Laura tilted back in her chair and sighed, she hoped out of hearing range of the intercom.

First Eugene Scherer is found murdered, then Addison suspects Karson of theft, and now she was about to get a visit from Devlyn O'Hare. This was turning out to be a very eventful morning.

Laura sat back and pulled herself together. She had to be in control for this meeting with Devlyn.

Laura had come to the office concentrating so much on looking through the files for information on the theater grant, that she forgot about Devlyn. She should have known Devlyn would certainly come to see her. Devlyn always wanted to know immediately whenever Laura came into the office.

Devlyn O'Hare. The name still made Laura stop and think.

Laura had hired Devlyn years ago. Devlyn was ambitious and talented. She understood the subtle aspects of fund-raising, and she kept her eye on the bottom line. She could instinctively tell the difference between a bona fide request for help for a worthy cause from a con job looking to deceive the foundation.

Laura was immediately impressed with her.

Together they had cochaired several successful charity events and had gotten much-needed funding to several struggling artistic programs and social causes.

They put in many late nights together working on projects. People had begun to talk about them as if they were the perfect power couple.

Devlyn had made Laura seriously consider breaking her personal long-standing rule against office romances. Nothing ever happened between them, but they both felt the attraction.

Laura had felt guilty back then about her flirtation, but Devlyn had been very hard to resist.

Then Laura met Slick, and that permanently closed the door on any possible romantic involvement with Devlyn. Laura lost her heart to Slick almost instantly.

After that Devlyn never had a chance with Laura. Her relationship with Devlyn cooled and became nothing more than professional.

After a while, it became very apparent to Laura that she had made a wise choice by not getting involved with Devlyn. Devlyn could be cold and ruthless with an infinite capacity for small, subtle cruelties. She was the soul of treachery.

Laura had found true love with Slick and had moved on. But Devlyn refused to give up trying to get closer to Laura. Her involvement with Slick hadn't cooled Devlyn's pursuit. For Devlyn it seemed only to heighten the challenge.

Laura wondered sometimes why she kept Devlyn on the payroll when she caused so much trouble. She told herself it was because Devlyn was only a nuisance to her that Laura knew she could handle.

To give the devil her due, Devlyn really was an asset to the foundation. The irony of it all wasn't lost on Laura. How could someone with the personality of a copperhead snake work for a charitable foundation?

Laura prepared herself to see Devlyn again. She inadvertently glanced over at her father's picture as she got herself together. She stopped cold. Owen would have loved Devlyn, she thought. Even more irony. Devlyn was more like her father than she was.

Laura sighed, then spoke into the intercom.

"Send her in, Sara, and buzz me again in five minutes and remind me of my meeting."

"Yes, Miss Charles."

The door opened and in walked Devlyn O'Hare. A more accurate description would be that she burst in. She was five-foot-nine, with dark eyes and dark gleaming chestnut-colored hair falling down past her shoulders. She was still gorgeous. She reminded Laura of Demi Moore at the height of her beauty on a good-hair day. Devlyn also had that smokey, whiskey-soaked voice thing, too.

When Devlyn moved, it was like watching a panther on the prowl. She had a natural feline grace and always appeared to be moving in slow motion, like she was stalking something.

She was wearing a very smart, very professional-looking black business suit, but it didn't matter. Whatever Devlyn was wearing, she looked like she just stepped out of a Victoria's Secret catalogue.

Everything about her was frankly sensual. Fully clothed she held the promise of untamed sexuality; naked, as all her lovers could swear to, she delivered it. And her hair always seemed to be blowing in a breeze. She could be in a remote, windowless, closed-off janitor's closet in the basement, and her hair still moved as if she was carrying her own little wind fan.

"Hello, Laura. So good to see you."

Devlyn walked over to Laura's chair and started to give her a kiss on the lips. Laura moved her head and held out her hand instead.

"Hello, Devlyn," she said politely.

Devlyn gave her an exaggerated look of disappointment at having been refused a kiss.

"Oh now Laura, is that a greeting for an old friend? We go way back."

"I'm preoccupied, Devlyn, and a little pressed for time."

Devlyn took the cue and shook Laura's hand, but she kept her lips very close to Laura's face.

"Who was that gentleman I just saw leaving your office?" she asked casually, still holding on to Laura's hand.

"Just an old friend of the family," Laura lied. She pulled her hand back and changed the subject.

Devlyn backed off, stood up straight, and gave Laura some space.

"You have something for me, Devlyn?"

"Yes. Here's the file you wanted," she said. "I took the liberty of looking through it. Seems pretty routine to me. Addison and Karson Taylor applied for and were approved for a grant of twenty-five thousand dollars for their theater. Is there a problem?"

Devlyn brushed Laura's hand with her fingertips and let them linger there as she handed her the file. Laura ignored it and took the file quickly.

"No problem. I just wanted to check a few things, that's all," Laura said guardedly.

Devlyn looked at her closely. She could always sense when Laura wasn't telling the whole truth.

"Well then, Laura, are you here checking up on me? Are you checking in to see how I'm running things?"

"Not at all. Everyone is pleased with your work. I've gotten nothing but good reports about you, Devlyn."

"Thank you, Laura. I've tried my best to manage things here without you. I think you know I'd do whatever it takes to keep those who work under me happy."

Laura said nothing, but Devlyn knew she had hit a nerve, so she continued.

"I find it very interesting that you haven't been here for ages and now you breeze in asking to see this file. And only this file. I find that very interesting indeed."

"I don't need to be here every day, Devlyn. You're the best

business manager there is. That's why you work for me," Laura said as smoothly as possible.

"I work for the board, too," Devlyn reminded her. "If there's a problem we need to solve it right away. Since you're in a hurry now, maybe we can get together for a drink later. Do some catching up. Strictly business, of course. Are you still drinking Absolut martinis? I know a place where they make them almost as good as Judson does."

Laura felt uncomfortable at this reference to her personal life, but did her best not to show it.

Devlyn sat down in the chair directly in front of Laura's desk. The same chair Addison had occupied only moments ago, Laura noted. Devlyn crossed one fabulously shapely leg over the other.

She made herself very comfortable.

"Excuse me, Devlyn, I need to review this file in preparation for a meeting later today," Laura said politely. She hoped that would be enough to send Devlyn on her way.

"Certainly," Devlyn said, settling in, crossing her arms, not budging from her seat.

Laura's body stiffened. She hadn't expected this would be so difficult. She was relieved when Sara buzzed her again.

Thank you, Sara. You're a lifesaver.

Laura looked at Devlyn and tried her best to maintain a conversational tone in her voice.

"Well, Devlyn, if there's nothing else, I've got to go. Like I said, I have to be at a meeting later. I'll have to look this over on the way."

Laura got up from her chair, picked up the file on The Broad Street Players and walked to the front of her desk.

When she was directly between her desk and Devlyn's chair, Devlyn sprang from her seat and pinned Laura to the front of her desk. Laura was forced to jump up on the desk just to give herself some space from Devlyn.

There was nothing professional about the look in Devlyn's eyes. She moved in as close as she could to Laura and spoke passionately.

"Laura, I miss you. I miss working with you. I think about you all the time. We were good together. You can't tell me you never think of me. There was a time when we could have been so much more. You do remember that, don't you? Let me show you what we could have had together. I want you here. Now. Just lay back and let me take you. Let me taste you."

Devlyn ripped open her suit coat and exposed her naked breasts. She let her suit coat fall to the floor. Then she put her hand on Laura's leg and started moving it up underneath her skirt.

"Ohhh, Devlyn . . ." Laura sighed.

Laura raised her hand and lifted it toward Devlyn's breasts. Without stopping there, Laura took her two fingers and gave Devlyn a Three Stooges-style poke in the eyes.

More stunned than hurt, Devlyn backed away.

"You have got to stop reading those trashy romance novels, Devlyn. I don't do dyke drama. I love Slick, and I will be with her for the rest of my life. So please get used to it."

Laura got off her desk and fixed her clothing.

"Let's just forget this nonsense. Maybe I'm a little to blame for this. But don't ever try that again, Devlyn, understood? If you do, no matter how good you are at your job, I will have you fired. Now get dressed and lock my office when you leave."

With that Laura walked to the door. She looked back at Devlyn. She was finishing buttoning up her jacket. Laura couldn't resist one last parting shot.

"*I want you here. Now,*" Laura said, laughing softly. "Get some new material, Devlyn. You're out of date."

Laura, continuing to laugh, opened the door and stepped out. Devlyn could still hear her laughing in the hall.

Devlyn went behind Laura's desk and sat down. She looked at the computer screen. It hadn't been turned off. She wrote down the address for the theater.

Devlyn was certain something was going on there. Something the board would not like. They were very scrupulous when it came to giving grants. They didn't like even a whiff of impropriety. They wouldn't tolerate any infractions. Not even from the great Laura Charles herself. The best part, Devlyn thought, was that she might be able to bring Laura down and it would all be due to her precious Slick.

Devlyn smiled to herself and leaned back. The chair tilted backwards to accommodate her.

She looked out the bank of windows and enjoyed the view. Devlyn made herself very comfortable in Laura's chair. She would check out this theater and see what was going on there.

She could wait.

Having the last laugh was always worth the wait.

16

Any setting, at any place, at any time has the potential of becoming a crime scene. Even though the instances and variables are too numerous to list, once a crime has been committed the areas where they are committed typically fall into one of four categories.

The first is the planned or organized crime scene.

In this instance the perpetrator has plotted the crime. There is premeditation and the effort to escape capture. The target may be known to the killer, or may be a stranger who has inadvertently wandered into the killer's scenario, but there are specific reasons why the killer has chosen a particular time, place, and setting.

The killer has allowed for time to remove the body, hide the weapons, or in some way scrutinize the area to remove incriminating evidence.

The second is the unplanned or disorganized crime scene.

This is a spontaneous crime. The killer has acted emotionally and hastily in a moment of passion and frenzy.

The scene is sloppy, with clues left everywhere, the biggest clues being the body of the victim, the weapon, and fingerprints.

The third type of crime scene is a combination of the organized and disorganized.

This could indicate that there was more than one perpetrator, or that there was a single killer who was interrupted. Or the single killer arranged the scene, planting objects of deliberate distraction to throw the police off.

The fourth type is the atypical crime scene. It can't be classified or categorized by the facts at hand. Investigators may have to do some searching of crime databases to see if the scene matches other crime scenes.

In the age of computers, all police departments are online. Even the most remote Mayberryesque class, Andy and Barney—run forces, have internet access.

Tapping into the database could give valuable information. For instance, was this unusual crime scene the work of a serial killer? Is the murderer evolving, planning more murders? This kind would be the hardest of all to catch, a freelance criminal, never having served time, never fingerprinted, and never having posed for a mug shot.

It was funny how quickly the regulations came back to her.

Slick summoned up all her years of training and expertise. She did a by-the-book inspection of the area. She walked around the parking lot of the rest stop, carefully and gingerly avoiding the yellow tape.

She cleared her mind and tried to center herself and get in touch with the instincts that had never failed her. Her sixth sense. She knew that most of the obvious evidence had already been gathered, photographed, and labeled.

But crime scene analysis is more than just preserving, documenting, and bagging and tagging. It's about reconstructing the crime. Some evidence always stays at the scene.

You just had to connect the clues.

Slick carefully approached the huge dark splotch on the ground. She knelt down to get a good look. It most certainly was made by Scherer. With all the blood that was lost, Slick was sure the murder happened here.

If Eugene had been murdered somewhere else and the killer dumped his body here, there would not be as much blood.

The rest stop was definitely the primary crime scene. Slick could see in her mind how the rest stop must have looked last night when the police got to the scene; bustling with uniformed blue motion and yards of yellow tape, the crackle of police radios and the cry of sirens.

Even though the scene had been crawling with police and forensic technicians, there would have been very little chatter. There would be somber concentration on the job at hand.

She could visualize how the hit-and-run itself had happened.

Hit-and-runs were bad. The damage done from metal smashing into flesh; the bone crushing, skull cracking, blood splattering mutilation was always the same. It didn't matter if it was the result of icy road conditions, or the adverse effects of alcohol and speed, or if it was intentional. Arms and legs were mangled, rib cages were wrenched out of shape.

Slick was used to it. She had seen it all. She pushed the sickening images from her mind. She was toughened by years of experience. She would not allow such thoughts to interfere with her concentration. Slick took pride in being a good detective. She still had the self-discipline of a good detective.

No matter how vomit-inducing the images were, a good detective had to stay clinical and stay focused. A good detective took command of the scene and meticulously searched it for hair fibers, tire tracks, footprints, glass, broken branches, blood trails. A good detective took the time to be thorough, orderly, systematic, and methodical. A good detective could use her superior intellect to get inside the mind of a killer.

Slick could feel her every fiber tingling, her senses pushed to high alert like a force of nature gathering strength. It had been a while since her last investigation, but Slick was up to the challenge.

She stood up and took the pair of latex gloves from her pocket. She put them on slowly, deliberately, almost as if the act of putting them on was part of a religious ritual.

The gloves felt good on her hands. She flexed her fingers and concentrated.

A good detective . . .

Just then a gust of wind came up and interrupted Slick's "A Good Detective" mantra. Garbo came running toward her, barking and chasing a piece of paper. Slick reached down, grabbed the piece of paper and examined it closely.

It appeared to be a page from a script. Lines of dialogue had been highlighted in yellow magic marker.

Slick looked from the page in her hand and looked down at Garbo with narrowed eyes.

The dog was frolicking around on the ground, rolling over on its back, legs moving in the air, demanding to be petted, wanting to play.

Without benefit of years of comprehensive training and study, without a highly evolved brain or access to the internet, without fanfare, and worse, without even trying, Garbo had managed to uncover a piece of evidence.

And now the little bitch sat licking herself, almost as if in self-congratulations.

Slick felt suddenly deflated, cheated, like a moment of cosmic greatness had just been yanked from her. It was a lesson in humility. Slick was certain that on some canine level, the dog was mocking her.

"Show off," Slick muttered under her breath.

She picked up Garbo, got in her car and headed for the theater.

Sometimes a good detective just got lucky. Even if it came by way of a little wise-ass dog, a good detective knew a clue when she saw one.

17

Death is a life-altering experience. Certainly for the departed, but also for those left behind. Although death is inevitable, it always comes as a surprise. It doesn't matter if it happens after a long life or after a fatal disease; it is always a surprise.

Never more so than an accident or a murder. The randomness, the feeling that a life was taken prematurely, all those thoughts that come to mind following a death.

Accidents can be more easily rationalized away as a twist of fate. But murder, the deliberate taking of life, is harder to accept.

Many murders are committed in the heat of the moment, without premeditation. The killer in this situation is often brought to justice.

More successful are the murderers who plan their crime beforehand. The police files were bulging with unsolved murders of this kind.

In the battle of wits between murderer and police, the murderer has the advantage. The findings in statistical studies may vary, but the conclusion is inescapable. Most murders go unsolved. Most killers go on living their natural lives quietly and in peace, having benefited from their crime.

Slick drove to the theater remembering how on several occasions she had watched autopsies of dead naked bodies on stainless steel tables without flinching. She had even found it fascinating. But she would balk at having to deliver the sad news to the surviving families.

It was the one thing she had liked least about being a police officer. Standing in the home of a stranger and watching their reaction was the most difficult thing she had to do. The few times she had to do it, she left the home as soon as possible. Sam had always been better at it than she was. Sam could give them the bad news and elicit information from them at the same time. Thank God for that!

She was about to turn on the radio when her thoughts were interrupted by the ringing of her cell phone. It was a welcome distraction. The number readout on her phone showed that it was Laura calling.

"Hey, Fox. What's up," she answered. She pulled the car over to the shoulder of the road to give Laura her full attention. Laura gave her an earful.

"Addison suspects Karson of the theft," Slick said into her cell. "That's interesting. While I was at the station looking over the background checks on the cast and crew, I read that Beautee Holsom recently made a twenty-five-thousand-dollar deposit to her bank. And when I went to the rest stop, I found a page from a script."

Laura was impressed.

"Oh, it was nothing. Just some good old-fashioned detective work."

Slick glanced over at Garbo who was in the front seat chomping blissfully on a squeaking chew toy.

Slick cleared her throat and changed the subject.

"Where are you . . . yes I'm on my way there now . . . I'll meet you in the theater parking lot. 'Bye."

Slick and Laura entered the theater and watched as Addison addressed his cast and crew. He looked deeply saddened. He looked like he didn't have enough strength in him to stay standing, much less lead his troupe that looked to him now for guidance. But somehow, he met the challenge.

He spoke gently and fatherly.

"I want to thank you all for agreeing to continue on with the show. Losing Eugene suddenly is a terrible shock and we will miss him. He was a talented, dedicated actor. I think he would want us to go on with the show. We'll dedicate this show to Eugene, and there will be a memorial writeup of him in the program. I'm sure you all have special memories of Eugene. Let's be thankful we had Eugene with us, even though his time here was too brief. He was very special to us all. There will have to be some casting changes, of course, but we can get through that."

Just then David Castrato burst through the crowd.

"I can't stand it anymore, Addison! You spoke so beautifully. I can't go on. I killed him! I did it. I murdered Eugene. I have to confess."

David's words hit Addison right between the eyes. Where was it going to end? He seemed to be involved in one atrocious scandal after another. His problems were rolling up and pounding him like surf.

First the thousands of dollars that he found hidden among Karson's things. Now one of his troupe was about to confess to murder.

He had never faced anything like this before.

He had lost theater companies in the past for more mundane reasons. But this was insane.

His universe was crumbling quickly around him. He would be left broken and discredited. All his dreams, all his intentions on how he wanted to spend the rest of his life, teaching theater, were dissolving.

The strain of it all showed on his face, in his eyes.

He steeled himself for the next blow. The knot in his stomach tightened.

David ran sobbing to Addison and threw himself at his feet. He wrapped his arms around Addison's legs.

David held everyone's enthralled attention.

They were alarmed, yet there was something very provocative about a confessed murderer being among them.

Most of the cast and crew thought of David as an ever-smiling, ever-singing flunky. He was only the ASM, for Chrissakes. Most of them had barely acknowledged his existence.

The thought that this basically ignored, insignificant nonentity could explode into violence and commit a murder was captivating. Now, from a safe distance, they couldn't take their eyes off him.

David spoke passionately. There was a touch of madness in his eyes. His entire body trembled like a Chihuahua's as he revealed his tortured soul, and spilled the terrible emotions in his heart. He looked angry and frightened. The strange expression on his face deepened and hardened. His voice quavered as he spoke.

"Every night I had to watch Eugene from the wings. He was more concerned with his hair and makeup and lighting than he was of the play. I couldn't help myself. He was so smug and so self-involved. He never gave his all for the part. He had no respect for the romance that is Theater. Eugene was the real murderer. Every time he walked out on the stage he committed a murder. The victim was theater. I couldn't let him get away with it another night. So I stopped him. It was dramatic justice. I killed him! I killed him! May God have mercy on me!"

David buried his head in his hands and had a watery collapse. He wept uncontrollably.

An absolute hush overtook the theater. They all felt so guilty. Maybe if they had talked with David more. Maybe if they had made him feel like an important member of the crew, like he belonged, he wouldn't have done such a horrible thing.

They all waited and watched as David pushed himself away from where he knelt before Addison and rose from the floor.

"GOTCHA!" David jumped up and started laughing. "I really had you going. I made you believe me, didn't I? I didn't kill Eugene. I wanted your attention. I just wanted to show you I could act. There's an opening in the cast now, and I thought this was as good a time as any to audition for it."

The looks of awe on the faces of the crowd suddenly changed to ridicule.

Someone started up a slow hand clap and soon the room was filled with the sham applause.

David looked around, nonplussed.

"This wasn't a bad time, was it?"

Addison stared at David as if in shock. He had been struck speechless. He shook his head and gave a long, heavy sigh. He didn't know whether to laugh or cry at David's antics. Inside, he did a little of both.

Actors, he thought. When would they stop surprising him with the lengths they would go to just to land a part? There was some truth in the story of *Rosemary's Baby.* Not that a woman had given birth to a demonic child, but that an actor was to blame for it. An actor would sell his soul to the devil if he thought it would help.

Then Addison continued, trying very hard to keep the sound of impatience out of his voice. His face was enigmatical.

"All right, that's enough," he said.

The counterfeit applause died down and stopped.

Addison turned and faced David.

"Thank you, 'America's Most Wanted,' for that brilliantly acted confession. You had me believing you were a one-man crime wave. It was an astonishing performance, which I hope I will never see again. Before you interrupted me, David, I was going to say that there would be changes in the casting. Randall will now have the lead role of Michael Ashton."

There was a flurry of comments. The room was filled with a chorus of whispers.

Randall said nothing, but nodded gravely, and waved, looking like a superhero who had just been summoned to save the world.

Blair's smile beamed. She looked extremely pleased. She looked in the direction of Dale and Sindee with an air of triumph.

Dale and Sindee immediately put their heads together and were talking privately.

Addison continued over the murmurs.

"You, David, will take over the part of Phillip Sinclair. Please go try on his costumes to make sure they fit."

"Oh, they fit, trust me!" David said gleefully, looking like he had just been handed the Tony.

"What was that?" Addison asked.

"Oh . . . I mean . . . I think they'll fit without a problem."

David then walked as quickly as he could to the men's dressing room.

Slick watched the reaction of the crowd. They seemed disappointed that David wasn't the killer. In truth, some were jealous that they hadn't thought of auditioning for the role themselves.

Addison continued to address them.

"We'll give David time to try on all of his costumes, then we'll run the show from the top in a half hour. Hopefully, that gives you all enough time to collect yourselves and prepare. I know it's going to be difficult, but we'll be just fine."

Addison looked over to Blair and tapped on his watch to make sure she was marking the time.

"Thirty minutes to places, people," Blair called out.

When Slick was sure Addison was finished she stepped up to him and asked if she could have a few moments of their time. Addison agreed to this.

"Ladies and gentlemen, I'm a private detective investigating the death of Eugene Scherer."

Everyone looked at her skeptically.

First David enacts a false confession and now the woman who had been introduced to them as a backer for the show was claiming to be a private detective.

They weren't about to get fooled again.

Sensing their suspicion, Slick said, "No, I really am a private detective. I can prove it."

She pulled her ID out of her pocket and flashed her badge for all to see.

When she was sure she had their attention she said, "I'll be talking to each of you tonight. You're not under any obligation to talk to me, of course. But I'd like to get some understanding about Eugene, and maybe get some leads to anyone who may have wanted him dead.

"Just a few questions. I'm sensitive to what you've been through. I'm sure you'll all want to cooperate and help capture Eugene's murderer.

"I'll try to stay out of your way as much as possible and not interfere with the rehearsal. Does anyone have a problem with talking to me?"

Glances were exchanged, then there were silent indifferent shrugs all around.

Now that's the kind of unrestrained spirit of cooperation I was hoping for, Slick thought to herself.

Alicia Beavers had been watching Slick the whole time, and now she came running up to her, eager to talk.

"Me first, me first! I'd love to talk to you! Ooooh! So you're a detective. That is so sexy."

"Yes I am and I'd like to ask you a few questions about last night."

They sat down on two front-row seats.

While Slick pulled out a pen and notepad Alicia licked her lips and looked Slick up and down like she was a tender tasty morsel to be devoured.

Alicia was fantasizing that Slick tasted like black cherries.

Slick didn't notice, but Laura did.

Laura read Alicia's mind thoroughly, and in the unexpurgated version.

Alicia moved in closer.

"Are you going to strip search me? Press charges against me?" Alicia winked at Slick.

Slick looked at her in disbelief.

"I bet you do your best work undercover. You know what I mean?" Alicia asked seductively.

"No. I don't know what you mean, you're far too vague for me. But thank you for using all of those stock phrases. I never get tired of hearing them," Slick said sternly. "Can we get back to last night? What happened after you left the theater?"

Having been rebuked, Alicia rolled up her hankering tongue and told her story.

"Well, first I went out for a drink with Sindee and Dale. Yawn. Boring. Dale drank like a fish and kept rambling on and on about Eugene. Sindee and he left. She said she was going home to give her cat Staccato her insulin shot. The cat's diabetic. Then she was going to drive Dale home. They left a little after ten. After that, I hooked up with Richard and . . ."

"Who's Richard?" Slick asked, looking through her notes.

Alicia sighed and sat back in her chair despondently.

"He's just someone I had really horrible sex with last night. He's one of the dancers in the show. He's got the smallest penis

I've ever seen. At first I couldn't even find it. I thought it was an optical illusion. But then I managed to find it with some tweezers and we started going at it."

Slick looked at her, wincing at the mental image in her head.

"Okay, I'm kidding about the tweezers part, but jeez, what a disappointment that was. Getting vaccinated took longer. And it was more fun. I should have skipped the whole thing and gone right to the part where you smoke the cigarettes afterwards. I'm gonna kill Sindee," she concluded.

Slick looked at her with raised eyebrows, her pen poised above her note pad.

"Oops! Probably shouldn't say 'kill' to a detective who's investigating a homicide, huh?"

Then Alicia got that wanton look in her eyes again. She thought of a new tactic to use for her seduction. Flattery. She moved forward in her chair.

"Has anyone ever told you that you look just like Halle Berry?"

Slick shot Laura an "I told you so" look.

Laura just rolled her eyes heavenward and groaned. Sometimes God chose the most irksome ways to demonstrate His infinite sense of humor. She knew Slick would never let her hear the end of the Halle Berry thing now.

Alicia caught their exchanged glances and, sharp as a steel blade, it suddenly dawned on her that they were a couple. Her eyes brightened with a lusting curiosity.

"Say, have you two ever had a threeway?"

Slick was losing her patience. "Can we please stick to the subject of Eugene? Do you know of anyone who'd want to kill him? Disgruntled lovers? Wacko fans? Anything that might help?"

Alicia gave up. These two were strictly business. There was

no chance of anything else with them. It looked like another night of watching "College Girls Gone Wild" videos. She tried to clear her head.

"What were we talking about?"

"We were talking about Eugene's murder."

Bummed, she let go of her fantasies of Slick and Laura, and answered the question.

"Eugene was annoying, yes, but not to the point where anyone would want him, you know . . . homicided. I can't think of anyone who hated him that much. He was like a lot of leading men, full of himself. Everyone was used to him."

Alicia continued to think aloud. "The only person to benefit by any of this is Randall. He wanted Eugene's role from the very beginning. Now he gets what he wanted."

Then Alicia looked very sad.

"Poor Beautee. She must be devastated. Out of all of us, she absolutely adored Eugene."

"Was there ever any trouble between Eugene and Beautee?" Slick asked

"No, never. They loved each other. But it was such a waste. He was so gay, and she's so, you know, Beautee-licious."

A thought entered Alicia's head. Maybe Beautee would need comforting. Alicia perked up a bit.

Beautee was straight, but things happen while offering solace and comfort. Alicia's face brightened.

"Are you done with me? Can I go now?"

"Yes, I'm finished with you for now. You can go. I may have some more questions for you later, though," Slick answered.

And like a heat-seeking missile, Alicia Beavers shot from her chair and started for her next sexual target.

Unfortunately, she was intercepted by David Castrato. Now that David was the second lead in the show he would be unable to be assistant stage manager. Since Alicia had the smallest part in the show and was only in the last scene, she would take over the duties of assistant stage manager.

This came right from Addison himself David told her.

Alicia didn't mind. It was for the good of the show. She didn't like the idea of being bossed around by Blair, but she didn't mind.

She would offer Beautee a naked shoulder to cry on later. She and David walked off together discussing what she had to preset for the start of the show, the set changes, and her other new duties.

Beautee Holsom was sitting and singing with the orchestra, finishing up the last few bars of "Michael Row Your Boat Ashore." They were just about to start up on "Kumbayah," when Slick and Laura approached her.

"I know you already gave a statement to the police, but I'd like to hear it from you in your own words. What you tell me will not be privileged. I'm just a PI. I'm not a priest or your lawyer or your doctor."

Beautee's mouth turned upward in a slow smile.

"Please ask me anything you like," she said

"Why don't you tell me again what happened."

"I got a call from Eugene. He wanted me to pick him up. He had too much to drink and didn't want to drive home. He knew he could count on me. I told him after the rehearsal I would come to get him. He called me after two a.m. I went to pick him up. When I got there he was injured. I thought he was dead. I called the police and an ambulance, but it was too late. He was dead."

No matter how many times she told the story, it still upset her. She seemed to wish it would end differently with each telling, but it didn't.

Slick decided to change the subject. She hadn't questioned

anyone about the theft yet. So many of the theater group had access to the money. Maybe it was time to start stirring the waters.

"You recently came into a large sum of money, didn't you?"

Beautee looked at Slick very surprised.

"How did you know that? What has that got to do with Eugene?"

"Maybe nothing at all," Slick answered. "Why don't you tell me about it."

"I can explain the twenty-five thousand dollars that was recently deposited into my account. I am the treasurer for my church group. We are going to build a Christian theme park. That money is what we've collected so far toward our building fund. Are you familiar with Bowcraft on Route 22?"

Slick and Laura both indicated they knew the place.

"Our theme park is going to be a small one like that for young children," Beautee continued. "It will be fun for the whole family and honor the Lord at the same time. For the very young children we'll have Bible story readings by the Good Samaritan and Noah. The kids will be able to play updated versions of old favorites such as 'Hide and Seek and Ye Shall Find.' There'll be great rides like 'The Holy Ghoster Roller Coaster,' 'The Holy Mother Mary-Go-Round,' and the 'Little Lambs of God Petting Zoo.' Thrill seekers will be able to have fun while cleansing their souls on our 'Crash Car Confessionals' and find salvation on the 'Ferris Wheel of Forgiveness,' then fly with a birdie to the Heavenly Kingdom in 'Putt Putt to Paradise.' It will be divine."

Beautee smiled, hands clasped together, looking far away at something only she could see, totally entranced and as dedicated to her vision as if she had started a quest for the Holy Grail.

"Um. Okay. That's all for now. I think I've got enough."

Slick scratched her head and looked at Laura. Beautee's expla-nation of the money in her account could be easily checked out.

Slick suddenly felt dirty, like she would burn in Hell for all eternity for even thinking Beautee had taken the money. She made a mental note to start going to church more often.

"Thank you. Before you leave tonight please give me the number of someone who can verify this." Then Slick added, "Just one more question, please."

"Of course," Beautee agreed, returning from her spiritual flight.

"You're obviously a deeply religious person. How is it that someone like you would form such a close bond with an openly gay man like Eugene? Usually people like you would be condemning his lifestyle?" There was an edge in her voice.

Beautee looked at Slick thoughtfully.

"People like you? So many prejudices, so little time to feed them all, right, Detective? Eugene was my friend, and he was gay. That's all there is to it."

Slick suddenly felt ashamed. Beautee had put her in her place without raising her voice and without rancor. She spoke with all the sincerity of a child praying at midnight. Slick could practically hear the gates of Heaven clicking into locked position against her. She would definitely have to put in some quality church time now.

Beautee went back to playing the guitar, and Slick and Laura turned their attention to Dale and Sindee.

Dale was washing down two Advils with some Diet Coke and Sindee was smoking a cigarette.

"Do either of you know who might have wanted to kill Eugene and why?" Slick asked.

"No," Dale answered. "He was such a stiff actor, killing him is almost redundant."

Slick and Laura looked at him with obvious expressions of shock on their faces.

"Oh, please. I feel just as bad as anyone that Eugene is dead. I really do. But I'm not going to spend a lot of time showing fake grief. And guess what, his death might even be good for the box office. You know, all that morbid curiosity. People may be more interested in the show now," Dale said unapologetically.

"Besides, I'm sure that right now, even in his current state, he looks better than I feel." He held the cold bottle of Diet Coke against his forehead and prayed that the Advils would kick in soon.

Laura and Sindee were quiet, not knowing what to make of Dale's statements.

Slick had seen this before. People handle bad news in different ways. Delayed shock, or denial. She was certain that Dale was acting out.

"Why aren't you asking these questions at the rest stop?" Dale asked gruffly. "Maybe he had sex with the wrong man." Then he turned his head away in anger.

Still Slick said nothing. She waited for Dale to start talking again. Finally he did.

"There were times when I would beg him not to go there," he said softly. "I used to follow him after rehearsals sometimes just to make sure he was safe."

Dale's eyes started to swim in tears, but none fell.

"You were in love with Eugene," Slick said, gently.

Dale said nothing. He just stared straight ahead. He was silent for so long that the answer to the question had to be "yes."

"I felt so sorry when I heard this morning that he was dead. I was out drinking. I wasn't there for him."

Sindee exploded, clearly thrown by Dale's revelation.

"What? You never told me you were involved with Eugene! That's why you'd run right out after rehearsals! You were going to be with him. How could you keep that from me? You lied to me!"

"I didn't lie to you! I would never lie to you." Dale thought about this for a second then added, "I *may* customize the facts once in a while to my specifications, but I don't lie! There's a difference."

"You told me you weren't seeing anyone special!"

"Well, it wasn't special." Then Dale added, a little sadly, "Not to him anyway! Eugene could never get enough sex. He got more ass than a bus seat. We'd have sex, then later he'd go out for more at the rest stop. I was beginning to feel like his 'fluffer.' But he could be so damn charming. He could talk the square pants off Sponge Bob. I was ready for something more. I'm tired of one-night stands, of chasing after chorus boys in every show. But Eugene . . . Let's just say we didn't last long." Dale's earlier flippancy about Eugene's death had completely disappeared. Now he looked angry, hurt, and sorry all at once.

"Wow! Well no wonder you two had such a horrible fight the night he died. You really have to love someone to be able to fight like that," Sindee said offhandedly.

Dale shot Sindee a look.

Sindee looked at Dale and then at Slick and Laura.

"No, No! I didn't mean to imply that Dale would *kill* Eugene. I just meant their fight was very passionate and now I know why." Sindee said this with a trace of a giggle, the kind that people make to ease the tension.

Sindee was about to light another cigarette when she nervously dropped her lighter on the floor. Slick reached down and picked it up. She looked at the masks of Comedy and Tragedy on the front. She read the inscription.

"Very clever," she said as she handed the lighter back to Sindee.

"Thank you," Sindee said. "It was a gift from Dale."

Dale smiled faintly.

"What happened after you dropped Dale off, Sindee?" Slick asked.

"I went straight home."

"Did anyone see you?"

"Just my cat."

"What about you, Dale? What happened after you got home?"

"I don't remember anything. I had had quite a bit to drink."

"Did you have a blackout? Is it possible you went out again on your own after Sindee dropped you off?"

"You told me you had to go meet someone later," Sindee said. "Was it Eugene?"

"I don't remember!" Then the memory of the strange phone message came back to him with crystal clarity.

"Oh my God! There was a message on my answering machine. I thought it was just a prank."

"What did it say?"

"It said 'I know what you did. I saw you.' "

"Did you recognize the voice?"

"No I didn't. I couldn't even tell if it was a man or a woman."

There was a long pause. Dale started to panic. He looked at all the faces looking at him and suddenly he couldn't breathe.

"No! I didn't do it! I couldn't have done it! I don't have to put up with this. I don't think I want to talk to you anymore.

You're trying to pin Eugene's murder on me because I was involved with him." Dale's tone changed from fear to defiance.

"I'm trying to rule you out as a murder suspect. I haven't accused you of anything," Slick said calmly.

"No. Don't listen to her, Dale. You don't have to talk to them anymore. Neither one of us has to talk to them," Sindee said. And they both hurried away, clearly shaken.

"Dale may have been the last person to see Eugene alive, and he doesn't even remember it," Laura said to Slick after they had gone.

"Either that or the first one to see him dead," Slick commented.

Blair and Randall were talking when Slick and Laura approached them.

Before Slick could ask any questions, Blair said, "I don't know how much help we could be to you. Randall and I were together all night at my place going over the script."

Randall said nothing. He just nodded in agreement with Blair.

"Really?" Slick asked, looking at them very closely. "I saw the way you two were talking in the parking lot. You left separately."

"We had a little fight, that's all. No big deal. Randall called me later and apologized. He came over and stayed the night."

"What time did he call you?" asked Slick.

"Look we don't have time for this right now. I've got to set the stage and Randall has to get into costume and take his medicine," Blair said and started walking away.

Randall said nothing and followed closely behind Blair.

Rachel was talking with some of the stage crew when Slick and Laura approached her. She knew they wanted to speak with her so she excused herself and turned to face them.

"I didn't have anything to do with Eugene's murder. I don't have a car. I wasn't out driving my father's last night. You can check my father's car if you like. After you dropped me off at home I was there all night. My father can verify that I was home," she said softly.

"I'm sure that will check out, just as you say," Slick assured her. "We know you took the money, Rachel, and now we know why. You did it for your father, didn't you? You might as well tell us what happened." Slick looked her directly in the eyes. Rachel knew it was time to tell the whole truth.

Laura sensed it was very difficult for her. She stood behind Rachel's chair and placed a reassuring hand on her shoulder. Rachel looked back into Laura's encouraging smile.

Then Rachel bowed her head, but it wasn't lowered in shame, it was as if she were beneath a great weight. Staring at the floor, Rachel began to tell her story.

"My father has been in jail twice for robbery. He was guilty both times. But he's changed. It was difficult for him after my mother died, trying to raise a daughter all alone. He made some mistakes.

"About a month ago there was a robbery of a store. One of the witnesses identified my father as a suspect from some police photos. He was picked up, but he didn't do it. He was at work at the time. But he was picked up anyway. Because of his prior arrests, the lawyer told me he might have to post bail. He figured it could be as high as $25,000. I didn't have that kind of money. I believed him, but I didn't have the money to help him. I didn't have anything for collateral. I took the cash from the theater's safe. It was the only thing I could think of.

"By the time of his arraignment, the real thief had been caught. All the charges against him were dropped, and I put the money back in the safe."

Rachel lifted her head and asked, "How did you know about my father?"

"A friend of mine recognized you. He saw you in jail visiting your dad. I had him ask around about you."

Rachel looked at Slick steadily. Now it was her turn to ask the questions.

"This friend of yours didn't by any chance get into my apartment the other night and then leave through my bedroom window, did he?

Laura looked at Slick stunned, but said nothing.

"Yes, that was him. I asked Mr. McDonough to do some checking around on you as a favor to me. He went a little overboard. I didn't ask him to sneak into your apartment. I apologize for that. He used to be a thief, but he's a good man. He's made some mistakes. I'm sure you can understand that."

Rachel nodded reluctantly. She understood that very well.

Slick resumed her questioning.

"Do you think someone from the theater knows you took the money?"

"I don't know. But it would have been so easy to do. Addison let everyone have access to the theater account. Sindee and Dale were talking about that not that long ago. There was a lot of gossip about the money that was spent on the show."

Slick became very interested.

"Who was talking about it? What did they say?" she asked.

Rachel told Slick and Laura all about the conversations she had overheard on Christmas Eve.

Later, when they were alone at home in their bedroom, Laura pulled the covers off the bed and said, "Assume 'spoon positions.' " Then she asked, "So, what do we do next? Do we have a plan?"

"Yes. We're going to break into the theater. That's the plan," Slick answered casually. "Do you want to be the inside spoon or the outside spoon?

"Outside spoon." Laura's eyes snapped open. "Wait! Did you just say we're going to break into the theater?" Laura was frozen in place beside the bed.

"Yes. We've got to look there for clues. That's the plan," Slick said as she slid under the blankets.

"That's the plan! Breaking and entering! It's illegal! Do we have a plan B?"

"Sorry. I didn't mean to sound so cavalier about it. As a former police officer I still have a very healthy respect for the law, but sometimes the only difference between a private detective and a criminal is that the detective gets to ride in his own car to the police station. The criminal arrives in the back of a black and white."

It occurred to Slick just then how her moral compass had shifted somewhat from being a police officer to being a private detective. She wasn't proud of it, but it was true. When she was a cop, the world was clearer. There was right and wrong. As a detective, things had gotten a little gray. She wouldn't allow herself to dwell on that just now. There was a murderer on the loose and she still had a theft to solve.

"But it used to be a convent; a place of prayer and contemplation and charity. Breaking into it seems sacrilegious somehow," Laura said, feeling her own moral doubts.

"There's been a murder, baby, and there's nothing sacred about that."

Slick took a slight pause, then asked, "Are you worried about what the media would do if they found out that wealthy socialite Laura Charles was found breaking into an old convent? That's a valid concern. I would understand if you didn't want to do it."

"I'd be lying if I said it didn't concern me," Laura said thoughtfully. "Plus I've got Devlyn on my case. She'd do anything to make me look bad in front of the Board. She's practically salivating for an opportunity. I'm sure she suspects there's something going on. I'm not concerned about the clam company so much. At a time when insider trading, stock fraud, and money laundering are running wild, what would life be these days without a corporate scandal about one of the officers? There's absolutely nothing going on there. That place is squeaky clean. But we've done some work at the Foundation that I'm very proud of. I wouldn't want to do anything that would tarnish everything we've accomplished."

"It's your call, Blue Eyes," Slick said. "You're the one with the good name and reputation. You only signed on to help Judson and Rachel with the theft of the grant money. You had no idea that murder and mayhem would ensue."

Laura was silent for a while as she thought this over. It was an uncertain journey for her with clearly troubling aspects to it.

She had been a very good daughter to her father.

Until now, she had never realized how much she had tried to emulate him and surpass him. She had done well with the business he left her and had even made it better than he could have imagined. She had set up the foundation in his name, and the good it did every day was something her father never would have done.

Because of Laura's efforts, her father's name would be associated with charitable work he never would have performed in his lifetime. She had done all she could to sustain and even enhance his name.

Laura was a very independent woman, but she still lived in the home her father built, living on the fortune he had made.

Maybe it was time to stop living so much in his shadow and make her own mark.

And the thought of a possible adventure with Slick attracted her. She was ready to take a chance.

Slick said nothing. She knew Laura was working things out in her own way as she always did. Slick would support Laura whatever Laura decided. She would not push her either way.

So, for several moments they lay next to each other with Laura's decision hanging silently, waiting in the background.

Then there was a deep calmness inside Laura.

Finally she asked softly, "What does one wear to break into a convent? A habit and camouflage paint?"

Laura laughed against Slick's ear. The laugh revealed so much.

"Think of it as a field trip," Slick said, smiling. "A learning experience for private detectives in training."

Slick's smile went unseen. It was an outward sign of her mute admiration. Admiration for the lady next to her, whose body fit so perfectly against hers, whose mind never failed to amaze her.

Laura was a positive force, she had a secret source that radiated courage. She had a sweet inner strength that always impressed Slick, but never surprised her. Laura moved in mysterious ways, and Slick loved every one of them. She was magnificent.

Slick knew their lives would go on precisely as before, but in that instant, it all had changed.

Slick turned over to face Laura, opened her arms and took her in. Laura went into her arms willingly.

"Good night, Laura" was all she said.

It was all that needed to be said.

18

Slick parked the car a few blocks from the theater. Then she and Laura and Garbo walked in silence to the theater's rear entrance. The streets and the parking area were eerily quiet. The hush of twilight seemed to muffle the city.

When they reached the back door, Slick pulled a mini-toolkit from her pocket to pick the lock, and then she looked at Laura. It was a signal that Laura still had a chance to walk away if she didn't want to go through with the plan. Laura's face was expressionless. It held the resolve Slick was accustomed to seeing when Laura made up her mind. They said nothing, but Slick understood.

Slick bent over the lock and carefully cracked it. She leaned against the door frame; nudging the door gently and slowly, she opened it, and they quietly stepped inside, closing the door behind them.

Garbo trotted in ahead of them, sniffing the air.

They stepped into total blackness.

"Can we at least light a candle?" Laura asked in a whisper. She started going through the backpack she had brought with her. It was filled with supplies she thought might come in handy. Never having done a B and E before, she wanted to be prepared.

"No. No candles, no lights. We'll just have to curse the darkness. Close your eyes for a moment. That gets them ready for the absence of light. In a few seconds your eyes will adjust. I think my eyes have already adjusted. I can see clearly. Follow me." Slick started walking.

"Ouch! Damn it!" Slick said, cursing not only the darkness, but the wall she had walked headfirst into as well.

"Okay, maybe one candle," she said as she rubbed her head. She could already feel the beginning of a lump. "I forgot this was a theater. Set pieces and walls get moved around."

"Super sleuth! Ha!" Laura ha'd.

She pulled a candle our of her bag and lit it. She lifted it up over her head and looked around. There was a little circle of light around them. Beyond the light the big room was all blackness.

During the day, the convent looked stately and majestic. In the dark, it just looked creepy. Shadowy forms surrounded them.

Outside there was a clap of thunder that rattled the glass in the windows. A blaze of lightning flashed and momentarily filled the darkness. Then everything went dark again. Even darker than before, it seemed.

The wind gusted and shook the convent. It blew its way into the pipes of the old organ, causing it to play an ominous chord, and rain started pounding down.

It suddenly became very cold, and Slick and Laura could see their breath drifting from their mouths like smoke. The bell in the old tower reverberated with a sonorous chime.

Out of the darkness there came a fluttering of wings. A bat whisked passed them. It darted around them for a few seconds, its teeth bared, soaring and swooping in tight little arcs. Then, as suddenly as it appeared, it flew away, back into the darkness from which it had come.

Slick and Laura exchanged looks of disbelief.

"Is it getting creepier in here, or is it just me?" Laura asked.

"So far, so mysterious and spooky," Slick said.

"I vote we get out of here. Like now," Laura said, looking around for the bat. "Did you see something move over there?" She thought the bat might be coming back to dive-bomb at them again.

"You keep the candle and look around out here in the theater. Garbo and I are going to go have a look in the men's dressing room. Maybe there's something personal of Eugene's in there that could help."

Slick made her way slowly to the men's dressing room and opened the door.

It was pitch black inside.

She found her way to the refrigerator and opened the door. It gave just enough light to the room for her to be able to see. In the refrigerator was water and soda, a few cans of beer, and a bottle of wine.

There was also a medicine bottle. It contained insulin and the prescription had Randall Garret's name on it.

Next Slick moved to the counter with the assigned seating for the actors. There were several scripts there.

Slick took the script page she had found at the crime scene out of her pocket. At the bottom it had the number 37 on it. She looked at the scripts and compared them with the page. When she got to Randall's she noticed that it was a match. The same lines of dialogue had been highlighted, but page 37 of his script was fax paper, not regular copy paper.

Slick found a loose brick in the wall. She grabbed hold of it and started to dislodge it. Maybe something was hidden behind it.

Garbo had been sniffing at the area and now started a low growl. Slick tried to quiet her as she continued working on the brick.

"Shhh, you! There might be a clue in here. You're always sticking your cold wet nose into my business."

Garbo would not be quieted. She continued to protest as Slick got closer to removing the brick.

Garbo got up on her hind legs and tried to push Slick away from the wall. She started to bark loudly as Slick removed the brick.

Slick looked inside the open space. Her eyes widened and she started to scream in horror. She was not prepared for what she saw inside the wall.

She instinctively picked up the dog and ran.

"Why are you running?" Laura whispered loudly.

"I'm being chased," Slick said, matching Laura's whisper, as she whizzed by.

Slick had been decorated three times as a police officer for bravery. The first time was when she purposely stepped into the line of fire and took a bullet that had been meant for her partner Sam. It wasn't as foolish as it sounded. Slick knew Sam wasn't wearing his bullet-proof vest. She was.

The second time was for going out a twelfth-floor window of a twenty-story building and talking down a jumper. The third time was for rescuing a family from their burning home. She faced fear every day on the job. She never let it get the best of her.

Now she sat on the floor babbling, her face ashen with fright.

Laura understood at once.

"Why do they need so many legs, anyway? Why? Why? It's obscene . . . crawling nightmares . . . furry monsters . . . monsters!"

Slick suffered from severe arachnophobia. The sight of a spider left her weak and helpless. Only Laura, Sam, and Slick's mother knew of her fear of spiders.

Laura watched as her "She-ro," her Warrior Princess, sat

curled up in a corner fighting to take back control of herself. She stared in a dazed way at everything, regaining her faculties.

She struggled to her feet, needing Laura to support her.

"I didn't find anything out here. Did you find anything in the men's dressing room. Besides spiders, that is," Laura asked.

"Yes," Slick said. She was back to normal. "I found out that Randall is a diabetic and the page I found at the rest stop came from his script."

"Can we go home now?" Laura asked, looking around. She still wasn't over the bat attack.

"I left the refrigerator door open in the men's dressing room. I should go back and close it."

Slick looked like she might faint. It meant going back to the spiders.

"Never fear," Laura said. She handed her candle to Slick. Then she pulled a can of Raid out of her backpack.

Slick smiled gratefully. "Have I told you today how much I love you?"

Laura smiled and led the way to the men's dressing room.

Once inside, she sprayed the area behind the brick and put the brick back in place, while Slick held the candle. She closed the refrigerator door, and just as they were about to leave, they saw something that stopped them both in their tracks.

On the dressing room wall there was a portrait of the first Mother Superior of the convent, Sister Deanna Sympathy. The face smiling at them from the portrait looked exactly like Beautee Holsom.

They walked over to examine it. Slick held the candle up to get a closer look.

It was clearly decades old, and not painted recently as a prop.

The resemblance to Beautee was uncanny.

"Maybe the Mother Superior was a great aunt of Beautee's."

"Did you see that painting before?" Laura asked softly.

"That painting wasn't there before," Slick answered. "It wasn't here when Addison and Karson gave us the tour, and it wasn't here when I checked this room a minute ago."

"Karson said they had ghosts."

"I'll debate that with you later. Let's just get out of here."

"Come on, Garbo! Let's go."

They all ran for the door.

19

Devlyn O'Hare sat alone in her office. She looked at the clock on her desk.

Eight twenty-three.

Most, if not all of the employees had gone home for the night. Devlyn had a few things she wanted to take care of.

There was a knock on her door. She had been expecting it. She knew who it was, but asked anyway.

"It's Bob Johnson, Ms. O'Hare. From Security."

Devlyn walked briskly to the door and opened it.

A tall man in a gray uniform stood in the doorway, tipped his hat and said, "Here's the tape from the security camera you asked for."

Bob gave Devlyn a good looking over.

She was crazy hot, he thought. He knew who she was, but she had never taken notice of him.

Bob rarely left his post at the security desk. So it was a big deal to get a call from her and be invited to her office. The office of the manager.

Bob stood there and looked around, he hoped, without being conspicuous. It was pretty fancy, all right.

Devlyn took the cassette from his hands. It was in a clear plastic box. There didn't seem to be much tape on the spools. She knew it wouldn't take her long to review it, not even a half hour of her time.

"Has anyone else seen this?" she asked without taking her eyes from the small package.

Trying to sound very commanding, he answered, "No, Ms. O'Hare. No one. Not even me."

Ms. O'Hare seemed to like that a lot. Bob felt encouraged.

Bob pulled himself erect to his full six-foot-three height and hooked his thumbs onto his belt. Might as well try to score some points with the boss while he had an opportunity. Besides, Bob thought, he wasn't a bad looking guy. He was alone with a beautiful woman in her office after working hours. There was no one else around.

Maybe she wanted a little something more from him. Powerful women had inner urges. Urges that weren't always satisfied. He had read about that kind of stuff, spontaneous sex stuff, in *Penthouse* magazine. You never know. Maybe he was about to get lucky.

He hoped his breath wasn't sour, just in case.

"You see, Ms. O'Hare, this is a pretty standard monitoring situation. We have cameras in most of the offices, conference rooms, and corridors. They're turned on and taping twenty-four hours a day. But if there are no obvious incidents that require an immediate security intervention, the tapes are logged in and filed away, just in case someone may want to review them later. It rarely happens that someone asks to see them, but we keep them anyway. It's part of the job."

Then Bob leaned seductively against the door frame, insinuating himself with much suggestive familiarity, so she could see his muscular body. He let his eyes roam over every inviting curve of her.

He spoke slowly and softly.

"If there's anything else I can do for you . . ."

"There isn't," Devlyn said.

She slammed the door in his face without ever having once looked up at Bob Johnson.

Devlyn thought she may have heard a barely audible yelp of pain from the other side of the door but she instantly dismissed it and forgot about it.

She walked over to her office television and slipped the security tape into the attached VCR. For the longest time there was nothing on the tape of interest to Devlyn, so she kept fast-forwarding it until she found the section she wanted.

When she found what she wanted her lips moved slowly into a smile. It was the only part of her face that did smile. Her eyes were the coolest onyx, watching the tape intensely.

Devlyn hadn't been sure about the quality of the security tape, how it would play in her VCR, but it was perfect. Every sound, every image came through with perfect clarity and fidelity.

Devlyn rewound the tape and played it again.

There it was, caught on camera. Addison Taylor walking into Laura's office and saying:

"I'm here about the grant money. I think I know who stole it. God forgive me. I think it was Karson. I think Karson took the money."

And a few frames later when Devlyn entered the office and asked:

"Who was that gentleman I just saw leaving your office?"

Laura had answered:

"Just an old friend of the family."

Yes, it was all there on black-and-white videotape, with sound no less. Devlyn was infinitely grateful that Slick had talked Laura into installing the security cameras. It made the moment so very special.

Devlyn walked to her office wet bar and decided she would treat herself to an Absolut martini.

She was playing in her mind how she would present the tape to the board.

It was going to be wonderful.

Here was proof of Laura Charles herself practically in collusion with the theft of grant money.

The board would certainly be reluctant to dismiss Laura, but what else could they do in light of the taped evidence.

Life was good.

Devlyn kicked off her shoes and jumped backward onto her soft leather couch. It caught and cradled her perfectly. She didn't spill one drop from her drink.

She thought of the different angles she could play this game. Her mind started clicking. This tape gave her great power.

She could, of course, let Laura know she had the tape. She could approach Laura on the pretense that she was shielding her from the board, that she had taken the tape from Security to show her that she was looking out for her. She could try to gain her confidence. It could be their little secret. It could be the basis for a nice silent relationship in the future.

No. Laura would never buy that.

Devlyn took a sip from her martini.

She could offer to sell the tape to Laura.

Blackmail? No.

She didn't want Laura's money. She wanted to be ahead of Laura at the foundation. She belonged ahead of Laura. She was the one who was there every day, not Laura. To get there she would have to gamble big time. It would have to be an all or nothing game. In the end the losers would weep and the winners would count their chips.

It was Devlyn's turn to count her chips. She was the kind who came out on top.

Her eyes looked around the office in a sweeping gaze of triumph. It was a great office, but soon she would have Laura's office. She raised her glass in a toast to no one. Then she stirred her drink with the swizzle stick, to get more of the olive favor into it.

Devlyn was sucking on the olive when she heard:

"Laura, I miss you. I miss working with you. I think about you all the time. We were good together. You can't tell me you never think of me. There was a time when we could have been so much more. You do remember that, don't you? Let me show you what we could have had together. I want you here. Now. Just lay back and let me take you. Let me taste you."

Devlyn turned back to the television and watched the tape.

She saw herself trying to climb all over Laura. She'd never seen herself on video tape doing soft porn before. She had to admit that she looked good.

She fleetingly wished there was a zoom on the security camera that had gotten close-ups of her gorgeous breasts. Laura was a fool to resist her. It was almost a shame to sacrifice this section.

But, the board didn't need to see that, Devlyn thought.

She picked up the remote and erased that portion of the tape. She rewound the tape to make sure that spot had been wiped clean. When she replayed it, there was nothing there but static. Devlyn walked to the TV set, ejected the tape and placed it securely into her Louis Vuitton briefcase.

Then she settled back snugly into her couch. She took a big sip from her drink. She ran her fingers through her long hair, tossed back her head and put her feet up. She let the warmth of the martini overtake her.

Devlyn sat alone in her office smiling to herself and feeling positively serene.

Serenely ravenous.

20

No one can betray you like a trusted friend or loved one. There is such an intense feeling of pain and incredulity, like you've given yourself away completely only to be hurt.

Disappointing. Shattering. Unspeakable.

They accuse you of horrific things. Murder. Stealing.

You can't stop shivering. They keep shouting at you "What have you done? What have you done?" Angry and derisive, the words are spit at you.

At first you feel nothing, only your face burning. Then they keep dangling the truth in front of you. Poking you with it. Poking you with the truth like needles. Making you choke on the truth. It's obscene.

Stung, you draw back and stare with disbelieving eyes at a face that suddenly seems unfamiliar to you. Your time together falls away, cold and dead like the tears falling down your face. You still can't stop shivering.

You beg them to keep your secrets You plead, but they say no. They're so ready to tell your secrets, but not ready to face their own. How dare they judge you?

Now the pain of their betrayal is cutting you, slicing you like razors, almost doubling you over.

You stand very still now, only half listening to them, trying to look repentant, but thinking about other things. The shivering has stopped.

You start to back away knowing what you have to do. You

have to take the problem into your own hands. You can't wait to be betrayed.

Barely listening now, you have a dreadful thought and a warm sick sensation starts inside you.

You've killed before, you think. You can kill again.

You try to resist, but you have no choice. They've given you no choice.

Slick and Laura went to the theater to watch the first rehearsal of tech week. This was the last week of rehearsal before opening night. This night would be the first time all the sound and light cues would be put into effect.

When they arrived at the theater it was pulsating with activity.

The crew was everywhere making sure things were plugged in and functioning.

Karson waved to them from the balcony, and Slick and Laura went up to the balcony to watch with Karson and get out of the way.

Blair and several stage crew members were setting up for the first act.

None of the actors were onstage. They were in the dressing rooms getting into costumes and make-up.

The orchestra was warming up in the pit. Slick noticed that Sindee was walking frantically around the orchestra looking under chairs, and under sheets of music. She spoke questioningly to several of the musicians. They only shook their heads and looked back at her blankly. She seemed to speak to them with much insistence. The warm up stopped and they all stood up and turned their pockets inside out.

Angrily, she loudly asked if anyone had taken her lighter from the piano. Startled by her outburst, everyone present, even Addison, responded that they had not. Bewildered, she took a box of matches from her purse and anxiously lit a cigarette. She sat down at the piano smoking, trying to get her nerves under control.

Addison called out to Blair and she hurried over to him. He was talking to her frantically. Then Blair ran backstage, and Addison climbed up to the balcony and joined Karson, Slick, and Laura.

Addison took out a handkerchief and mopped his forehead.

He explained that Randall hadn't arrived yet and he had to send Blair backstage to tell Dale he would have to play the lead role until Randall showed up.

Blair came from backstage and climbed the stairs to the tech booth. The stage crew disappeared backstage.

Soon the set lights dimmed and the house went dark.

The first act went smoothly.

There were a few dropped lines and it was easy to see the actors were nervous, especially Dale.

At the first act intermission Randall had still not arrived.

When he hadn't arrived by the second act intermission, the actors were visibly shaken by his absence.

As the big birthday cake was wheeled on stage for the act three finale, Alicia Beavers started to scream in terror from inside. All the dancing and music stopped.

Something was definitely wrong.

Alicia crawled out through the trap door under the cake still screaming in a panic.

The top of the cake sprung open and there was Randall's dead body dangling from the inside top of the cake.

His legs were akimbo and his arms were twisted in unnatural positions. He looked like a marionette whose strings were disastrously tangled.

The cast stared at the body, transfixed. Someone screamed onstage and it spread to the orchestra.

Addison, Karson, Blair and Slick scrambled down from the

balcony for the stage. Laura had jumped to her feet with them, but Slick told her to stay put.

Laura did so not knowing what Slick had in mind, but trusting that she knew what she was doing.

Slick jumped up on the stage, pushed through the actors, and examined the body.

She felt for a pulse. There was none. Randall was dead.

Slick carefully looked around the inside of the cake. On the bottom of the cake was the inscribed lighter Dale had given to Sindee and a syringe.

She carefully searched Randall's clothing.

Inside Randall's pocket was a receipt for a $25,000 down payment on a property in Maplewood, New Jersey.

She asked Laura, who had stayed in the balcony, to take the house lights down and operate the spotlights.

Addison called out directions from the floor.

Laura walked to the tech booth, played around with the knobs and switches and eventually the lights came on.

Slick called Detectives Rafferty and Simpson from her cell phone and told them to come to the theater. Then she instructed Addison to wait backstage with Randall's body until they arrived. Addison went to the cake and rolled it away.

Everyone in the room was still. Slick walked amongst them regarding them all very closely. All her suspects were right in front of her.

She started thinking out loud.

"Ladies and gentlemen. I was called here to investigate a theft. And now there have been two murders. I believe the thief and the murderer are here on this stage."

There were audible gasps.

"Let's start at the beginning, shall we?"

She saw Rachel and walked over to her. She signaled Laura and a spotlight came up on Rachel.

"Rachel took $25,000 from the theater's safe to post bail for her father who was wrongly accused of a crime."

Rachel looked around at everyone, clearly embarrassed.

"An associate of mine recognized Rachel when she went to see her father in jail. Rachel replaced the money. She is not a thief. She's just someone who found herself in a desperate situation and, loving her father, she did whatever she could to help him."

Slick placed her hand gently on Rachel's shoulder.

Then she continued.

"But someone else knew Rachel had taken it, and *they* stole the money. I had some background checks done on all of you. You're a very interesting bunch. And there were some overheard bits of conversations on Christmas Eve that give motives for theft and murder."

There were glances exchanged all around. They all had secrets.

Slick walked up to each of them. The deductive wheels were spinning in her head.

Was the thief Karson, who wanted to complete the renovation of the church and finally have a stable home with Addison?

Was it Sindee, who was working on a personal project with Dale?

Was it Dale, who owed a lot of money to people in Florida?

Was it Beautee Holsom, who had plans of building a Christian theme park?

And who killed Eugene? A page of Randall's script was found at the scene. Did Randall kill Eugene? Then who killed Randall? Sindee's lighter that Dale had given her was found near Randall's body. Was it Dale and/or Sindee who killed Randall?

She let them all sweat as she walked around them.

Finally she got in Sindee's face and asked, "What is the project you're working on with Dale?"

Laura turned the spotlight on Sindee.

Flustered, Sindee said, "I'm working on a one woman show as a fund-raiser for the theater. It was going to be a surprise for Addison. Karson was in on it. We had several phone conversations about it. We didn't talk in the theater because we wanted it to be a big surprise for the company. I needed Dale because I can't dance. I thought I could make money for the theatre and for us as well."

"And how did you get the money to do this? Did you take it from the theater's safe?" Slick was pressing her hard.

"No! Of course I didn't! I raised the money myself by winning karaoke contests throughout New Jersey." Sindee blinked and squinted, trying to shield herself from the light.

Slick continued to question her.

"Randall had wanted to be the leading man all along. You said his voice wasn't good enough. Did you kill him after he got the lead because you didn't want him ruining your music?"

"No! No! I didn't kill Randall! I didn't! I swear!" Sindee was nearly hysterical.

Slick didn't let up on her.

"Then how do you explain your lighter being inside the cake? You were very upset earlier that you had misplaced it. Maybe it fell inside the cake when you were hiding his body."

Sindee's fear grew. She could feel everyone staring at her.

"And what about the syringe," Slick continued. "Randall was a diabetic. I found a bottle of Humilin in the men's dressing room refrigerator. Humilin is a brand name of insulin that is used both on animals and humans. You have a diabetic cat. It would have been very easy for you to give Randall an overdose of insulin."

"Someone's trying to frame me! I didn't steal any money and I didn't kill Randall." Sindee was sobbing now.

Slick walked over to Dale. All eyes turned to him as he was lit up with the spotlight.

"You amassed quite a debt in Florida after you were fired from Disney World. Did you steal the money to cover what you owe?"

"No, I didn't," Dale answered calmly. "I've been sending payments regularly out of what I've earned here doing this show. You can check."

"I'll do that," Slick assured him. She stepped closer to him. "You were too drunk to remember whether or not you killed Eugene. Do you remember if you killed Randall?"

"I didn't kill Randall. I had no reason to kill Randall."

"But you did have a reason to kill Eugene, didn't you? Love and sex are two great reasons to kill Eugene, aren't they?"

Dale looked at Slick defiantly, but said nothing.

Just then Addison returned and walked over to Slick.

"Those two detectives are here, Slick. They're taking care of Randall's body."

Slick nodded, looked past him at Karson and walked toward her.

"Did you steal the money after Rachel replaced it, Karson? She would have been the perfect fall guy for you. You had her confession that she stole from you."

Addison turned to face Karson, hoping his suspicion didn't show on his face.

"Goodness, no! I wouldn't steal from the theater! This has been our dream."

Slick was silent for a moment. She stared at Karson thoughtfully.

"You're a writer. Did you have other projects on the side that you didn't tell Addison about? Did you have extra income that you kept hidden from Addison?"

"Yes," Karson said quietly, squinting from the light in her face. "I have money hidden in the house. It was for the completion of the renovation and for the theater workshops."

Karson went to Addison and looked deep into his eyes. "After all the moving around we've done, I didn't want to move any more. I want to stay here. This is our home now."

Addison understood at once and took Karson into his arms, sorry that he had ever doubted her.

Next Slick approached David Castrato. He started to tremble. He finally got his wish of being in the spotlight.

"You confessed to murdering Eugene. Maybe you really did it. Maybe you killed Eugene *and* Randall."

"No, I didn't! I just wanted to be in the play, but I wouldn't kill to get in it."

"Maybe. Maybe not."

Slick crossed over to where Beautee Holsom was standing.

Beautee Holsom was never really a suspect. How could she be? She's like Mother Theresa without Mother Theresa's penchant for evil, she thought.

Slick approached Blair and Blair took a step back. The light was tight on her.

"On Christmas Eve, Randall told Rachel that he was going to break up with Blair. Maybe he said the same thing to you, Blair, after having had sex with you all night."

Slick started pacing around her.

"Randall said he was interested in someone else. You thought it was just part of your break up/make up routine until the night of the disastrous rehearsal. On that fateful night, I watched as Randall stormed off in his car and I saw you, Blair. I saw you follow him in your car."

Blair remained motionless.

"I'm thinking you followed him all the way to the Montvale rest stop, Blair. It's a well known gay pick-up spot."

There was a stunned reaction all around. Everyone knew Eugene was gay, but the news that Randall was too was a bombshell.

Blair looked around nervously at the crowd.

"That's outrageous! Randall was straight!" she insisted. "Every one here knows we were in love. Randall told you himself that he was with me all night the night Eugene was killed."

"A page of Randall's script was found at the rest stop, Blair, the morning after Eugene's murder," Slick said softly, but she didn't let up. "Randall left immediately after having sex with Eugene. He didn't want to be recognized at the rest stop. After all, he had been the leading man for years at this theater. He didn't want it to get out that he was really gay."

Everyone in the theater was riveted. Their eyes on Blair

"Randall left but Eugene waited around for more action. When Blair saw he was the last to leave the rest stop, she ran him over with her car."

The theater started to buzz with whispered conversations about Blair.

"My guess is that Randall felt bad about leaving Eugene drunk and alone at the rest stop. I think he went back to offer him a ride home and found him dead before Beautee Holsom got there. Of course Randall didn't know that Blair killed Eugene when he went to Blair that night to ask for her help. He confessed to her that he was having homosexual feelings for Eugene. Randall asked Blair to cover for him. He promised he would never again have sex with anyone else but Blair. Blair agreed to be his alibi, thus giving herself an alibi, too. Isn't that right, Blair? You killed Eugene because he took Randall away from you. Then you killed Randall and I'm sure it has something to do with that receipt for twenty-five thousand dollars in his pocket."

"This is preposterous," Blair screamed. "I didn't kill Eugene. And I loved Randall! I wouldn't hurt him!"

Blair ran to Sindee and pointed an accusing finger in her face.

"It was Sindee! Sindee hated Randall! You all saw what a hard time she gave him during rehearsals. She mocked his singing voice. She never liked him. That's her lighter in the cake. Sindee killed Randall, probably with her cat's insulin."

Sindee face went bloodless white. She started to cry.

"I didn't. I'm innocent."

"You are innocent, Sindee," Slick said. "Blair killed Randall. The syringe in the cake was Randall's. It's for fifty units of insulin. Obviously it was a timed release dosage. Fifty units of insulin is too much for a small animal. A cat or dog would take only twenty units. Thirty units max."

Blair felt trapped, but there was nothing she could do.

"It's true, every word of it. I loved Randall! I would have done anything for him. I hated that he was having sex with Eugene."

"What about the call to Dale? The call left on his answering machine?" Slick asked.

Dale stepped forward to hear Blair.

"Randall knew that Eugene was having sex with Dale. He thought of Dale as a rival. Years ago Randall's little brother saw Dale having sex with Prince Charming at Disney World. Randall saw it, too After the murder Randall left the message on Dale's answering machine to scare Dale and implicate him in Eugene's murder."

"And this receipt I found in Randall's pocket?" Slick asked.

"I stole the money from the theater after Rachel replaced it. I put a down payment on a building in Maplewood that I was going to convert into a theater where Randall and I would always be the leads in the shows we did there. Randall found it. I told him I had taken it from the theater safe to start our own group. After all the time we had spent here doing shows for free with the Taylors, I said we deserved the money. Randall disagreed. He thought that was disloyal. He said he was going to tell the Taylors that I took money from the safe. When I couldn't talk him out of it, I killed him with an overdose of insulin and put his body in the birthday cake. I put the syringe inside, took Sindee's lighter from the piano and tossed it in there, too. I didn't know he had the receipt in his pocket when I killed him.

"Yes, yes, I killed him! But he should have suffered more. He should have suffered more for the way he humiliated me."

Then Blair went silent. She saw all the eyes staring at her and decided to run.

She broke through the crowd, not caring who was in her way. She was about to reach the back door of the theater when from above a portrait fell down. Slick and Laura recognized it as the portrait of the Mother Superior that they had seen in the men's dressing room.

The portrait fell squarely on Blair trapping her in its frame.

Later, when the police were taking witness statements, and Blair was taken away, there were many who said they had seen the portrait fall, but the police never found any evidence that it had been hanging in the theater and Slick and Laura never found out how it had been moved from the men's dressing room.

21

Opening night.

Addison made a last check of the lobby. It had been spotlessly cleaned. The chairs were arranged carefully, and the pillows on the couch were fluffed and in place. The floor had been swept and the rug was vacuumed.

He checked to make sure the bureau that held the refreshments was stocked with fresh cookies and candies. What a difference.

During rehearsals it was usually in a state of chaos with used coffee cups, napkins, and crumbs everywhere, but tonight it was all arranged very attractively.

Addison got the coffee urn going, then checked the programs. They were neatly stacked on a table by the door ready to be passed out with the ticket purchases.

He checked the reservations book. Seventy tickets had been sold for opening night. A crowd of seventy was terrific for a community theater.

Addison remembered when they first opened eight years ago, his company was so small that four actors played fifteen parts. For most performances there were more members in the cast than there were in the audience.

He looked around the lobby, confident that everything was ready and in place. He was about to go through the checklist again, but decided another check was utterly pointless. Everything was done. He was just nervous, but he knew his cast was ready. The show was ready, he said to himself, hoping it would make him stop sweating. After all these years he still got opening-night jitters.

He lit his pipe and enjoyed the calm and quiet of being alone in the lobby.

He looked toward the door that separated the lobby from the theater and imagined the flurry of activity that was going on just beyond it in the dressing rooms.

Actors getting into makeup and costumes. Actors checking the stage to make sure their props were preset. Actors getting ready to bring to life characters only they understood intimately and hoping to make them real for the audience.

They had to make them so real that, even though they had immersed themselves into these characters for weeks, they had to act like the events of the play were unfolding to them for the very first time.

Starting tonight, it had to look like the first time three times a week for the next five weeks.

Addison wanted to go backstage and reassure them. He wanted to tell them a story from his many years in the theater that would inspire them and get them through the next few hours. But he couldn't. The show was in their hands now. He had brought them as far as he could, and now they were on their own.

His thoughts were interrupted by a gentle hand on his back. He turned to look at Karson. Beautiful sweet Karson. She knew exactly what he was feeling. She was feeling it, too. It was her story that was about to be brought to life. Her words, her characters.

Addison kissed her forehead and her eyelids. They held hands, sharing this peaceful moment, each knowing that whatever happened this night and every night afterward, they would face the future together.

Always together.

There was a knock on the theater door. Addison forced himself away from Karson and looked out the window.

Outside there was a line of people waiting to get in. It went around the block.

Karson straightened Addison's tie and brushed off his jacket. She wanted him to look his best.

"It's show time!" they said in unison.

Together they opened the doors, and the first wave of the audience came pouring in. With them came the excited expectation that came on opening nights.

Addison and Karson led them to their seats.

When everyone was seated, Addison walked out into the theater, and all the before-show conversations died down.

He stepped up to the floor mike that was left there for him, gently tapped it to make sure it was live, then he greeted the audience and thanked them for coming. He gave them a brief description of the show, piquing their imaginations. Afterward, he shut down the mike and returned it to the lobby.

Then he flashed the lights in the lobby to let the stragglers know the show was about to start. It was also a signal to the cast that the show was about to start.

Addison darkened the lobby, locked the doors, and climbed the stairs to the balcony where Karson was seated, to watch the show.

Moments later, the lights in the theater dimmed, the orchestra started the overture, and the red velvet curtain started to rise.

It was the perfect evening. The Friday opening night of *Sorry I Missed Your Birthday* was dazzling. The cast took full command of the stage. The orchestra embraced every note of the score. The dancers seemed to glide across the stage. They

moved gracefully through all the intricate movements, seam-
less and cohesive.

The show ran flawlessly from the first dimming of the lights
and the opening notes of the overture to the final bringing
down of the curtain.

The musical numbers were funny and poignant. There were
three show-stopping tunes in Act One alone. The musicians
and dancers were extolled. The performance received a wildly
exuberant standing ovation.

The show was written to give each of the actors several
scenes to display their singing and acting abilities, and they
had performed brilliantly.

There was so much cheering and whistling from the audience that the cast had to come back twice for more bows after
the curtain call.

The house was jam-packed. There were many more in attendance than the seventy reservations that had been taken at
the box office. Many of the audience members just followed
the crowds outside the theater indoors, anxious to see what was
going on. They were glad they stayed to witness the opening
night. Quite a few made reservations to come back and see it
again.

The investors, most of whom were present for the performance, were relieved, practically delirious with the favorable
reaction, and the good buzz that they knew would be coming
from the word of mouth of those in attendance. Several were
already talking about putting up money for the next show. The
delicious *Ka-ching Ka-ching* sound of money rolling in played
over and over in their heads.

The *Star-Ledger* had sent a reviewer and a photographer.
The reviewer spent the night spewing praise and flattery on
Addison and Karson, and expressing how the show had lifted
the world of community theater to a new level of excellence.

He used words like *exciting* and *vivid* to describe the play, and he called the writing and directing team of Taylor and Taylor brilliant.

It was correctly assumed that the review in the *Sunday Spotlight* would be a laudation. The successful run of the show was a given.

The photographer loved the staging and the costumes and kept snapping pictures at every opportunity. He wanted to meet Cheri Boone-Blume, but she was tucked away in her cubbyhole working on costumes.

In the lobby there were head shots of Eugene and Randall with a grateful tribute to them beautifully written by Karson. It was done in a way that would honor them and give those who wanted to remember them a few moments of quiet reflection, but not take away from the joy of the evening.

Blair's head shot had been removed and destroyed.

The sign-in book provided for audience members who wanted to be put on the theater's mailing list was filled.

Laura had arranged a champagne reception after the show for the cast and the backers and their invited guests. The room was overflowing with people. Addison and Karson slowly worked their way through the large crowd. They were stopped at every step by fans and well-wishers who wanted to congratulate them on the start of what would surely be their most successful season.

When the cast had changed back into their street clothes, they came out single file into the theater and got even more applause. They graciously accepted praise from everyone.

Dale was overwhelmed by the interest in him. *The Star-Ledger* wanted to do a story on how this successful dancer, who, according to his bio in the program, had risen to head choreographer at Disney World, then chucked it all to return to his roots in New Jersey.

He was seen drinking many bottles of Diet Coke through-out the night.

Sindee was busy passing out fliers about the upcoming fundraiser for the theater. All the fliers went home with the people they were handed to. Not one of them ended up on the theater floor or in the trash baskets.

Off in a quiet corner of the room, Rachel, her father, and Judson were talking and taking the first tentative steps at be-coming a family.

David Castrato was surrounded by a group of aspiring actors. He was lecturing them on how he had worked his way up from assistant stage manager. His advice to them was to learn every bit of the show they were working on because they could be called on at any moment to step in. The actors listened to him as they would a prophet, hanging on his every word.

Richard was approached by members of a neighboring the-ater troupe and asked if he would care to come to a dance au-dition for a musical they were planning soon.

Slick and Laura sat up in the balcony away from the noisy chatter watching everything.

Slick picked up a glass of champagne and toasted Laura.

"I am the first to admit that I was wrong. It was a very good show. I wasn't sure it would all come together but it did. Despite my original doubts, I really got caught up in it. Your foundation helps bring these productions to life. You must be very proud of the work it does."

Laura was about to respond when she saw Snatch McDonough and Desk Sergeant Stanley Ames from Slick's old precinct walk-ing up the balcony stairs toward them. She waved.

"Hi Laura! Slick! Thanks for the tickets to the show. It was great," Snatch said enthusiastically.

"Yes, it was terrific. Thanks," Sergeant Ames added.

Slick invited them to sit down.

When they were seated comfortably she gave them each a tulip-shaped champagne glass, then pulled a bottle of champagne from the floor-standing ice bucket beside her in the aisle. She poured some into the glasses, then said, "We're very glad you enjoyed the show, but there's another reason why we invited you here tonight. That's why we wanted to talk to you both up here, privately, away from the party for a while."

Slick paused, looked at Laura, and then took a deep breath and continued.

"Laura and I have a business proposition for you two."

Snatch and Sergeant Ames exchanged puzzled looks.

"I'm going to be stepping down from running Laura's clam company," Slick explained. "I'm going to get back into detective work." Slick smiled broadly. "This time with a partner."

She raised her glass, indicating Laura.

Laura smiled back and they held hands.

"I guess you could call us partners in crime," Laura said.

Stanley and Snatch both rose to their feet and shook Slick's hand, excited by the news that their friend was getting back to what she loved most.

"Slick, that's great!" Sergeant Ames said. "I couldn't be happier for you."

"Wait. Here's where you two come in. If Laura and I are working together, that will mean that neither one of us will have time for Laura's company," Slick explained.

"We were hoping that you two would look after it for us," Laura said.

"You'd really be doing us a big favor," Slick urged.

Snatch and Stanley Ames looked back at them in disbelief. An ex-cop and an ex-thief running a company together? They dropped back into their seats stunned.

They each started talking excitedly at once.

"Are you crazy?"

"I don't know anything about the clam business."

Slick tried to calm their doubts.

"I never knew anything about running a business, either. But don't worry, Laura's got the company so well structured, you'll do just fine. And remember, Laura's still going to be the President and CEO; if you have any problems just ask her. This business has been in her family all her life. We wanted to turn the management of it over to people we could trust. We trust you. And what you don't know about running a business, you'll learn. Believe me. If I could do it, so can you. So, what do you say, guys?"

Snatch and Stanley exchanged looks briefly.

Sergeant Stanley Ames was ready to leave his job at the precinct. He had wanted to be a good cop and he had been one. He had seen enough there to last him a lifetime. The misery in his life had become an all too comfortable companion. Now it was time to move on. Time to shift gears. Time to get his world in order. He wanted to look at life from a different angle, from outside the bottle. He was grateful for the opportunity.

"I'm in," he said.

"Then I'm in, too," Snatch replied. He got a little choked up and wiped a tear away. He'd just gone from stocking shelves at Wal-Mart to running a company. He wished his mother was alive to see he had done more with his life than being a thief.

Slick and Laura were very pleased. They all hugged and shook hands, and champagne glasses were clinked all around.

"Gee, I do hate to interrupt such a tender moment. So sorry to intrude on your group hug."

They had all been so involved with their conversation that they had not seen Devlyn O'Hare walk up the stairs to the balcony.

"I know Laura and Slick, but I don't know you two gentlemen. I'm Devlyn O'Hare. I work with Laura." She rapidly shook hands with Snatch and Stanley, but didn't give them an opportunity to introduce themselves. She'd have forgotten their names at once, anyway.

"Ohhh! Champagne! I'd love some!"

Devlyn didn't wait to be asked. She picked up a glass and grabbed the bottle from the bucket. She poured some into the glass. She took a sip and savored it while the four friends just looked at her.

"What do you want, Devlyn?" Laura was annoyed.

"Pol Roger. Excellent choice, Laura! God, I love this stuff! This is great champagne," Devlyn said, ignoring her. "It's the perfect way to celebrate an ending to a perfect gala evening. I saw the show," Devlyn continued. "It was pretty good. I don't care much for musicals myself. My taste tends to run more toward *The Vagina Monologues,* but it wasn't a bad show."

"Devlyn, I'm not going to ask you again. Why are you here?" Laura was firm.

"Okay, Laura, that's one of the things I really like about you. You get right to the point. So I'll skip the social amenities and cut to the chase. I'm here because I have some news for you. There's going to be a meeting of the board on Monday. Ten a.m. sharp. Your presence is requested. I've called this special meeting to show them a very interesting videotape I've acquired of Addison Taylor coming into your office discussing the theft of the grant money the foundation had given them."

Devlyn winked at Slick and raised her champagne glass.

"Thanks, Slick. I couldn't have done it without you. Adding the security system was a brilliant idea." There was a gleam of satisfaction in Devlyn's black eyes.

Laura was speechless.

"Oh, now. Don't look so shocked, Laura. Smile. You're on *Candid Camera*," Devlyn joked. Then she tossed her head back and laughed loudly. No one laughed with her.

"Oh, come on, you guys. You have to admit that was pretty funny."

Devlyn reached into the bucket and added a little more champagne to her glass.

"That money has been accounted for and returned to the theater. It's being used as stipulated in the grant," Slick said stonily.

"Oh, I'm sure it has. But the board will be interested to learn that the head of the foundation didn't report the fact that she knew money was missing. And I think they will also find it interesting that the head of the foundation may have had a personal reason for not reporting it. Judson has worked for Laura for all of her life. I'm sure she'd do anything for him. I've seen Judson down there talking to one of the actresses in the play all night. Judson doesn't get out too much. I'm sure with a little digging I could make a connection between him and the actress.

"You may have started the foundation and all, Laura, and it may be named for your father, but still the board may have a little something to say about malfeasance. I don't think they'd like that at all. I'm sure they'll vote to relieve you of your duties."

Slick and Laura looked down into the theater to the corner where Judson was talking with Rachel and her father. He looked happier that they had seen him look in years.

"And what do you think will happen to this show once it gets out that Addison and Karson Taylor misappropriated the foundation's money? Oh, look! There they are!"

Devlyn pointed her glass in their direction. She waved at them and called out "Addison! Karson! Great show! Loved it!"

Addison and Karson heard her, looked up, and when they saw Devlyn with Slick and Laura, assumed she was a friend and smiled and waved back appreciatively.

"Aren't they sweet," Devlyn said, smiling. "Too bad they're about to get crushed. Bad publicity, an investigation of their books. That's not the kind of thing that's good for a show. It really is too bad."

Devlyn turned up her glass and finished the champagne, steadily watching Laura over the rim.

Laura looked at Addison and Karson talking and laughing with the cast and crew. They were glowing. They had all worked so hard on this show. They had come through so much together to get it up and running. Laura wasn't concerned about herself. Devlyn was after her, not the Taylors. The Taylors were just collateral damage. Their pain would be a source of entertainment to Devlyn. Nothing more. Whatever happened at the board meeting on Monday, Laura would still be well off. But Devlyn was playing with the Taylors' livelihood. Laura couldn't let that happen.

She took a step toward Devlyn.

"Devlyn, please . . ."

"No, no, Laura. I can't stay longer and have more champagne, no matter how much you beg me. I've got to go now and prepare for that meeting on Monday. And I want to say good night to the Taylors and to Judson before I go. I couldn't leave without saying good-bye to them. That would be rude. Thanks for asking, though," Devlyn said.

The four watched in silence as Devlyn walked down the stairs from the balcony.

"T.T.F.N.," she called back cheerily, without looking at them.

Snatch looked puzzled by this.

"Ta-ta for now," Stanley said softly.

Slick and Laura watched helplessly from above as Devlyn, true to her word, stopped and chatted with Addison and Karson, then made her way to Judson. At both stops Devlyn made sure she was seen from the balcony. She waved up at them and made sure that Addison, Karson, and Judson did so as well.

And just before Devlyn walked out the door to leave, she stopped and blew a kiss up to Laura.

No one on the theater floor knew what had happened in the balcony or had any idea of the havoc that was coming, thanks to Devlyn. They continued to party and celebrate the opening of the show, mercifully unaware.

There would be shock and awe when Devlyn was through. She was like a weapon of mass destruction pointed at them, ready to launch.

The celebratory mood had definitely died in the balcony.

Laura immediately set about trying to make Snatch and Sergeant Ames feel comfortable. Her eyes showed worry, but she turned to them with a big smile. And Slick fell in line beside her.

"I'm sorry for the interruption. Devlyn has a talent for being unsettling, much like a dentist's drill touching a live nerve ending," Laura said with gracious good humor. "Please, let's not let her spoil this evening. We've enjoyed a night of good theater and we were celebrating your taking control of Clam-de-monium. I'm very happy about that."

"Yes," Slick said, reaching into the ice bucket. "We have some champagne left. Who's ready for another glass?"

Snatch and Stanley looked at each other and then looked at their hosts. They both stammered out fake reasons why they were leaving.

Slick and Laura asked them to stay but they both declined.

They both knew Laura wanted to be alone with Slick and that Slick needed to comfort her.

They made a date to get together to discuss their new job positions and then said their good-byes.

When they were alone, Slick and Laura put their arms around each other and held on to one another as tightly as they could.

It took a few moments, but from below they heard the sound of metal tapping against glass. They separated and saw that Addison was about to make a speech.

"Ladies and gentlemen, Karson and I want to thank each of you for a job well done. This production has had its share of problems and heartache, but we all worked together and made it happen. If tonight is any indication, I think we've got a winner. I think we are in for a very successful run."

There was a round of applause and shouts of enthusiastic agreement. The gleeful noise reached a crescendo then fell away as Addison continued to speak. The love he had for his company shone through.

"As we begin our next season, Karson and I are grateful to all of you who have worked with us over the years. We appreciate your talent, your time and your commitment. We treasure you. As we go forward, we will remember those who worked hard here whom we have lost. We will continue to celebrate the art of theater and the glorious impact it has on the lives of those who perform it, and the lives of those who come to see it.

"Each year we find new friends who help us along this path. This year I want to give a special thanks to our friends in the balcony, Laura Charles and Cassandra Slick."

Addison lifted his champagne glass in a toast.

"To Laura and Slick, everyone!"

A spotlight was pointed at them so everyone could see them.

There was applause and cheers, then everyone lifted their glass in a toast.

Slick and Laura looked down at the sea of happy smiling faces shining up at them.

They looked at one another and their hearts sank.

22

The following Monday morning, Devlyn was up with the sunrise. She got out of bed filled with the joy of being alive. This was very uncustomary for her. She was not a morning person. In fact, she thought that anyone who got out of bed naturally perky and zippy was very disturbed.

But this was not the start of just another day.

She went to the windows and looked outside. The forecast from the night before had predicted that it was going to be an unusually mild winter's day. So far that appeared to be the case.

She opened the windows to let in some fresh air. The sun streamed into the room. The sky was a dazzling blue.

"What an excellent day for an inquisition," she said aloud, after inhaling deeply.

She slipped out of her pajamas and got into her sweats. She went to the other bedroom that she had converted into a workout room and looked at the array of computerized exercise equipment inside. She turned on the classic rock station and walked past the stationary bike and the treadmill and to the shelf against the wall. She would hit the bag today. She taped up her hands.

They were in the middle of a great set on FM104.3. By the time she put the tape on and positioned herself in front of the punching bag, Led Zeppelin's "The Immigrant's Song" was starting up. Next was "Rocking the Casbah" by the Clash.

Devlyn punched and jabbed the heavy bag with punishing

combination cycles for a full hour. The bag bounced and swayed on the heavy chain. She strained with the effort, and the shock of each punch traveled up her arms. But her face remained impassive. She was perfectly disciplined, as if she were in competition with the bag. She refused to show any weakness.

This morning exercise was a ritual for Devlyn, bordering on obsession. She did it for the usual reasons everyone had for working out like keeping weight off, sex appeal, and relieving stress. But Devlyn also was convinced it kept her focused, lean, and hungry.

When she exercised, Devlyn didn't have a dainty glow of perspiration, she would sweat like a champion racehorse in training for the Kentucky Derby. Her entire body was soaked head to toe with beads of moisture.

When she was finished beating the bag, she wiped the perspiration from her face with a towel, scrubbed her hair with it, and then let the towel hang around her neck. Then she walked into her kitchen and put some coffee on.

She was starving. Her adrenaline was pumping, ready now for the meeting. She needed to feed it.

She looked in the refrigerator for something to eat.

Why did she bother? Nothing but vegetables rotting in plastic bags, a desiccated wedge of lemon, some fuzzy yogurt, milk well past the sell-by date, and an expensive unopened bottle of white wine. Not even a container of edible leftovers.

Housekeeping wasn't her strong suit. She tossed it all, except the wine, into the garbage.

Devlyn didn't eat at home much and she cooked even less. She decided to grab a little something on the way to the meeting. She drank two cups of strong black coffee and put the cup in the dishwasher, then headed for the bathroom.

She decided that instead of her daily shower, today she

would treat herself to a bubble bath. She kept a large wicker basket close to the tub, filled with oils and scented soaps. She ran the water and poured in an expensive bath oil that she saved for special occasions. Billows of scented steam filled the room. She slipped in under the bubbles and felt the velvety water caress her body.

Devlyn lay back in the tub enjoying the sensation of it and then turned her mind to what she would say at the meeting later.

She would have to be appropriately respectful of Laura while showing the board that Laura was no longer deserving of heading the foundation. She would also have to convey tremendous sorrow that Laura had put her in the position of having no choice but to assemble the board and call for Laura's removal. After all, the good work of the foundation could not be compromised by Laura's misconduct with the Taylor grant.

Her presentation and arguments would have to be top notch. All professional, nothing personal.

Sincerity was the key. There were a few board members who, Devlyn knew, would vote to remove Laura at once. They were extremely conservative and had no connection to Laura or her family.

Devlyn had to win over the others. Most of the members were old enough to remember Laura's father.

Devlyn kicked around a few other thoughts, then began to bathe herself.

She washed her hair with the showerhead attachment, grabbed a towel from the towel rack and turban-wrapped it around her head. She used another towel to dry herself and then put on her robe. She blow-dried her hair, shaping it with her fingers and tossing it back into place.

Afterward she went to her closet and picked out the clothes she was going to wear to the board meeting with great care.

She wanted to look very professional and businesslike. It had been a long time since she had addressed the board. She had to be at her best, especially for this meeting. It wasn't every day one asked them to consider removing the head of the foundation.

She carefully sifted through the rows of expensive clothing bought at exclusive boutiques, mentally rejecting every item for one reason or another.

Finally she picked out a dark blue suit. She lifted the hanger from its place and gave the suit closer scrutiny.

It was attractive yet conservative. It conveyed a sense of professionalism and dignity.

She took a pair of Donna Karan panty hose from her dresser drawer and found the perfect shoes to match her outfit.

She combed her luxurious hair straight back into a smooth topknot, not a strand out of place. She opened her jewelry box and picked among the rings, bracelets, and necklaces until she found what she was searching for. She inserted some modest looking earrings into her earlobes.

Next, she put on her makeup more carefully than usual. She did it so carefully it looked as if it had been done professionally when she was finished. It was almost invisible. Then she applied a subdued shade of lipstick. She put on the pair of glasses she kept on hand for those occasions when she felt it was to her benefit to look studious.

After she had all her clothes on, Devlyn looked at herself appraisingly in her full-length mirror and smiled at what she saw reflected there.

She was tastefully and modestly dressed. She could have passed for a librarian. A very hot, steaming, smoldering-with-sex librarian.

Even though she was dressed in a more toned-down manner than usual, on Devlyn the most sober of business suits implied contradictions to the look she was aiming for. Devlyn didn't mind that. She couldn't help it. At least the board would see that she took the meeting and the situation very seriously.

She looked at the time. It was still early, but Devlyn wanted to get to the office well ahead of time to make sure the conference room was set up properly and comfortably for the board members. She wanted to check the conference room microphones, television, and VCR herself.

She put on her coat, and just before she left, she remembered to close the windows. When she went through the living room, she saw the window in there was open, too. She stopped in her tracks. She didn't remember opening that window. Had she opened it and forgotten about it?

She looked around her apartment. She knew it was crazy, but she checked each room.

There was nothing missing. No one else was there.

Then Devlyn had a very disturbing thought. She went quickly to her briefcase and looked inside. She smiled at herself. She must be more nervous than she realized about the board meeting. She sighed in relief. The tape from the security camera was still inside, just as she had left it.

Devlyn closed the living-room window, picked up the briefcase, slung her bag over her shoulder, and headed out the door.

Laura didn't greet the start of this particular Monday morning with the same anticipation Devlyn did. She had spent most of Sunday night tossing and turning in bed, unable to sleep. Every time she closed her eyes she kept seeing the faces of Addison and Karson smiling up at her from the theater floor.

When she wasn't trying to sleep, she was pacing around the bedroom, wracked with worry about the trouble Devlyn was going to make.

Slick gave her verbal support and encouragement, but she

knew it wasn't much of a comfort to Laura. Slick felt useless. And frustrated.

She couldn't feel Laura's pain, but she could certainly feel her own as she watched Laura. All she could do was be there if Laura wanted to talk, and give her space when she didn't feel like talking.

To add to Laura's heartache, a beautiful floral arrangement had arrived Saturday from Addison and Karson, thanking them for their help. The attached card was signed by the cast and crew. Addison had also left a message that the Saturday night performance and the Sunday matinee had been as well received as the Friday opening.

Laura hadn't called him back for fear that he would detect the sadness in her voice. She knew Addison and Karson were enjoying some tranquility from the epidemic of troubles that had plagued them.

Laura didn't have the heart to tell them that more bad news was on the way.

Slick managed to get a few hours sleep, then woke up with the bed feeling empty. She knew Laura wasn't beside her before she'd even opened her eyes. She couldn't remember the last time the bed felt that way. She hoped she wouldn't have to experience that blankness very often.

Slick went into the bathroom and splashed some water on her face. She threw on a robe and made her way downstairs. She knew that Laura would rather go down to the main kitchen than risk waking her. Slick walked down the long staircase and made her way through the corridors.

Before entering the kitchen Slick watched for a few moments and studied Laura. Slick could tell she was distraught, but she still had poise and self-containment. She didn't give off any hint of trouble. But she seemed so small and alone.

Slick entered the kitchen and sat down beside her.

Evelyn was asking about the breakfast that Laura had asked for then hadn't eaten.

Judson had left Evelyn in charge. He had taken the day off to spend with Rachel and her father.

"Is there something wrong, Miss?" Evelyn asked. "Do you want something else?"

"No, really, Evelyn, it's fine. I'm just not very hungry," Laura said, pushing the plate away.

The doorbell rang and Evelyn excused herself and went to answer it.

When Evelyn was gone, Slick took Laura's hand.

"I missed waking up next to you. I didn't like it. The room felt so empty without you."

"I knew I kept you awake all night. I left so you could get some sleep."

"A package came for you, Miss."

Evelyn was back. She handed the package to Laura.

Laura opened the small box. It was a videocassette. There was no label on it. Laura didn't know what to think until she saw the note inside. It was a carefully folded piece of paper.

Laura and Slick,

Here is the tape you may have been worrying about. I promise it's my last job. Just so you know, I switched it with another one. Before I got sent up Dorf was really popular. That Tim Conway cracks me up. I hope you enjoy seeing it today at the board meeting.

Snatch

Laura broke into tears of relief and handed the note to Slick. Slick read it and felt a flutter in her heart knowing that Laura and the Taylors were going to be spared from Devlyn's machinations.

She held Laura in abandon until her tears turned into laughter. At that moment it was the sweetest music to Slick's ears.

Evelyn quietly slipped away as the sound of laughter through kisses echoed throughout the kitchen.